DRAMA QUEENS WITH LOVE SCENES

"Something that makes me fond of Drama Queens with Love Scenes is that it flouts m/m convention throughout." 4 STARS - Ulysses Dietz, Prism Book Alliance

"Kevin Klehr has crafted a wonderful new world for these characters—a glittery, fabulous, and just a little bit catty eternity that lends itself to the seeds of theatre pop culture, history, and themes he weaves into the narrative." Nathan 'Burgoine (author) for his review in Chelsea Station Magazine

"Klehr has created some wonderful characters and his prose style immediately pulls us into the story and into the characters who actually become our friends." Amos Lassen, Amos Lassen Reviews

"Kudos to author, Kevin Klehr, who has penned the most original love story I've ever read. Drama Queens and Love Scenes is amazing in that the characters are dead, yet full of sass and mystery." 5 STARS – Morgan Wyatt, Goodreads

DRAMA QUEENS AND ADULT THEMES

"It is not exactly what I expected, but ultimately this story offers a powerful love song for readers willing to listen." "…I found myself pausing as I read, thinking back over my own long lifetime as a gay man in a rapidly shifting world." 4 STARS – Ulysses Dietz, Prism Book Alliance

"There are lovely vivid images evoked in the story…" "My best analogy would be the sensation of funhouse mirrors where art imitates life imitates art…" The Reading Addict

"…despite the complexity of the weave, the story doesn't feel complex when you're reading it. It has a good flow and a three-dimensional feel to the characters and the story." 4 STARS – Nephy, Nephy's World

"Klehr certainly knows how to tell a story, but I am still not sure if we were laughing at the characters or at ourselves." Amos Lassen, Amos Lassen Reviews

NATE AND THE NEW YORKER

"The writing is what really got to me. This starts out nice and slow, like a good orchestral piece and you're thinking "nice" and then the other instruments start to chime in, each one at its exact moment in queue, until I was surrounded by a full crescendo of such rich characters, each one developed exactly right for the story, not overdone or lacking in any sense." 4.5 STARS – O.J. Cast, O.J. He Says / Goodreads

"So, let's just get the bottom line out of the way: this is quite possibly *the* best novella-length story I have ever read." 5 STARS – Jaycee, Goodreads

"Blind-sighted. That's the only way I can explain what just happened to me. I mean...holy cow!" 5 STARS - Elaine White (author), Goodreads

"I think it is fair to say that Klehr has joined the ranks of other gay men that are writing about our lives." Amos Lassen, Amos Lassen Reviews

Up to this point, I had enjoyed Nate and the New Yorker, but it was Klehr's simple, but clever, way of shifting the emotional momentum of the story which totally won me over. 5 STARS – Kirsty, Joyfully Jay

Drama Queens with Love Scenes

Actors and Angels, Book 1

Kevin Klehr

Published by
NineStar Press
PO Box 91792
Albuquerque, New Mexico, 87199
www.ninestarpress.com

Print ISBN #978-1-945952-94-4
Cover by Natasha Snow
Edited by Jason Bradley

Acknowledgements

First off I'd like to thank my partner in life, Warren Brown, who showed me more than deserved patience and encouragement on this endeavor.

Endless thanks to Angus Gault, who has read, reread, and basically shared this adventure with me, as well as coming up with some of the best one-liners in the text. His contribution is immeasurable.

Thanks also to Brett Tyler and Carmel Keohan who shared their enthusiasm in the early stages of the project. Without it, I'm not sure I would have gone anywhere beyond my handwritten first chapter.

The best line in the second paragraph comes courtesy of Chris Jones, who said it in polite conversation. I was quick to ring our home voice mail so I wouldn't forget it. It still makes me smile.

Cheers to Nicky, who in a way became my first fan. Just in being spellbound in my story meant a lot to me. It helped me believe in myself.

Dr. Anita Heiss and Dr. Janet Hutchinson have both been inspirational and open to sharing their knowledge on writing, and the industry. I've learnt a lot.

Many thanks to the late Mary Belk who was a great teacher in the art. There was a lot to learn and hopefully, I took it on board.

Thanks to Mum, Krys, Mary, and Steve, who always wanted to know how my novel was shaping up.

And to Ethan Day, Jason Bradley, Val Hughes, J.P. Bowie, Adrian Nicolas, Raevyn McCann, Kristin, April Blackburn, and Alison.

Finally, thanks to Dad, who watched me silently at work.

ONE

SHE LOOKED LIKE Jayne Mansfield without the attributes. Her cherry-colored wide-brimmed hat complemented her black unbuttoned jacket. A low-cut white dress completed the look. She seemed overdressed and would have looked better wearing a casual pink T-shirt and torn jeans, like a pinup girl sparking the imagination of a lusty army boy. Her pleasing smile said she had been waiting to greet us.

An angel stood next to her, barefoot in old blue jeans and a ripped-sleeved khaki shirt. While he didn't have the glam factor of the female, his striking dove-gray wings drew focus. They spanned his height and then some, towering above his head by at least an arm's length. He rarely made eye contact with us and stood hunched with his hands lightly clenched below his navel. His demeanor implied a vanilla hint of gayness.

Just what did we actually get up to last night?

My friend, Warwick, and I safely considered this scene from the doorway of our tiny room.

A moment ago, we had said goodbye to my uncle and his girlfriend, and now we were facing two strangers on what looked like the set of a Greek epic.

Our confused oohs and ahs echoed off the marble black and white tiles, which stretched so far into the horizon they became gray as they met a set of stairs. Each step alternated in color, again black and white. Someone had overdosed on 1980s pop videos when they conceived this design.

"What do you make of the red velvet curtains, classic or uninspired?" I asked my friend.

"Allan, they're lush. Just lush."

"Don't be alarmed, gentlemen," the Jayne Mansfield look-alike said with an air of whimsy.

As we nodded awkwardly, she shot a concerned glance at the angel and whispered, "Don't smile like that. It doesn't match the décor."

Discouraged, he rolled his eyes and mislaid his smile.

I began biting my thumbnail as my eyes darted between our hosts and the opulent aspects of this room.

"A sex kitten and an angel," I timidly said to Warwick. "Does this mean...?"

Warwick stepped through the doorway and addressed the angel. "Those wings? Please tell me they aren't real."

The angel gracefully flapped them three times before shrugging. I switched my denial into overdrive.

In the past week, Warwick and I had left our chaotic beach-town lives for a little break. My dead-end job was getting me down, and my partner in crime suggested a holiday would be the best remedy. Until this point, he was right. All had been going as planned. We'd visited my uncle Bryant and his new love interest in Melbourne before considering a driving trip around Tasmania. Who could have imagined this strange twist in our plotline?

Our hosts seemed to study us like a diplomat about to shake hands with a head of state. The angel endeavored to smile again, while the blonde bombshell gave us a moment to gauge our bearings. Then her arms extended in greeting like Jesus in a biblical painting.

"My name is Samantha, and this is Guy. We're here to welcome you."

"I'm Warwick, and this is Allan," my friend said. He gestured back in my direction.

I stepped into their lavish space. Five-meter-high crimson walls screamed at me; several burnt-caramel marble arches signposted entrances to other rooms, each shielded by more red velvet curtains. It was lavish in a color-blind sort of way. All that was missing was a harem.

"It's nice to meet you, but where exactly are we?" I asked.

"You're in the Limelight Quarter," announced Guy.

"I'm sorry, but I really don't understand what's going on. Where did you say we were?" I was fearful of the answers.

"You're in the Limelight Quarter," replied Samantha. "We've been sent to show you to your new home."

She stood confidently, owning the floor beneath her. I mouthed the words "our new home" as she read my lips. The more our hosts tried to enlighten us, the more obscure this setting became.

Warwick courted my short attention by subtly pointing above us. I was already feeling nauseous at the combination of colors, but by looking straight up, I saw something that made me picture Liberace and his piano bringing this room to life. Projecting rainbow colors throughout the space was a mammoth chandelier, even though there were no rays of sunlight streaming into the room. I could sense the echo of ivories entertaining an audience of women with their best years far behind them. His grand instrument dazzling us with reflected hues. Was this camp heaven or decorator hell?

"You're in pleasant company. Don't be alarmed," Samantha continued.

She beamed in what seemed an attempt to win us over. Her feminine charms began to work.

"You realize all of this is going over our heads," Warwick explained. "We've never heard of the Limelight Quarter, and we don't understand why we have new homes."

"You've arrived in our little sector. A place we like to describe as the theater district," she replied.

"So why are we here?" I was desperately piecing together the moments before our arrival.

"Your resumes tell us that you're both comfortable treading the boards," explained Guy.

Yes, it was true that we both dabbled in acting, but at that point, we were hardly household names.

"We welcome new visitors to our theatrical paradise. That's our job," said Samantha. "We know about your thespian tendencies, so you've been assigned to stay here."

"So that means the Limelight Quarter is just *part* of this unique location?" Warwick asked.

"Definitely!" answered Guy. "People from all walks of life inhabit their sectors of interest. We match new visitors to their hobbies."

"So the Limelight Quarter is part of *what* other place?" I rubbed my chin, not really wanting my doubts confirmed. This query seemed to stump our angel. Was he biting his bottom lip to avoid the question, or was it an attempt to work out an ambiguous answer?

"Sweethearts, you are here! That's all that matters," replied our hostess. Her charisma was working overtime. "Now, Allan and Warwick, we have to welcome you in the traditional manner."

"Which is?" I asked.

"A friendly cocktail at our own special bar," she replied. "Follow us. The Pedestal awaits!"

"I'll do anything that feels familiar," I replied. "Lead the way."

MY FEET WERE massaged by the cobbled streets as we followed our hosts. Striking sandstone apartment buildings, all about three stories high, sported luxurious balconies. The perfect setting for theatrical types to hide away between plays, soaking up the golden sunshine from the terrace while skimming through their lines.

Somewhere in the Afterlife, there were architects who knew what they are doing. I felt calmer. Around us, local inhabitants either strolled or rode pushbikes around the streets, enjoying the weather. Warwick placed his hand on my shoulder as he strode next to me. I was so glad I wasn't experiencing this alone.

A tall woman in a scarlet dress and black feather boa sauntered past me, closely followed by a couple of older stylish men in corduroy jackets and tortoise-shell glasses. They had a sexy lecturer look that made me want to share in their knowledge.

"How long have you all been here?" Warwick asked.

"Always," replied Guy.

"A fair while," said Samantha. "There are so many fascinating people here, it's not worth leaving."

"So who are they?" I asked.

"At any one time, our new arrivals are the most interesting souls. But our ever-changing cast of characters are sure to delight your intellect."

"Are these characters as intriguing as you?"

"My dear, no one is as intriguing as me."

Guy rolled his eyes as his wings flapped a couple of times. I wondered if this angelic gesture was similar in effect to a mortal coughing after hearing a lame comment. The banter continued for several more paces before we arrived at an art-deco building ruined by electric-blue paint and a multicolored neon sign flashing "The Pedestal." It was like someone had consulted Mr. Magoo for decorating tips. I welcomed the idea of drowning my bewilderment in alcohol, even if it was to just rid myself of this horrid image.

Samantha did an eccentric half twirl between us and the doorway. Guy glanced at the sky, seemingly underwhelmed by her flamboyant antics. Warwick huddled close to me as they ushered us inside.

We stood at the back of the bar as my friend rubbed my shoulders. I still had a far way to go before accepting our demise. I was wondering if the drinks here contained alcohol, or was that against the rules in the Afterlife? Did we need to be holier than thou?

The Pedestal was an artist's space, a nightclub in feel. Candlelight flickered from tables, accenting its distinct cast of creative types. Inspired conversation and polite small talk could be vaguely heard around the room. A fusion of sandalwood from burning wax, and other faint perfumes wafted past us. Diner-style booths graced the walls to the sides, as mismatched furniture in leather, denim, and assorted fabrics fought for attention. This varied seating arrangement littered about two-thirds of the available space, leaving a drink-stained bar to one side and a cozy dance floor and stage at the front. The performance space also featured a pair of those hideous red velvet curtains pushed to the sides.

But the main focus on stage was an eye-catching dark-skinned woman in a pin-striped man's suit. She was introduced as Nellie by one of her jazz band. This statuesque figure held her microphone as if it were some sultry extension of her body. Her soulful lips emitted a tone that could melt chocolate.

As she sang, a young lady in burlesque attire stood captivated in front of the stage, mouthing her lyrics. Nothing could mistake her glance—she was a lesbian waiting to happen. We perched ourselves at the bar, where next to us a woman in her late thirties gazed longingly at the barman as he poured a glass of red wine.

"Please keep the change. Just give me the look of love," she uttered as the barman grinned flirtatiously. It seemed a strange comment as I didn't see any exchange of currency.

"This place? Shabby or charming?" I asked Warwick.

"Charming, in a shabby sort of way."

Within this short space of time, there'd been a lot to take in. Two strangers posing as new friends leading us from ostentatious opulence to mix-and-match glam. If my friend was as guarded as I was, he definitely was not making it known.

I spotted several framed portrait shots hung between faded theatrical posters at the back of the club. Cheesy smiles and forlorn looks graced those faces. Some posters looked like cut-and-paste montages for school plays, while others embraced graphic concepts so out there, you'd swear Salvador Dali had set up a studio nearby. Elsewhere, this charismatic ad hoc décor laced with local creative types would have put me at ease.

"Warwick, look over there." I pointed to the booths. "That petite old Korean woman. She's arguing with her son." My friend squinted to focus.

"I think that's her boy-toy," said Samantha. "She's with a different one every time I see her."

"She has good taste in her vices," I replied. "Who is she?"

"Some extraordinary old star waiting to be rediscovered."

"Obscurity agrees with her."

I found solace in examining the characters around us. Not all of them looked like your average theater crowd. There was a sprinkling of actor-types wearing flashy clothes, and a middle-aged plump woman taking notes for what I assumed to be her next role.

Among the non-thespian crowd were two tree huggers solving the world's problems while sharing herbal cigarettes. Another hippie, who already had his share of smoke, danced like an epileptic octopus on valium, interpreting a beat only known to himself.

I was studying ghostly souls, a thought that started to unnerve me again, so I followed Warwick's lead to discover more about our hosts.

"Do you ever not like who comes through the door?" I asked.

"There was an old fortune-teller with a pet snake," moaned Samantha. "She freaked out as soon as she saw Guy."

"She screamed at me!" added Guy, shuddering.

"Nothing she had foreseen prepared her for this place."

"She just couldn't cope with life. That's what happens when you live alone for too long."

"But she *had* her pet snake," said Samantha, raising a brow.

"Where is she now?" Warwick asked.

"She finally found inner peace when an old friend arrived."

"Speaking of inner peace," I said, "where will we be staying?"

"That's all in hand," replied Samantha. "For now, just enjoy yourselves. We'll show you to your rooms later."

A metallic body clanked across the dance floor.

"Warwick, Roman gladiator at three o'clock. Overdone?"

Warwick studied the armored visitor, then made his assessment. "Maybe he's historically accurate?"

His assumption unsettled me. Had this soldier been wandering around aimlessly for centuries?

"Warwick," I whispered. "What's going on here?"

"Like I'm supposed to know?" he replied. The ancient warrior's armory squeaked as he took his seat. "It's like we're in a time-travel movie. But the only difference is the angel. A *real* live angel."

"I'd expect Bibles at the bar," I said. A small flame glowed from the corner. The toy-boy was lighting a cigarette for the Korean cougar. "What about her for instance? The priest would wash his *own* mouth out with soap after *her* confessional."

"Maybe God's not as judgmental as we think," Warwick replied.

"Or Buddha or Ganesha or whoever?"

"Maybe there's a VIP room where they all sit around chilling out?"

"Yeah, they spend their days singing religious chants with Krishna on honky-tonk piano."

Warwick smiled. He was usually the expert in not getting his feathers ruffled while I often grappled with the world, but in this instance, we both needed reassurance.

Only three days ago, he was prescribing this holiday while I was dealing with my own personal dramas. Warwick was making me a perfect cup of peppermint tea. He stood, devoted to this task, while I was mesmerized by his supple latte-colored skin. He looked as inviting as the homemade lime cheesecake that sat under glass on our kitchen bench. Which would be tastier? Maybe I could have the two of them at the same time? One bite here, one nibble there. When he mentioned a visit to my uncle, I dispensed with the fantasies, then looked up as he handed me my tea. But that was three days ago when the world made sense. Now we were guest-starring in a surreal reality show. If Samantha had broken into song or Guy morphed into a reptile, it wouldn't have dumbfounded me at this point.

"Are we staying here forever?" Warwick asked our hosts.

"Not necessarily. Stay for as long as you like," answered Samantha.

Her words only puzzled me more. Life was easier when there was just lime cheesecake to consider.

"So at some stage, are we going to return home?" I asked.

"Just think of it as a holiday, pet. Stay as long as you need to."

Nellie's crooning began washing over me like a comforting embrace, or maybe it was just the vodka and cranberry juice. The liquid additive was definitely diminishing my fears. Around me contented beings swayed to the singer's hum. She was the hypnotist, and they were captured by her trance.

"As much as I try, I just can't *get* jazz," said Guy in a hushed tone.

"You don't realize what you're missing," I replied.

A rousing applause followed. The saxophone's gentle notes invited us to free our concerns. The soothing voice of the large bass seduced us as the cheeky piano held us captive with its prearranged melody. Soon the cheerful flute made us ready to play. I was drunk, and jazz was now my mistress.

When I focused back on Warwick and our hosts, I noticed that Guy had gone to chat with a handsome man slouched on a formal coffee-colored sofa.

Warwick began moving his hips on the barstool, bopping around like a dazed Eurovision diva. Alcohol had definitely taken hold. Whenever he got like this, I had an evil desire to stick fake eyelashes on him, just to watch them flutter.

Shortly after, Guy returned with his friend. In this informal atmosphere, only Guy looked out of place. Maybe angels were not supposed to surrender to sensual pleasures like music? Before introductions were made, I asked about his deficient jazz gene.

"Why don't you like Nellie and her band?"

"I like songs," he replied. "Melodic songs. The band is okay, but they're not my taste."

This angel needed an injection of *cool*, unlike his handsome companion. I was a sucker for polo-neck jumpers, which his friend harmonized with a leather jacket and corduroy jeans. All in basic black. Color-wise, it was a lazy mix-and-match job. But who was I to argue as I was drawn into his hazel eyes and lips that were moist, rosy, and imminently kissable.

"Warwick, Allan, meet Pedro," said Guy. "You're going to share the stage with him."

I examined this man, hoping to share more than just the stage.

"He's even written the piece you're going to perform," said Samantha.

"Obviously, a man of many talents." I listed his possible abilities in my head.

"It's just something I've been working on," Pedro said in a faded American accent.

"And how long have you been working on it?" I asked.

"Since the 1920s."

"Really?" Had I just caught onto the one advantage of our fate? This man was thirty-something surely, while that Roman gladiator still looked buffed. Everyone who ends up here must stop aging. I glanced at Warwick, grinning like a faded movie star who'd found a discount plastic surgeon.

"Yes, the roaring twenties," explained Samantha. "That's when this delightful young man stumbled here from New York."

"Good thing too. I was penniless. I lived with rats in moldy public housing. I even gave gangster names to the two rats that slept by my bedside. Mr. Money and Mr. Death."

"Come on, Pedro, it wasn't that bad."

The writer was embellishing. He recognized he had a captive audience.

"Okay. It's true about the rats, but I had lots of friends, and lots of friends with cocaine to help me keep my sanity. My string of affairs helped me survive without a blanket. In between real life, I wrote. Mostly one-act plays about cheerful things, like alcoholic street workers and murderous cops. One of my plays was even performed at a chic uptown party."

"What was it about?" I asked.

"The night Santa was kidnapped."

"For his toys?"

"Yes. Knife-wielding youngsters set a bear trap down their chimney." A sinister grin spread over his face. "And Rudolph was served with mashed potatoes and corn."

"A lovely venison meal."

"That glowed in the dark. No candlelight needed!"

"You must have found fame after that?" I admired his originality.

"No, not really. It was a Christmas gathering. Mrs. Simpson made sure I was never recommended to any in her circle after she swore I made her die of embarrassment."

"But you're about to take the lead in your newly penned work," announced Samantha.

"What's it about?" I asked.

"It's based on the rats I shared my flat with."

Nellie introduced her next number. The raucous improvisation made it difficult to converse, so I closed my eyes. My mind and my tapping foot were taking pleasure in my own solitary nirvana. The saxophone randomly voiced its frustrations. In a jumble of emotion, I felt it scream out for liberty before it wallowed back into its comfort zone. Next, the clarinet took flight. With sharp notes, it took for granted what the saxophone was yearning for. I opened my eyes.

Pedro had returned to his comfy sofa. His eyes were closed as his head and shoulders swayed in rhythm and his hand slapped his knee in time. Warwick and Samantha had joined him on the couch, and after sharing a few words, they too copied his seated dance.

I also began to sway and turned to Guy to share in this infectious beat. He looked back at me as if I needed a toilet. I effortlessly moved my arms as if I was dancing with an invisible partner. He just shook his head like I was an idiot. This angel was no jazz fan, so I decided to converse instead.

"It must be marvelous to be able to fly."

Guy paused for a second, then answered, "I wouldn't know." He bit his bottom lip again, before the sides of his mouth pushed nervously into his cheeks.

"Am I asking you about something you don't want to talk about?"

"I wasn't brought up by my parents, so I never learned. I'm an orphan."

I wanted to ask more but chose to wait until he volunteered the information. I had a wicked urge to ask if he was hatched or delivered the normal way.

Nellie was now in torch-song mode, and the admirer who had been mouthing her words earlier patiently waited with the hippies. From where we were perched, we could take in the aroma of their joint. Recollections of Amsterdam were interrupted by the angel's decision to open up.

"I was brought up by my auntie Jemima. She wasn't really my auntie as she didn't have wings, but it wasn't until I was a teenager that I put two and two together and realized we weren't related."

"So who are your real parents?"

"I don't know. I had a fantasy about my father being some brave dragon slayer, while my mum would be some mystical woman, in love with life. I dreamt that she would return and show me the joy in everyday things. Aunty Jem was fascinated with other people, and I never realized at the time how special that was. I appreciate it now."

"So wasn't there anyone else who could teach you to fly?"

Guy took a mouthful from his wine glass before easing into his tale.

"I had a friend named Joshua who tried to teach me to fly, but I was too scared to learn. Everyone admired his spectacular black wings. He was always dying his hair, sometimes a white blond, sometimes golden, and to me this was daring.

"One day we walked toward a cliff, side by side with arms outstretched, hands on each other's shoulders. This was his way of forcing me to fly. We stepped over, and I flapped frantically. A couple of times I was able to keep his pace and fly beside him, but I kept losing altitude and dangled below as he tried to hold onto me. After a while he gave up, landing us both on the ground. We spent a bit more time together that day, but after that, we just drifted apart. I never understood why, and I never asked."

There was an awkward silence as I wondered if Joshua was a lover. Guy had bared his soul and seemed to be avoiding any more conversation on the subject, and as much as I wanted to, I knew I shouldn't ask. I didn't need to. Another sip for strength and the winged one continued.

"I knew almost everyone where we lived, but I really didn't connect. I just watched my life go by, not living it. I craved for things like a friend, or a lover, but when they didn't appear in exactly the way I expected them, I didn't develop the relationship."

Guy stopped at this point. Nellie was taking a break while her band played up-tempo lounge music. Warwick, Samantha, and Pedro were in animated conversation. Pedro sat self-assured as Samantha slouched in alcoholic bliss. Warwick was all arm gestures, almost communicating with the deaf.

"You like your friend, don't you?" asked Guy.

"He knows what to say to keep me serene. Like you, I've always tried to control things. I'm learning to let go and fall without the parachute."

"That's not what I meant, Allan. Of course you like your friend; otherwise he wouldn't be your friend. But you'd like to be *more* than just friends; that much is obvious."

I didn't answer. I had been exposed.

Aware of how I felt, the angel placed his hand on mine and waited for me to continue.

"Warwick and I met at work in our under-stimulating public service jobs about a year ago. We clicked immediately and enjoyed long lunch hours to alleviate the boredom. We socialized, met each other's friends, then shortly after we moved in together. Our flat became Grand Central Station, as people would drop in with drinks or other social additives. We enjoyed what life had to offer.

"Then came the week from hell! Warwick had the flu, and I was simply burnt out. I crashed in bed and didn't raise my head unless my stomach rumbled. That was six months ago, so we decided there was only one solution. A sea change!

"We moved our public service jobs to Port Macquarie and tried to slow down. It was like *The Golden Girls* but with half the polyester, and our feet nowhere near the grave. The chemical additives stopped, but champagne became the substitute. Our city posse was replaced by our regional mob, and those fabulous parties started up again.

"Maybe it was the salt air that cleared my thinking in between hangovers, but over that time, I found myself viewing Warwick in a different light. The thoughts were subtle at first. A simple caress from his waist to his shoulders. An impulsive beard rub to the back of his neck. But over time, full cinemascope scenarios barged in during routine tasks.

"One night, while cooking Peruvian curried chicken, I envisioned Warwick entering the kitchen wearing nothing more than a white apron. He'd saunter over to check if I had enough spice. Once while polishing the furniture, I imagined him placing one hand on mine, assisting me in rubbing in the oil. These circular motions would reduce, as we found more appealing places to rub. I won't even tell you what vacuuming the apartment conjured up."

By Guy's wry smile, I knew he understood exactly what I was talking about. I had learned nothing about Joshua, but Guy was discovering all there was to know about my unrequited passions.

"Then there were *those* moments. Times when I thought fantasy would become reality. Three months ago, we were celebrating the news of our friends' engagement at our favorite little drinking establishment. Warwick and I had plastered ourselves with a blend of orange liqueur, soda, and lime. Curtis and Carmel were equally soaked as we kept raising glasses to an endless supply of causes. We toasted Port Macquarie, a milder lifestyle, and possibly every individual grain of sand on the beach. As the lovebirds gradually overlooked our presence, they began to demonstrate the foreplay that led to the proposal. We were convinced theirs was a shotgun wedding, and this was a reenactment of how they got into this predicament.

"We left our soft-porn friends at the pub and staggered home where, although the details are sketchy thanks to alcohol-induced amnesia, we both rested in my bed. We cuddled the way friends do when inhibition is laid to rest. He positioned his head on my chest. With sleep being the last thing on my mind, I kissed his scalp and caressed his neck. The scent of faded cologne reminded me of how much I had come to appreciate his distinctive tastes. The smart jacket draped on my bedpost would never be out of vogue. The burgundy shirt, which was half-unbuttoned, spoke elegance and style. I guided my hand under the shirt and caressed his defined torso. His silky chest hairs helped my fingers slide over his upper body. He wriggled briefly in that endearing way people do to gesture that they like what you're doing."

Guy quickly ordered another glass of wine while I shared the sordid details.

"I wish I could tell you that the yoga classes we had been taking came in handy. The term 'downward dog' may have had a new meaning. Frankly, I don't remember. I woke several hours later, head feeling like a battered boxer down for the count, but with Warwick still in position. I didn't move. I concluded that we didn't do it and prayed that I wouldn't throw up."

For a moment, I felt I had said too much. Guy was staring past me in the direction of our other companions. I swiveled on my barstool and watched Samantha wander back to us. Beyond her, though, another story was unfolding. With intense fervor, my friend and the brooding writer were sharing saliva. As I scrutinized their kiss, I was more taken back by Warwick's uncharacteristic display of public affection than the desire to take Pedro's place.

In one word, Guy summed up my emotion. With his hand still on mine, he squeezed, then simply said, "Ouch!"

TWO

I SPRAWLED OUT on the plush red sofa, gazing at the antique harlequin money box in the display cabinet. Samantha and Guy had shown me to our lodgings the night before, sadly without Warwick, and my erratic sleep patterns put me in a zombielike state.

This apartment was almost a match for our rental back in Port Macquarie. A fusion of subdued primary colors coated the walls in the living space, making way for bolder pigments in the bedrooms. Vintage and modern ornaments sparked curiosity amid the classic furniture. A glass devil dancing on one leg, a bronze cubist sculpture, and cheeky Norman Lindsey prints celebrating old-world Eros were near perfect matches for collectables we had at home.

In renovation terms, it was "grandmother meets gay boy." Its welcoming décor could include a cultured old woman working on a crossword, with her grandson seated next to her checking out male models in *Cosmopolitan*. The crisp aroma of Beef Wellington, which either might have prepared, would fill the room.

Seeing this carbon copy of our home gave me a fresh perspective on our tastes. I couldn't wait to hear Warwick's view. Without him there, I felt something was missing. Fearful thoughts that our friendship would dissolve echoed in my head. When I needed a companion to deal with this strange adventure, my spirit would be void of his comfort. I wanted to hear his reassuring voice in all its theatrical tones. I missed seeing his glossy, curly black hair and noticing how tight those little ringlets were. I wanted to admire his light brown skin and his alluring dark brown eyes enhanced by the furnishings.

I kept telling myself that I had no right to be jealous. After all, if the shoe was on the other foot, I'd have whisked Pedro's clothes off him so fast he'd be in danger of a nosebleed. Even the harlequin figurine glared at pathetic me. I closed my eyes and focused on the events of the past day. We couldn't have landed ourselves in a campier setting if we tried. A saucy blonde, a gay angel, and a set to rival any Hollywood epic. Then, within minutes, a trip to a club with a sultry drag king. Throw in the Ziegfeld Follies and this truly would be heaven!

I cast my mind back to the beginning of this adventure. The details seemed sketchy for a moment, even though they had happened just a few days ago. It was like trying to remember the details of a dream from the night before. The longer you are awake, the more the dream fades.

I recalled three days ago, Warwick handed me a cup of peppermint tea he had prepared with loving care. "You know, Mr. Incompetent is getting you down at the moment. You need to stop waiting for your fortunes to change. Allan, you need freedom!"

There was silence. His luscious maroon lips had a point. I let his words sink in. Here was an opportunity to not only break the monotony but to chill out with my friend. Perhaps taste those luscious lips. It was time to be selfish.

In a world where work opportunities were limited, I was putting up with an insecure baby boomer. He was the type of boss who came from the "if it ain't broke, don't fix it" school. No promotions meant no hassles. Loyalty was a foreign concept, unless aimed at the endless string of nubile under-twenty-ones he'd hire for jobs that didn't exist.

"What do I tell Mr. Incompetent? I can't just march in there and say I'm having a holiday!"

I could see it. His assistant, Natalie, in that pink breast-hugging jumper of hers, sitting on his desk, legs crossed, and notepad poised. She'd carefully trace the tip of her tongue around the shape of her mouth. I'd make my demands, standing over him, while his downstairs stirrings would make him too self-conscious to stand up. Natalie would have no trouble in helping me set this up, if only I had the guts to play out my rebellious fantasies.

"Allan, you could be a coward and just not show up for work. After all, your uncle has been complaining that you've never visited him since he moved away." Warwick paused to let his words sink in. Then came his demand. "Come on, let's leave today!"

I tended to plan every aspect of my life, not always achieving the results I expected. So what if I didn't arrive at work? I looked up at Warwick who was verbally going over what to pack. My internal argument was about to be resolved externally. We went to his bedroom where he unzipped his favorite navy sports bag and slid open his wardrobe. I contemplated the temperature down south. Deciding that clothes for all types of weather might be best, I followed his lead and charged to my own bedroom. My much-loved black suitcase was flung onto my bed as I took pride on my first radical deed since I had rigged my sister's pregnancy kit to reveal a positive result.

ALTHOUGH I WAS snoozing, some part of my brain zeroed in on the sound of a key jiggling around in a lock. My subconscious was spying on Warwick. Samantha or Guy must have caught up with him to give him a key. As the doorknob turned, I checked the room for a magazine or book, anything to obscure the fact that I'd just woken up. Nothing. It was time to stare at that harlequin again.

"What are you looking at?" asked Warwick. He strode cocksure into the lounge.

"An antique money box."

He went to pick it up. As with the one back home, he needed both hands to raise it, as the nineteenth-century child who might have owned it could never lift its weight. Its painted metal surface had become lackluster over the years. The harlequin smirked as if keeping a wicked secret. Maybe he was having a torrid affair with the bearded lady? Perhaps he'd given her hair remover disguised as beauty cream? Whatever the reason, his spirited smile intrigued me.

"That's almost like the one you bought in New Zealand," Warwick said.

His gaze guardedly scanned the living area right before his head turned to follow its lead. He let out a nervous sigh while numbly pointing at various items in the room.

"What the...?" he mumbled.

"That's what I said twelve hours ago," I replied. "Come check out the antique in the dining room."

Warwick wandered over to a gramophone. He had one just like it back home, which we affectionately christened Edgar. He commented in disbelief about it having the same 78-rpm record on the platter we often displayed—"Island in the Sun" by Harry Belafonte.

"What do you make of it?" he asked.

"Spooky," I replied. "And that's not the half of it. There's a laptop with the same video-editing software I was thinking of buying, and a video camera similar to mine. There's even more weird stuff in our bedrooms."

As I led him to my room, he noticed several other items that matched the décor in our rental back home. His modern surrealist pictures hanging in the hallway and the wood grain doors with brass doorknobs all raised disturbed remarks. Even the kitchen with its burnt-orange tiles and aged-ash cupboards were doing their best to stop us from feeling homesick.

I made my way to my wardrobe and presented exhibit A, a black shirt with a Chinese collar. It didn't button up in the middle. The buttons were to the right of the shirt and worked their way up to a scarlet triangular flap. This meant nothing to Warwick, but I explained that it was like one I'd been given as a teenager. I had a fascination with 80s new-wave bands like the Models, Deckchairs Overboard, and Japan, so a neighbor had made it for me. Now and again it came out to parties.

My next exhibit was recognized instantly. A hand-me-down checkered western shirt from my brother. He didn't fit into it anymore, so Warwick and I often took turns wearing it. A gray-and-white knitted beanie was next on display. A friend had knitted this for me as a gift for letting him stay over when he was in town. How it had made its way to our modest 1970s-replica style apartment in the Limelight Quarter stumped us both.

Warwick darted to his bedroom as I followed. His heavyset wooden bed was an accurate match, except for the color of the lacquer. Back home it was a deep mahogany; here it was maple. At least the Afterlife spies got some things wrong when they decked out this place. However, his classic black leather jacket was displayed prominently in front of all other garments, exactly as he'd left it days ago before our trip. As he thumbed through his much-loved attire, he uttered several unrelated vowels before sitting on his bed.

"I've had a whole evening to get used to it," I said. I perched myself next to him. "But last night when Guy and Samantha showed me around, my head was spinning."

"What else is there?"

"Most of your pots and pans. Almost all my music collection. But to cap it off, my digital photos are in an album in my bedroom."

I left Warwick and fetched them before jumping back on his bed. As soon as I turned the cover, the images haunted me as much as they did the previous night. We peered at artistic monochrome shots of chess pieces taken for high school art class. There were family party photos featuring childhood versions of my now married brother. Some publicity shots from my high school play. An old lover. An old friend. An old friend who became a lover. A photo-booth strip of my sister and I making each other laugh.

By the time we found the images of Gary's hospital-emergency-themed party near its back pages, Warwick recovered his composure. He placed his hand on my knee, but I was self-conscious at how clammy I was. Seeing these pictures again unnerved me. Had someone broken into my home and reviewed my life by printing my photos?

Loser? Artistic wannabe? What would they have thought?

Warwick looked up and smiled. I wanted to savor his maroon lips. Their sheen was highlighted against the claret-colored wall. I wanted to reach behind his head and slide my fingers through his thick curly hair, before leisurely moving his lips to mine.

"I'm astounded!" he said.

I paused my daydream to compute what he'd uttered.

"Reassuringly 'feels like home' astounded, or unnervingly 'what the frig' astounded?"

"More like 'stunned, I need answers but not jumping to conclusions' astounded."

"Warwick, at this stage, we have no choice but to jump to conclusions. Where are we?"

"In the Limelight Quarter," he replied, blank-faced.

"Very funny. You know what I mean."

My friend wandered to the window. I watched him, unrealistically believing he could give me all the answers. He viewed the flourishing garden outside before turning to me.

"They all seem secretive," he said. "The only answer I seem to get from people is the Limelight Quarter. I don't feel we're in danger, though."

"What choice do we have? After bonding with Guy last night, I feel pretty safe, too."

"I guess it makes sense to find comfort in an angel. He's the only one who has to be a true local."

"Comfort, yes; answers, no."

"Allan, I thought you'd find him sort of a geek. He's a bit, Gomer Pyle. When we first got here, you were admiring Samantha's outfit and gawking at Guy's."

There was not much I could keep secret from Warwick.

"Okay, I did at first, but you left me so I had to get to know him. In some ways, he reminded me of what I was like when you first met me. A bit of a lost soul. Our chat helped take my mind off this bizarre place."

"Yes, Allan, I went home with Pedro to take my mind off this *bizarre place.*"

That repeated phrase reverberated in my head. I stared at Warwick. He stared back. The thought of my demise was hard enough to face, but this version of the Afterlife with no link back to concepts favored in religious texts made it harder to accept. There was not an omnipotent being in sight. We had one angel surrounded by a cast from different eras of earthbound time, going about their business with no qualms. And still, no one wanted to elaborate.

"Heaven or hell?" my friend asked.

"Perhaps limbo, or maybe we're just having a weird dream?"

"Of course, Allan, at exactly the same time." Warwick winked at me.

"Yeah maybe. Your wet dream with Pedro and my, my..."

"Your buddy-genre dream with an angel."

He made me smile. As he looked out at the garden again, a more believable explanation came to me.

"Warwick, maybe I'm just in a coma, and somewhere near my hospital bed, you're talking to me, trying to wake me up."

"Allan, if I am talking to you from your hospital bed, how will I know you can hear me?"

"Look, Warwick, I'm wiggling my toes."

My friend turned to see me lift my legs and shake both feet.

"Allan, what if you're covered by a blanket, and I can't notice your toes?"

"Don't be silly. You'd notice my toes wiggling under the covers."

"Maybe there's a serving tray or a hospital chart on the sheets?"

I thrashed my legs more violently, just in case there was some truth in my theory.

"Allan, you're not in a coma."

"How can you be sure?"

"Because from my point of view, I might be the one in a coma."

My legs stopped kicking.

"Warwick, either way we should keep conversing, so no one ends up pulling the plug from our life support."

A chill ran up my spine. I looked past my friend to glimpse the garden outside. It flourished with an assortment of trees and bushes, all leafy and in full bloom. Dark purple flowers blossomed in several makeshift pots, welcoming visitors who wandered along the brick pathway leading to the building. I pictured a lion and a lamb taking in the scent of the buds before regarding each other with kindness and lying on the grass. As serene as this thought was, it did little to pacify me. Warwick came back to the bed and sat beside me.

"There's going to be a lot to get used to from now on," he said.

I nodded. "If that's the case, Warwick, I have something else for us to get used to." I raced to my bedroom, grabbed a makeshift bound manuscript, and returned. "This is Pedro's script. There's a copy for you in my room as well."

"What's it about?"

"A team of gangsters trying to outwit each other. One of them wants to become a partner in a lucrative moonshine business. You're playing the head gangster's moll."

Warwick looked as if our landlord had just burst in for a surprise inspection.

"Well, okay. I always pictured myself as RuPaul. So what else do we need to get used to?"

"I read through the first few pages last night before going to bed." I thumbed through the script to show him the page I was up to. "This morning, while I was getting dressed in front of the mirror, I recited those lines."

"You mean with the script in your hands?"

"No. I read this once last night. Today, I remembered the lines as clearly as if I was reading them off the page."

"If only you could've done that with our theater society back home." Warwick was right. I usually paraphrased and was grateful if the director didn't mind. "What's Pedro like as a wordsmith?"

"His play is corny as all hell, but hopefully it's meant to be. What's Pedro like as a lover?"

"Maybe a two-star rating out of five. His equipment reminds me of a turtle retreating into its shell."

"You could always coax it back out with a lettuce leaf," I replied. I knew this would be territory Warwick wouldn't be keen to revisit. "So was he devoid of passion?"

"Oh, he's passionate, but not in the bedroom. Foreplay is A-plus, but coming up with the goods, C-minus."

"A bit like his script. What do you make of Samantha? Simply sex kitten, or is there more to her?"

"Well, she's definitely in charge around here. At least she is with the people we've met. I think there's a side of her we've yet to discover. What about Guy? Self-doubting angel or mystery man?"

"There's definitely something mysterious about him. I've found out a lot. He's more open when he has a few drinks, and somehow more attractive as well. Or maybe he just gets more attractive when I've had a few. There was a revelation in our discussion at the bar."

"Do tell."

"He can't fly."

"That explains his lack of confidence."

"Yes, he tries to mask that, but it results in him looking uptight."

We smiled, soon becoming absorbed in our own private thoughts. The way friends do when they know each other well enough to just be still. I mused over the Roman gladiator I'd been admiring the day before. How interesting it would be to chat with him about his life.

Warwick placed his hand on mine. I felt coy and prayed I wasn't blushing. I reached over with my other hand and placed it on top. He wriggled his hand, sliding it away. My heart sank, surprising me. Had I overstepped the mark? He picked up his script and flicked through the pages.

"Who do you play?" he asked.

"I play Mr. Money, the gangster who's trying to muscle in on Pedro's empire. He plays the lead, Mr. Death." For a moment, I considered whether to ask my next question, but it fell out of my mouth of its own accord. "Do you think you'll revisit Pedro, in the biblical sense?"

"Only if I'm desperate. Who knows, maybe *you* can find a way to light his fire?"

This idea didn't entice me to the extent it had the day before. For the rest of the afternoon, we retired to the lounge and learned our lines. One reading pretty much did the trick, but between scenes, my private thoughts became fixated on my overdue romance. Maybe his interlude with Pedro was my wake-up call? Memories of the last few days on earth were flooding back. My mood had been similar just before our visit to Uncle Bryant. Like some lost puppy dog on a busy road, too scared to make a move in any direction, hoping someone would come and claim me.

I usually wasn't keen to visit family when I wanted a proper break, but Warwick felt I had to reconnect with my mob before we spent time alone. If truth be known, he could have suggested anything by that stage, and I would have blindly followed to avoid routine. A flight on a space shuttle? Sure! I'll sell my siblings for the tickets.

*

Uncle Bryant was one of the more blessed members of our family, having won a large amount of money with a lottery ticket given to him for his birthday just three years prior. After the win, he chose an upmarket relocation. Why a bachelor of his vintage needed a penthouse was beyond our family's understanding, except maybe to fuel his addiction to clutter.

The smell of musty books permeated the living area. There were piles of them on makeshift bookshelves, of which about half of them my uncle admitted he hadn't read. He always claimed he had some obscure job to do around the apartment that prevented him from sitting still and reading. But it never stopped him trawling through secondhand bookshops.

Anywhere else, this décor would look appropriate in an attic. Old board games and train sets I'd swear had never been played with. Archival documents stacked on top of an early color telly that stood proudly on its own wooden legs. A 1960s portable record player sat with its lid open, playing the LP of an AM-radio-inspired soft-rock band.

I didn't want to look too closely at the cornices in case there were insects trapped in spider webs, begging to be devoured just to escape the sight of this dust trap.

There were also five cats, Misty, Fred, Lipton, Sam, and Pike, and one goldfish he forgot to name. My uncle often had to replace his goldfish if he overlooked feeding the cats, but fortunately his cats were now too old to climb onto the shelf where this new fish looked out at the world.

The other notable newcomer in Uncle Bryant's apartment was an elderly woman elegantly poised on the tan upholstered sofa. She was introduced as Pamela, the retired poet. Pamela lived in a small flat downstairs and often visited for company. In front of her was half a cup of tea and the remains of a slice of homemade carrot cake.

"How long are you planning on staying?" asked my uncle. He always claimed guests are like fish. They go off after three days.

"Not long," Warwick replied. "Allan has this odd desire to visit Adelaide."

"Why? It's a country town with its own miniature Melbourne in the CBD. You moved to Port Macquarie! Aren't you sick of small towns?"

Pamela came to my rescue. "But there's a sense of the creative in Adelaide." Uncle Bryant lifted his head and passively looked to the ceiling. "Oh sweetheart, I know that look. Just because I don't agree with you doesn't mean that you'll ration our hanky-panky."

"True. I wouldn't survive. I'm more of an Errol Flynn than a—"

"Please, let's not go there," I said. "Now my other choice is Hobart. We've never been there." Luckily neither had our hosts, so no debate was entered into. "We were wondering if we could leave the car here, fly over, and come back later."

"Absolutely. I have a spare car space. Pamela insists on driving me everywhere."

"Bryant, tell them where your car is."

My uncle hesitated, then informed us that he sold his trusty old Ford Falcon.

"And tell them why you sold it." This time no reply, so Pamela filled us in. "He can't see."

"I can see!"

"Just not very well."

"I can see what I need to see!"

Pamela then mouthed the words "license renewal," shaking her head. The problem was, my uncle was old-school. He came from a generation that would rather die than wear glasses.

This affectionate banter entertained us for the rest of the evening. Between cups of tea and slices of carrot cake, we heard all about Bryant and Pamela's love in bloom. They first met in the elevator, comparing groceries and chitchatting about prices. Pamela had bought three T-bone steaks on special, but my uncle still felt she was ripped off. He recommended his little Greek butcher just down the road a few blocks, next to the funeral home. The retired poet shrieked in horror at the cost of Bryant's leg of lamb and swore with hand on heart that her Polish butcher was cheaper. And so began a romance. Taking turns to cook meals, it was my uncle's honeyed carrots that initiated the courtship. One taste and she was under his spell.

We listened to their story, glancing at each other with wry smiles as each absurd twist of their culinary courtship unfolded. Maybe there was a lesson to be learned from them? Maybe food was *our* missing sensual ingredient? I made a mental note to rush to the supermarket once we arrived in Hobart.

Conversation continued through dinner, ironically take-away. In that time, Pamela graced us with a few recitals including "Ode to Honey Dipped Carrot," "T-Bone Teaser," and "The Love Butcher." The latter was ripe for a theater restaurant, with dubious references to rump steak and marinated heart. It was soon after this rendition that she dropped the "clanger."

To me, it felt like the sky had fallen. It tumbled so effortlessly from her tongue, it simulated polite conversation. There was no consumption of alcohol to blame for this error in judgment.

With a straightforward glance, summing us both up, she inquired, "So, are you two shagging?"

I turned to my uncle, expecting him to set his lover straight. Warwick emulated my plea. Bryant and Pamela beamed like drunken newlyweds before he asked, "Well, are you? If you're not, it's about time you did!"

THREE

I TRIED TO dress in a fashion that matched my temperament. A T-shirt covered with the craters of the moon meant that I was in "creative mode," and Warwick knew how to handle the anxieties of this "artist at work."

Through one of the velvet-clad entrances of the room we first encountered was a large theater. The seats, the floor, the walls, and the ceiling were all a dazzling white. A giant scarlet curtain with black trimming was the only splash of color, besides the newly enlisted thespians. How this theater stayed spotless was beyond me.

"Ostentatious or elegant?" I asked although my question was redundant. I liked it.

"White seats, red curtain. It's like rows of teeth facing a giant tongue, and we're the bits of food waiting to be flossed."

"I've always wanted to perform on a stage like this," I confessed.

"Me too," replied Pedro from the front row of seats.

He turned and smiled at both of us, so Warwick strolled over to chat. It was the polite thing to do. At least that's what I told myself. Inside, I felt as isolated as an Oscar nominee who didn't win. Guy crept over. I assured him all was okay, and that there weren't any real fireworks between my best friend and the writer. Samantha was there as well, although not in the role of director as I'd assumed from our chat at the Pedestal. That honor went to a middle-aged woman named Maudi.

She was an old-world actress from London's Gaiety Theatre, back in the nineteenth century. She sported an ankle-length hooped dress in pastel blue and stood in front of the stage with her arms gently crossed, as still as a statue. Soon she made her way to a desk to the right of the stage, pulled out the chair, which had a blue parasol hanging from its back, and sat. She then thumbed through a glossy magazine, aptly titled *The Stage Door*.

I took this action to mean that we were wasting her time, so I sat in the second row. The rest of the cast followed.

"Now, now, fellow performers," she declared while clapping three times in quick succession. "I trust that you've all read the script. Of course I know *you* have, Pedro." We all nodded. "Well then, I want you to each give me one word that describes your character."

I was first, and after careful analysis of Mr. Money, I decided that he was "apprehensive." Warwick was next, believing his gangster's moll, Betty, was "caring." Samantha thought of her loving streetwalker as "devoted." Pedro described Mr. Death as "calculating," while Guy saw his henchman persona, Bullet, as "spineless."

"Now don't forget, my dears, that one word you've each given me is not all that your character is. Everyone is a walking contradiction, and so are the people you are playing. They may face the world with their one characteristic mask, but behind that mask are many complexities. Everyone exhibits subtext!"

We began a reading of the play. I was in my comfort zone. My unrequited passions, my pangs of jealousy, and my confusion over what the heck the Afterlife was about all seemed so distant. As if I was moving on. Of course, I knew this wasn't true, but for the duration of this line run, I'd be suspended in time from my worries, working toward a goal I had the skills to accomplish. I was back in control.

Warwick sounded like a cartoon hyena on heat as he tried his best falsetto voice to give life to Betty. We all attempted Bronx accents to fit the piece. Then it was time to block the play on stage. Again, I was dumbfounded at how easy it was to remember my moves. By the second run-through, we were all on automatic pilot when it came to stage business.

*

Crafted between plotlines of wheeling and dealing, Pedro's Mr. Death meets the kindhearted streetwalker played by Samantha in the first act. They start flirting. Warwick's Betty has always been loyal, waiting patiently for Mr. Death to make an honest woman of her for years. In the second act, Mr. Death comes clean to Betty.

"You know, Poopsie, I always loved the way your eyes twinkle when there's a full moon," says Betty played by Warwick, trying to seductively swing his hips as he enters Mr. Death's den. "I always look forward to the tiger within you, holding me down and making me a woman!"

I had trouble keeping a straight face at the lame dialogue, but having the words spoken by my best friend added a comedic touch that made it bearable.

"I have a confession to make, Doll," Mr. Death announces. "I've been seeing someone else." Pedro's melodramatic arm gestures could have landed a plane.

"Oh baby, don't kid me."

"No, darling. I'm not kidding. I'm a cad. A hopeless Casanova. An unfaithful brute."

Momentary silence as Betty takes in the news. With no verbal response from her, Mr. Death decides to continue his reasoning.

"Darlin', you're too good for me. You stay by my side. You support me. You're there when I need you. What is it you see in me?"

"I see a man who needs love. More than anything else in this world, I see a man who needs love."

"But you can do better than me. What good is a man who might be in jail, or worse still, dead!"

"Poopsie, even dead, I don't think I would ever leave you!"

Betty swings herself toward the door, stage right, and exits. At this point of the play, reality hasn't quite sunk in for the gangster's girlfriend. Mr. Death pulls out a gun from his drawer, which at this stage we're not sure will be used to bump Betty off or to eradicate an enemy.

*

"What was *that*, my dears?" proclaimed Maudi from the fifth row. Warwick re-entered the stage as Pedro glanced up.

"Warwick, sweetheart, you were fine, but Pedro, Pedro, Pedro!" Maudi's hands rested on her forehead. "Mr. Death *doesn't* just turn off a switch and decide he's no longer in love with Betty. They have history! Show me the love during next rehearsal."

A director who believes in broadcasting their notes is always confronting for any actor. Hearing "you're doing well" or "I like what you're doing in scene five, but just tone it down a bit as you're pulling focus," all within earshot of your fellow cast members is fine. Being told basically that you can't act is something that should be left for a private sitting.

Pedro looked to the stairs at the side of the stage, took a deep breath, and moved toward them. Warwick grabbed his arm to stop him before comforting him with a lingering hug.

Guy met my eyes. I shrugged it off. Inside, however, jealousy was subtly brewing in my subtext. What did this Pedro guy have that I didn't? It definitely wasn't dick size!

But I had no claims on Warwick, and Pedro was just a fleeting incident. There was no reason to dislike him. However, to my delight, the writer continued portraying his head mobster role with the sort of playacting associated with silent cinema.

Warwick and I learned more about our new associates during breaks. Over tea and biscuits, we both asked Maudi where in the Limelight Quarter she lived.

"No, my dears, I live in the Grand Sector," she told us. "Some refer to it as the Merchant Ivory Quarter, or at least, those from well after my time."

"Maudi, I think Warwick and I are going to enjoy our little exchanges," I said. "Afternoon tea at our place is definitely on the agenda."

"I'm always up for afternoon tea, but I think a gin and tonic would make me feel more at home."

She was an inspiration for my task ahead, and someone I was looking forward to knowing better.

During a scene between Mr. Death and his mistress, Guy explained that different visitors lived in various settings. He'd been brought up at the Carnival of Lost Souls, and let us in on an intriguing fact about his pseudo-parent, Auntie Jem.

"She was a very good fortune-teller. She was always there to give me advice on what was about to happen and how I should handle it, but I always felt that she was intruding. I couldn't skip classes, run away from home, or tell tales. I was too scared to touch myself as a teenager. Imagine the images in her crystal ball!"

"You would have steamed the glass, I'm sure," I added. "So there's the Limelight Quarter, the Carnival of Lost Souls, and the Grand Sector. Is that it?"

"There are plenty more, and I'm sure you'll have fun discovering them," continued Guy with the enthusiasm of a travel agent. "I think you'd both enjoy the ancient sectors. They don't dress the way they used to in their time, but when they do, the party begins! Pan's flute declares that it's festival time, so you borrow a toga to join their adaptation of the game Twister. But just remember to leave when they bring in the goats, no matter how smashed you are."

Warwick smiled at me, while our angel buddy shared the joys of historic rituals. I stepped closer to my friend and placed my hands on his shoulders. He didn't move away. I massaged him gently as he asked the next question.

"What can you tell us about Samantha?" We discreetly observed the lady in question.

"She loves her clothes. To be honest, that's all I know. Maudi just stepped down from the new arrivals committee a couple of weeks ago, and Samantha answered our ad. I only met her then."

We watched her shimmy, swoon, and seduce as her amorous alter ego.

REHEARSALS CONTINUED THROUGHOUT the day before I felt the shift in my universe. There are moments in life where you look back and wonder what would have happened if you had acted differently. Like the time my flatmate's girlfriend believed her object of desire had a bladder problem, just because I kept pouring a glass of yellow-tinted water on his sheets. What would have happened had I owned up? Would he still have that unfortunate nickname? You only regret the things you didn't do.

One of those moments was about to present itself. My ego was stroked severely when Maudi suggested Pedro and I swap roles. Maybe it was Pedro's lack of controlled dominance during a crucial scene that sparked this director's decision. Mr. Money, the opportunist played by me, confronts Pedro's character, Mr. Death, for the eighth time.

*

"I don't think I even play second best in your estimation at controlling this town."

"You're being paranoid," Mr. Death replies, even though he knows Mr. Money is right. "Why, you're my number one protégée."

Mr. Money pauses and holds back his anger at what he knows is untrue. He gives Mr. Death a filthy look. In a dismissive tone, Mr. Death asks Mr. Money to leave, as they have nothing more to discuss. Mr. Money refuses. Mr. Death pulls out a gun. Bullet, played by Guy, does the same.

"Are you immune to requests?" asks the underworld leader.

"Don't you believe in loyalty?" asks Money through clenched teeth.

"Don't you believe in respect?" replies Death.

"Only on my own terms."

"Then we have a mutual agreement."

They both pull their triggers, but it is Death who falls. From the director's chair, this was the writer's swan song.

*

Maudi stood up, strolled to the front of the stage, and delivered her thoughts in moderate tones.

"I've had a change of heart. I think for the purpose of good theater, Allan and Pedro should swap roles."

The moment of silence that followed felt like an eternity. The proverbial pin could have been dropped. Pedro turned to glare at her so fast, his neck cracked. I was still processing the news.

"Why?" demanded Pedro.

"I think you would have more fun in the role of Mr. Money," replied Maudi.

For a moment, Pedro seemed contained, but he started pacing like an amateur hit man about to make his first kill. He stopped in his tracks to glare at Maudi. His body grew as rigid as an ironing board.

"This has nothing to do with my sense of fun!" he yelled. "You think I'm hopeless!"

"No, but when I look at you, I see you more as a Mr. Money than a Mr. Death."

"How can Allan play Mr. Death? He wasn't alive in that decade!"

"Sweetheart, actors have played Greek tragedies and Shakespeare without a time machine to help them research."

"But it's my play!"

"And as the playwright, you should be interested in doing what's best for your play."

Pedro was struck dumb. He stormed off the stage toward the exit, smashing a water jug to the floor. Samantha and Guy leaped out of range of the flying shards. With wet trouser legs, the angry actor left the theater. To my horror, my best friend and confidant followed him. I would have expected Samantha to placate Pedro, as she knew him better. Even Guy would be an obvious choice.

I stood on stage staring at the exit. I felt like a child being punished, watching his favorite toy being confiscated. Warwick had marched through the velvet curtain to console the one person who was now my natural enemy.

FOUR

"YOU SHOULD BE charmed," said Maudi. "You have the lead, and deservedly so."

We were back at the Pedestal. The barman served chocolate-honey cocktails to Guy and me while our director sipped her gin and tonic.

"Maudi, I appreciate the role change, but Pedro is one tortured actor at the moment."

"Pedro's leading man material, don't get me wrong, but leading actor material, he isn't."

"But he did write the play. It's his baby."

"And I don't know how I'll survive hearing those inane lines over the next couple of months without slitting my wrists. At least my other actors know how to ham it up. Pedro thinks he's written a compelling masterpiece."

The strum of a solo guitar floated through the air. I breathed it in, trying to calm myself. The young musician sat as peaceful as a cherub, strumming her instrument like it had magical healing powers. Nellie stood next to her as poised as a model in her pin-striped suit, crooning into the type of microphone the Andrew Sisters would have used in their era. Its textured metallic surface reflected muted candlelight as the singer cradled it in her hand, dancing with it like an unfamiliar lover.

"Are you usually this neurotic?" asked Maudi. "For goodness sake, child, you have the lead."

"Look, I'm kind of happy about the role change, but..."

"But?"

"That's not what's worrying him," replied Guy.

Maudi thumbed through the pages of *The Stage Door*, searching for a particular passage. "Interview with New Playwright by Wilma Reading." Her finger rested firmly on the page, pointing with as much sarcasm as she displayed in her voice. "As this fine-looking writer cum actor reclined on his aged settee, I asked about his latest work. He told me it was his best play. More drama and intrigue on one page than most plays have in one act." Maudi sipped her gin before taking a dramatic breath. "I've tied shoe laces that have intrigued me more than that play!"

"He thinks he's written an intriguing drama?" I asked. I skimmed through the article.

"Yes, my dear. Even less of a reason for you to concern yourself with that useless writer."

"Maudi, that's not what's worrying Allan." Guy was flicking the stem of his cocktail glass. Its sharp pitch could not go unnoticed. "It's all about Warwick."

"Warwick?"

Guy proceeded to tell my tale of love on the back burner. The theater dame listened as if she was hearing gossip juicier than anything she might read in her magazine. I tuned out.

Some young girls in vampish black leather rocked gently to Nellie's soulful voice. One was bulging out of her tight-fitting skirt, while another was so thin she'd have to run around under a shower just to stay wet.

That Korean faded star had returned and was reclining on a velour sofa, bookended by two college boy types. I contemplated her success rate and wondered what was in it for them.

I shut my eyes to muse on these random thoughts, but soon reality knocked on the door. I was drifting in this world while my best friend and confidant was occupied with someone who had little reason to like me. I was being abandoned, dropped from the team because I had little to offer.

Guy tapped me on the shoulder.

"Darling boy," said Maudi, "it's about time you stop feigning confidence and actually be confident! Impress Warwick. Ignore Pedro's childish outbursts. We all know you have talent. Now seize the experience and relish your new role!"

"Pedro's not the problem," I replied. "I've been in plays before where temperamental actors ruin the tone of rehearsals. It doesn't bother me. But Pedro's outbursts are gaining Warwick's sympathies."

"And eventually Warwick will see those outbursts for what they are— Pedro's calls for attention." Maudi stared right into my eyes with maximum effect. "Pecking orders, petty jealousies, drama queens. My dear, they are all part of life."

A wicked grin emerged as I reflected on her wisdom. She swallowed the last mouthful of gin and continued.

"Yes, I am speaking from experience. While the men conducted their affairs, the women schemed in secret. That Claire tried to unnerve me many a night by carefully forgetting my cues. I cannot begin to tell you how many times I had to ad-lib after she fell silent. I'd try desperately to maintain the sense of the dialogue. If it weren't for my quick thinking, the audience would have never been able to follow the plot of the play."

Soon I'd have to interrupt, before she revisited the scandalous anecdotes of actors and actresses who lived and died a good century before I was born. "Did you ever try to heal the friendship?" I asked.

"What friendship? The battle lines were drawn quite early. Lord Edward Thorne was my beau. Both he and Claire just had to be made aware of that fact."

"Sabotaging the performance is not going to help me, Maudi."

"Ah, but it can add the spice you so lack, and the drama Pedro appreciates."

Game playing was not in my nature, but there was addictive mischief in her words. It was not advice I was going to embrace, but I could at least cherish her vote of confidence.

"Ms. Director," said Guy, "it's a heart that needs healing, not a play that needs sabotaging." Guy flapped his wings thrice in quick succession. "No one has seen Warwick and Pedro since this afternoon. They could be thrusting madly as we speak."

"Thanks, Guy," I said. The effects of alcohol had changed the shy angel into a brazen devil. "The images are a bit hard to swallow." Guy smirked, lifting his drink to his lips. "Besides, Warwick is commitment phobic. This little affair won't last long."

"Maybe. Maybe not," replied Maudi. She raised a finger to attract the barman's attention. "But why is Warwick consoling a man he's only known a few days, rather than celebrating his best friend's new leading role?" As the barman responded to Maudi's request, I asked for another cocktail, with a double shot of comfort.

ONLY TWO WEEKS passed before we were ready for dress rehearsal, the day before our first performance. Usually a rehearsal period was four weeks, but our mysterious sharpness of memory meant that opening night came sooner than expected.

"About your accent, Allan," said Pedro as we waited in the wings.

"What about my accent?"

"You do know what a Bronx accent sounds like, don't you?"

"Yes, I think I've done enough drama classes to know what one sounds like."

I averted my eyes to the stage where Guy's character was hiding stolen money. I wasn't going to let Pedro get under my skin. Besides, he might have not liked my accent, but he had a lot to learn about keeping in character.

The lights faded as I walked onto the stage, before coming up again for the next scene.

*

"Mr. Death, I presume," recited Pedro, inviting himself to my headquarters, upstairs from the illegal casino.

I, as Mr. Death, counted money as my henchman, Guy, stood beside me.

"Who's asking?" I replied, self-conscious about my Bronx accent.

"Let's just say I'm Mr...." Pedro paused as his attempt at a character searched thin air for a suitable pseudonym to keep his anonymity. "Mr. Money."

"I like it that way," I replied. "That way I can never tell the coppers who you are, or who you were."

"Trust me, Mr. Death, unlike many in this city, I don't see you as my enemy."

If only that were true.

"Good to hear. Only the ignorant *invent* their enemies."

There was a pause as my henchman and I shared a sinister glance. In my own head, I was thinking of ways to rub out this unfortunate actor. Take him out of the picture for good. I liked to take my method acting seriously.

In the play, our silence forced Mr. Money to speak.

"I'm here to offer you business. No doubt you've heard of Parke's Diner."

"Ah yes. Dear old Charlie. Never could pay the bills. The cops still don't know where he is."

"Well, I'm taking over, but I need a few supplies of the drinking kind to help kick-start the business. I believe you're the man to see."

"Who told you to see me?" I asked. Mr. Death is concerned that Mr. Money could be a detective.

"I have my sources."

"I think you heard wrong."

Mr. Money knows at this stage that there is no point debating the credibility of this information. If Mr. Death wants a piece of the action, he'll take interest sooner or later.

"Then I guess I'll see you for a bite at the diner," utters Mr. Money as he stands up to leave.

"Sure. And if I find someone who can help you, I'll send them over," Mr. Death replies. "Bullet, show Mr.—err, Cash was it?"

"Cash, Money, Profit. Whatever," Pedro's character replies, implying missed opportunity. Or at least he was supposed to. He sounded like he was reciting a shopping list.

"Show the nice gentleman out," my character responds, a little miffed. "He has a lot of work to do."

Guy, alias Bullet, escorts Pedro downstairs as I continue counting cash. The lights fade.

*

A few scenes later, Pedro and I found ourselves alone in the dressing room while the others were on stage. He was ignoring me, reading the article on himself in *The Stage Door*.

"So what's a nice guy like you doin' in a place like this?" I asked theatrically in my best Bronx accent.

"You still can't get it right." He peered over the magazine.

"I think it's a pretty good attempt."

"The operative word being 'attempt.'"

I wanted to scratch his eyes out. Whatever did Warwick see in him?

"But Pedro, what about character?"

"Character?" he asked. He was now eyeing his own picture in the journal like a centerfold.

"Yes, character. What do you think Mr. Money is all about?"

"He has to court Mr. Death into a deal."

"Right. That's what he wants to do in this play. But what's he all about?"

He ended his love affair with his own image and glared at me.

"Allan, I've written the piece. No one knows it like me. Instead of giving advice, why not ask for some. Do you understand Mr. Death?"

"His vice is status. He doesn't need the money, but it's the only thing that gives him power. In the meantime, there's a woman who loves him, and that's all he really needs to feel complete." The playwright didn't respond. "Am I right, Pedro?"

"I think you're overcomplicating it, Allan."

"I don't think I am."

"Humph."

Guy frantically ran through the door.

"You're both supposed to be on stage. Didn't you hear your cue?"

I bolted upstairs, but as I was halfway up, I heard Pedro say to our angel, "Sorry, we were caught up in polite conversation."

*

"I don't think I even play second best in your estimation, at controlling this town," Pedro said as Mr. Money.

"You're being paranoid," I replied as Mr. Death. "Why, you're my number one protégée."

Pedro tried to give me a filthy look, but I'd swear his pursed lips and clenched brow wouldn't frighten a baby.

"Money, this conversation is over. Come back when you've had a good lie-down with a girl or two."

Pedro pulled out his gun. I did the same.

"Are you immune to requests?" I asked.

"Don't you believe in loyalty?" Pedro said this through clenched teeth, sounding like an amateur ventriloquist.

"Don't you believe in respect?"

"Only on my own terms."

"Then we have a mutual agreement Sent."

I pulled the trigger on my prop gun. Before Pedro could fire his, an ear-splitting crash made the stage shake. There was nothing masculine about my yelp as I hit the floor, trembling.

*

The anxious murmurs of our director and the other cast members filled the air. I looked up to see Pedro shaking like a jackhammer still clutching the gun, before passing out with a thud.

I stood up. Warwick was pointing to the wall behind us, so I turned, noticing shards of glass covering the floor like the pieces of a jigsaw puzzle thrown in frustration. A large stage light had fallen from the ceiling, and its dented body was now part of the set. My friend jumped up on stage and clutched me like a long lost relative while I shivered in his arms.

As we eventually pulled away from each other, I noticed Pedro had come to. The others were huddled around him, questioning how this happened. As we stepped toward them, Guy turned and walked to us. He extended his arms and his wings, wrapping both around me. I felt as safe as a small boy hugged by his mother.

"What could have happened to us?" I asked under my breath. "I mean, if it hit one of us. We can't die if we're already…" I couldn't say that word.

"No, you can't, but just like in life, you could've been hurt."

"But what's the point of being hurt in the Afterlife?"

Guy didn't answer. He just held me a little tighter.

FIVE

THE CHAOTIC MELODY of carnival music echoed around us. Flames spurted from the mouths of brooding jesters, warming us from the icy mist that wove through the crowd. Snakes were charmed. Colored balls were juggled through the air. Odd collections of prose and rhyme were heard as poets poured out their hearts. A young man hit operatic notes that could send shivers down the spine of a corpse. We were at the Carnival of Lost Souls, a popular district of the Medieval Quarter.

It was about an hour after our dress rehearsal. Warwick, Pedro, Guy, and I took time to explore the Afterlife in an effort to calm ourselves from the accident earlier that day.

My mouth drooled at the odor of a well-crisped pig, glazed in fresh honey. It rotated on a spit, begging to be tasted. I hadn't noticed before but the opera singer had an ulterior motive. He was brewing fresh coffee. I think Guy was flirting with him while choosing between a golden custard tart and a glistening crème caramel. He expanded his wings a little, as a courting peacock might spread out its tail, while his face resembled a startled Marilyn Monroe. We drank our coffees as I watched this strange mating ritual. At least I wasn't the only one who lacked technique in winning hearts.

"Are you still as shaken up as me, Allan?" asked Pedro.

For the first time since we swapped roles, he was being nice to me.

"Yeah. More from a sense of confusion than anything else."

"In what way?"

"It just adds to the many puzzles of the Afterlife. I mean, we had a near miss, but although we wouldn't have been, been..."

"Dead?"

"Um, yeah, that's the word. What you said. We're like Wile E. Coyote who can get squashed by an anvil a hundred times, but he only gets seriously hurt. That fallen light could have damaged us in some way, yet here, we're supposed to be free from our bodies. Souls wandering through the hereafter. Why would we feel pain?"

"It's been a long time since I asked myself *those* questions."

"Yeah, that's what I find weird," added Warwick.

"Why would you find that weird?" I asked.

Before my friend could answer, Pedro replied.

"Warwick found it weird when I told him I've been here for seven years."

"But you're from the 1920s. That was almost a century ago."

"From your point of view, Allan, but not from mine. As far as I'm concerned, you're both from the future." Pedro placed his hand to his chin, rubbing gently before continuing his train of thought. "At the moment, I can feel my jawline, just as you can feel and sense this world around you. Why wouldn't you feel extreme pain?"

Guy had finished his attempt at winning a heart. With only a coffee in hand, he strolled over.

"But it's more than that, Pedro," I replied. "Why do we need to eat, to get drunk, to make love, and to feel pain? Can you answer this, Guy?"

"What's there to answer? Your souls still hunger for what makes them feel alive."

"But why? Isn't this the Promised Land? Why do we need to still feel pain, physically and emotionally?"

"Allan, it's what makes you *you*. Without those things, you'd just be a robotic soul. No highs. No lows. No passion."

Warwick met my eyes. He gently bit his bottom lip and nodded. Guy had a point. What kind of soulless creatures would we be in the Afterlife without everything that made us who we were? Although it was kind of eerie that some higher being thought physical pain was still warranted.

A loud clanking bell startled me. Its dull ring thumped in my head like a migraine. A dark-haired man with an oversized moustache called for riders on his Ghost Train while shaking that irritating bell. Warwick was keen, as he often loved anything of a horror genre, but Guy suggested that as we were still drinking coffee, the Ferris wheel was a safer option. Pedro got in first, followed by Guy who sat next to him. I'm sure the angel was coordinating the seating arrangement, leaving Warwick and me to share the other seat.

From our carriage, the pale gray and emerald structures of the Art Deco Sector were highlighted with soft shadows. Almost as if someone had lit the buildings for a romantic comedy about a flapper and an adventurer. She'd ask him for a light of her cigarette, and from there a steamy romance would begin. Their favorite nightclub would feature his daredevil friend, a rugged drummer who had often saved the adventurer's life on their many trips to the Amazon. Their much-loved café would be owned by Cecil, her uncle who made the best spaghetti outside of Italy. And their nights would begin by sharing a bath, gently lathering each other's backs and cheekily blowing soapsuds around the room. Sultry nights in the bedroom would follow, where going to sleep was never an option before midnight. How I wished I was that girl.

Warwick turned to look at the view as I placed my arm around his shoulder. The seating wasn't cramped, but I positioned my body as if it was. My dear friend gently nudged against me. The scenery became secondary. I wanted us to melt into each other. To become one entity that could never feel the fear from an uncaring world, no matter what demons or lovers would grace our path. I was about to press my body harder against his when Pedro pretended to clear his throat. We were like naughty schoolboys caught smoking by the headmaster. I quickly moved my arm from his shoulder as he turned to his lover, breaking the physical bond we had.

"Excuse me," said Pedro. His voice was monotone.

"Sorry," said Warwick.

I tried to smile at my friend, but he never met my gaze.

"You know, if you want to be with Allan, you can."

"Pedro," I said, "I think you're overreacting. We've known each other for ages. We're just close. And we're tactile. We always have been."

"There's a difference between being tactile and longing for more."

"But friendships can be just as close. A relationship is a relationship."

"Yes, but you don't go bonking all your friends. You listen to their relationship problems. You don't become the relationship!"

"But Allan and I are close enough that we can touch, hug, give each other a welcoming kiss," said Warwick. His palms pressed against his temples.

"And you both really can't see what's happening below the surface? Little glances. Little touches. Guys, give me a break!"

"Pedro, like Allan said, we're just old friends."

That last sentence made my heart sink. Guy discreetly mouthed "ouch" so that only I'd see it. As we left the ride, Pedro clutched Warwick's arm and marched ahead of us, tying himself to him as if they were in a three-legged race. I found this act petty.

For a while, we continued to explore, wandering past many eccentric characters with treasures to share. I frivolously commented on the assorted jewelry and clothing, trying to take my mind off my nonexistent romance. It didn't really work. I kept daydreaming that I was nestling my nose into the back of Warwick's neck, intentionally peeling off the same trinkets and garments I had remarked on.

Eventually we found a stand that brought childhood memories flooding back. Thick red toffee oozed from a cooking pot, spreading like tentacles of molten lava across the base of a shallow pan. Soon crisp apples were speared by little wooden sticks, before being immersed in the sticky goo.

A plump woman in a headscarf handed Warwick and me two luscious toffee apples. I put my nose close to mine, taking in the blissful scent of caramelized sugar, remembering how Dad used to tempt me with this treat every time I'd agree to get my haircut. I shattered its shell with a loud crunch.

"You look like you're making love to that apple," said Guy.

"This is a new kind of bliss," I replied.

"Is that true, Warwick?"

"Yep. The toffee apple has to be one of life's undiscovered aphrodisiacs. Share one with your partner instead of foreplay."

He offered his lover a bite, but he refused, stating that he found them too sweet. So I leaned over to take a mouthful while offering Warwick a taste of mine. His upper lip skillfully slid on the hard flat top of this delicious delicacy, before his teeth cracked its rosy shell. He moaned as he chewed. Pedro bowed his head before shaking it.

"Aren't you being obvious?" he said.

"Well, you didn't want a bite," replied Warwick.

"Yes, but if I did, I'd see no reason to pretend I was having an orgasm as I was eating it. Besides, you both have the same type of toffee apple. What is there to taste that's different?"

"It's part of the ritual," I said. "A substitute for foreplay."

"Come on, Pedro," said Guy. "You're overreacting again."

"Am I? A while ago they were chummy on the Ferris wheel. Now they're substituting toffee apples for their dicks. Come on! I wasn't born yesterday."

"Allan and I are just good friends," said Warwick. Pedro rolled his eyes. "We can joke about toffee apples as a phallic symbol. Moan to each other. It means nothing!"

As those last words resonated, I felt like I'd been punched in the stomach. Guy stretched out his wings, grabbing my attention as the lovers argued. He gave me a sympathetic look as I tried to smile back. It was no use. I'd never get to first base touching Warwick's soft coffee skin or inhaling his body's unique musky scent. I'd never be comforted by the kind tones in his voice while making love. They would only soothe me as a friend. I was losing something precious I'd never owned, but only borrowed when I needed strength.

"Allan, how do you feel about Warwick?" asked Pedro.

"I love him…as a friend."

"I don't believe you. You gaze at him like he was your own personal god or something."

"I don't!"

"Pedro, leave Allan alone," said Warwick. "He's my best friend."

"Yes, we're just friends. That's it." I found it hard to convince myself, let alone anyone else.

The writer stormed off. Warwick shrugged his shoulders before following. I took a breath and ran my fingers through my hair in frustration. We weren't alone in watching this mismatched duo bicker as they swept past various stalls, leaving surprised glances, and idle chatter in their wake.

"Is this really worth it, Allan?" Guy asked. "Chasing after a man who's not interested?"

"I ask myself that every day."

"And what's the answer?"

"I can't imagine him not being there. An extension of myself would be missing. The camaraderie we've developed would simply amount to nothing."

"But it hasn't, Allan."

"I know, and that's the thing I can't explain. I have him as a friend, but this fling with Pedro has made me realize that I could lose that friendship. I don't want the years to roll on and for us to become distant."

"But you might find someone better."

"Perhaps, but I've felt this way for the past year, and no matter how much I tell myself I'm being silly, my heart tells me something different."

Guy stepped forward and planted a soft kiss on my cheek.

"What was that for?"

"For being consistent over the past year."

His gesture made me feel terribly alone yet strangely understood. I wasn't the first person who'd struggled with unrequited love, and I definitely was not going to be the last.

"A kiss for being mixed up over the past year? It's a unique reward, Guy."

I wondered if he'd felt the same about his friend Joshua, when he was a lot younger. That being yourself wasn't enough.

"Samantha," he said.

"Samantha? What's she got to do with all of this?"

"Samantha," he repeated, pointing. "She's here."

Sure enough, there was the bombshell wandering with a man and a woman around the bookstall in the distance. As Guy stepped in her direction, I stopped him to ask about this cosmic universe.

"Samantha has more than a passing interest in 1950s fashion?"

"True."

"Pedro would have hit adulthood during the First World War. Maudi's from the late 1800s, and Warwick and I are from the early twenty-first century."

"Are we taking stock, Allan?"

"No, hear me out. I've seen a Roman gladiator from the Ancient Sector and all sorts of people from different periods of time."

"And your point is?"

"At first I thought we didn't age. That I would never grow older, but I'm not even sure about that anymore. Pedro believes that he's only been here for seven years."

"Correct."

"How can that be?"

"Just like you, he's here at a point when he needs to be."

"But we're all here at the point we left our mortal coil."

"I think you've just answered your own question, Allan."

As I gave Guy a puzzled look, Samantha strode toward us. Her cohorts, looking somewhat bored, trailed behind. The woman seemed familiar to me.

"Wilma, Peter. This is Allan, and Guy, my favorite angel."

"How many angels do you know?" Guy asked.

"Just you, darling. That's what makes you my favorite." Samantha's friends made no attempt to greet us. They just gave us one nod each.

"These fabulous actors are on stage with me in Pedro's new piece. You *are* both coming to our opening night tomorrow?"

Again they nodded and mumbled something.

"Wilma, what is your role in the Limelight Quarter?" I asked. She was a plump woman, probably early fifties, with no hint of self-consciousness about her weight.

"I'm the resident critic. I live for your performances."

Now I recognized her. She was the woman taking notes at the Pedestal when we first arrived.

"You'll get more than you've bargained for tomorrow night," I replied. My poker face was working overtime.

"Yes," added Samantha. "It's a shame what happened to Pedro the other day. That nasty role change business."

Guy and I subtly exchanged glances.

"Why? What happened?" asked Wilma.

"Our director, Maudi, didn't appreciate his talents. I mean, he wrote the play. He should be in the main role."

"Maybe the director knows what she's doing?" said Peter. "I mean, I'd love to get a lead role in a play. It's any actor's dream. Who did he swap with?"

"With me," I said sheepishly.

"Then you'll have a lot to live up to," replied Wilma. "I'll expect nothing short of brilliance."

So many thoughts came to mind. How could anyone find brilliance in Pedro's play? They'd have to use a microscope to read between the lines and still be overwhelmed by the mundane. But I kept my mouth shut.

"Wilma, just wait until I become a director," said Samantha. "I'll show you brilliance. That nineteenth-century old woman couldn't direct traffic, let alone a play."

Again, Guy and I discreetly glanced at each other.

"I'm sure you can do better," added Wilma.

"What would you direct?" I asked.

"More Pedro-penned masterpieces. Help him shine on stage."

Her walking companions seemed to agree. I wasn't sure how to take this remark.

"Is he writing anything at the moment?"

"He's researching genres. He'll type away madly when we've finished our run."

"A man of so many talents," I replied, grinning at Guy.

"Well, we must fly," announced the bombshell. "I need to soak in this area for inspiration. Toodles!"

After more unassuming nods from Wilma and Peter, our fellow cast member and her friends left us. They strolled back to the bookstand and flicked through some volumes.

"I'm sure there's crash test dummies with more personality than Samantha's friends," I said.

"I know what you mean. Did you feel the barbed wire?"

"What do you mean?"

"Her Maudi comment was directed at you, Allan."

"I wasn't sure. But I think I was a little sarcastic in my comment about Pedro."

"No kidding. That was obvious." My friend fluttered his wings. "Just a word of warning, keep an eye out for the subtext while you're here at Limelight."

"I'm noticing that very fast."

"There are people here who think they're god's gift to the arts, like Wilma."

"And Samantha."

"Correct. And Peter has been hanging out for a role larger than a bit part for ages."

"He's committed."

"Maybe? Maybe not?" We watched the three in question as they fussed over one book before putting it down and moving on. "Peter uses the Limelight Quarter like a security blanket. He's hooked on the glamour, waiting for his big break. Allan, you've got yours. After this, move on."

"I wouldn't call Pedro's play my big break."

"Still, Allan, listen to what I'm saying."

Samantha and her friends were now out of sight. We headed toward the bookstand where the assorted array sat disorganized on the table. The stale smell of dusty hardcovers overpowered any other scent. To my delight, Warwick was turning the tea-colored pages of an old Bible.

"Where's Pedro?" I asked.

"He went home, sulking."

"When did you get back?" asked Guy.

"Just now. I tried to talk sense to Pedro, but he wouldn't listen. He just wandered off without me."

"Do you want to talk about it?"

"It's not that serious. Or at least I don't think so. You know what a drama queen he can be."

I loved hearing his description of Pedro. It gave me hope.

"You know, Warwick," I said, "you can always come home tonight."

Before he could reply, we were interrupted.

"Guy!" proclaimed a woman at the bookstand. Her round turquoise glasses overpowered her face.

"Monique!" Guy matched her zeal.

"I need to tell you, my snake and I have calmed down a lot since we first met you."

Before introductions were made, I realized who this person was.

"This is that fortune-teller I told you about," said Guy. "The one who freaked out when she first met me."

"Terribly rude of me, I know, but you weren't quite what I was expecting."

"In this place, none of us know what to expect," I replied.

"You're Allan, aren't you?"

"Yes, how did you know?"

"I'm a fortune-teller, remember?" I grinned foolishly. "When you're done here, come and see me in that tent over there." She pointed to a small royal-blue marquee opposite the bookstand. "I feel I have something important to tell you." She turned to Guy. "Now, my beloved angel, can you fly yet?"

"One day I'll get there," he replied coyly.

"We should help you," I suggested.

"What do *we* know about flying?" Warwick pointed out the obvious.

"We've watched birds."

My friend peered down his nose at me like I was the class clown before we both laughed. Monique and Guy continued catching up on gossip. After a short while, they were caught up in their own little world, so I pretended to study a journal with a jagged leaf etched on the cover. Soon, curiosity started nipping at my heels.

"Does he ever bitch about me when you're alone with him?"

"He's too much of a gentleman."

"I guess you're staying with him for a while?" I braced myself for the answer.

"I don't want to drop him in a heap in the middle of this run. He's been through enough with losing the lead role. On the final night, I'll break up with him discreetly."

Inside, I felt like a bottle of champagne with the cork popped off, ready to blow.

"I'm glad. I miss having you around. After the run, I wouldn't mind leaving Limelight and exploring the rest of this, um, post-normal-life predicament."

"Post-normal-life? Allan, so much of our normal life has faded that this feels like normal life."

"Yeah, I know what you mean. I'm strangely comfortable with all of this now. Logic tells me I shouldn't be, but my frame of reference is vanishing, except for memories of you." I laughed nervously. "This play has given me something to focus on."

"Okay, Allan," interrupted Monique. "It's your turn to make sense of *your* world." She gestured once more to her tent. "Your future awaits."

I kissed my friend, telling him I'd catch up with him at home if he didn't sort things out with Pedro. Guy kissed me as well, bidding me goodbye before I followed Monique into what seemed a comic cliché of a clairvoyant's workplace.

All sorts of knickknacks littered the tables inside, including several crystal balls and various tarot decks. I was a little dubious about what she could tell me that I didn't already know, but I sat on one side of her paint-chipped worktable and shuffled the cards.

"You're suspicious of what I might say, aren't you, Allan?"

"A little but I'm keeping an open mind."

When I felt I'd finished shuffling the deck, I handed it to her. She carefully laid out the cards facedown in the shape of a cross, with four random cards placed to the side.

She turned the first card over, but before I could focus on it, my vision became blurry. The fortune-teller and her belongings were being seen through frosted glass. Her voice was just a low hum, serenading me through this peculiar vision.

Something slimy forced its way from my legs to my chest. Its oily residue stained my clothes like dank perspiration. Its face hissed at me, and its tongue licked my cheek, leaving slushy mucous running down my neck. The snake twisted itself around me and pulled me down where the ground once was.

Monique's voice appeared somewhere from the ether. "Don't let the snakes pull you away from your destiny, Allan."

"Did I need such a literal hint?" I shrieked.

A stainless-steel ladder appeared to the side of the snake. I reached out. The snake slithered away as I grabbed a rung. As it moved upward, I heard the ear-piercing sound of shattering glass. I peered down to see the gold and green squares of a Snakes and Ladders game. But one of the snakes had been crushed by the same stage light that had almost landed on me and Pedro hours earlier. The ladder jolted, forcing me to let go.

I bounced onto my chair, startled like I'd wakened from a bad dream. Monique turned the last card of her tarot deck. It was the Lovers, blissfully clutching each other for eternity.

"That's a good sign. It's me and Warwick together at last."

"No, it isn't." Monique brought her eyes closer to the card.

"It isn't?"

"No. There are snakes in the grass."

"And who are they?"

"It's whoever unhinged that stage light to scare you away. Keep you out of the picture."

"What do you mean?"

"My dear Allan, the lovers don't want you around."

SIX

"GUY, THERE ARE lovers out to get me."

"What? You think Warwick and Pedro are out to get you? Pedro, maybe, but not Warwick."

My angelic friend strolled with me to the theater about an hour before opening night.

"No, hear me out. It came out in my reading with Monique. That falling stage light was no accident."

"What?"

"Apparently there are 'lovers' who were responsible."

Guy gave me a puzzled look.

"Are you sure you understood what Monique showed you?"

"Pretty damn sure. She was fairly direct. There are lovers who were responsible for the falling light."

My heavenly chum stopped in his tracks. I almost bumped into him.

"Allan, the only lovers cast in this play are Pedro and Warwick. The light fell while Pedro was on stage. He wouldn't put himself in harm's way if he was responsible."

"Perhaps he knew exactly where to stand when it fell?"

"But if it was loosened, how would he know exactly when it would fall? He may have been walking directly under it when it came crashing to the ground. In fact, any one of us could have been under it. You can't orchestrate something like that."

He had a point. As the eccentric locals weaved around us, Guy stood stroking his chin.

"It's official. I'm neurotic," I said.

"A little around the edges, maybe, but you're not a raving lunatic yet, Allan. Now if Monique said something like that, then there's truth in it somewhere. Pedro might be out to get you, and he's one-half of the 'lovers'—but being clever enough to cause 'accidents'? I don't think so."

We began walking again. Old-world streetlamps lit the mild evening. A blond child, not more than seven years old, whizzed by in a bright red toy car, chased by what appeared to be his older brother. People leaped out of the way of his runaway vehicle. His cheeky cackle took me back to my own starry-eyed innocence, long before I reached puberty. Before the world *had* to make sense. I once told my angel buddy I was trying to fall without a parachute. This carefree young fella would be my role model.

"Allan, have you told Warwick about Monique's reading?"

"I haven't seen him since we were at the Medieval Quarter, yesterday."

"Maybe that's a sign to move on. His relationship is blossoming, and getting in their way will only fuel Pedro's resentment."

I wanted to cover my ears and hum loudly to drown out Guy's advice. My security blanket was being pulled away, and I was ready to break my nails if I had to before I would let it go.

We pushed through the heavy doors of the theater, and the rest of the cast greeted us. I cheerfully acknowledged Pedro who was rereading the article about himself in *The Stage Door*. His wimpy hand waved back.

We put on our costumes, chatted to the others, and soon heard the murmur of our waiting audience. Would we bore them with mundane dialogue or delight them with a farce? The vain playwright had put down the magazine, so I flicked through it. There was an interview with Maudi claiming the play's 'melodramatic style was an aspect missing from so many plays of the last century,' even though she accepted the realism that had taken over since she last took to the stage. It seemed she was putting the hard sell on this show.

The first act went over well although Pedro complained several times about the audience's laughter. He didn't see what was funny about his play.

At the start of the second act, my Mr. Death and Guy's Bullet have a little disagreement.

*

"So you think you can run this business?" says Mr. Death. "You've got delusions of grandeur."

"I pretty much run this business already. What do you do? You just rake it in!"

"I'm the brains. You're the brawn. It's that simple."

"I can be both."

"You ain't got the smarts. My empire would collapse in your hands."

"I guess there's only one way to find out!"

Guy barked that line with more venom than he ever did before. He was so worked up he even charged toward me, which he wasn't supposed to do. Mr. Death was meant to walk over and pick Bullet up by the collar.

"Whoa!" shrieked Guy.

He was no longer Bullet. He slipped, sending himself airborne like an acrobat. Confused gasps filled the theater as the angel fluttered madly. He hovered above the stage before carefully landing on his feet.

I mouthed "You can fly" as he nervously pointed to the floor. A clear gel with Guy's sliding shoeprint glistened on the wooden boards. I stepped over it and grabbed Bullet by the shirt.

*

Backstage, Warwick's fingers glided over his cheeks, touching up his ruby makeup. His wig was off, making him look like a failed cross-dresser. I would have done anything to share a soapy bath and a bottle of champagne, gradually wiping his face back to the image of the man I longed for.

"What happened on stage?" he asked.

"I slipped," replied Guy.

"And he flew!" I added.

"I slipped on some goo on the floor."

"And he flew."

"Allan, that something was meant for you. You're the only one who's meant to walk across the stage in that scene."

"Guy, who cares? You lifted yourself off the ground. You can fly!"

"Why would someone put goo on the floor?" asked Warwick.

"Because they wanted Allan to slip over."

"What?"

"Monique, the fortune-teller, told Allan that someone doesn't want him here. So the falling light and the goo on the stage were meant for him."

"It's Pedro for sure," I said.

"I know you two have stepped off on the wrong foot," said my old friend, "but seriously, he's not that vindictive."

"How would you know? You've only dated him for a short while."

"Because he was on stage with you when the light fell. He was just as shaken up as you were."

"But look at the way he smashed that jug of water when Maudi made us swap roles."

"Yes, in anger. He was reacting. This is different. You're accusing him of going out of his way to cause trouble."

"But he's got a motive. What do you think, Guy?"

The angel scratched his head.

"Allan's right. He's the only one with a motive."

"Think about it," said Warwick. "Really think about it. Why would Pedro sabotage his own play, even if he's no longer playing the lead? This show is his baby!"

Guy's wings slackened. The tips rested on the floor as he continued scratching his head. I smiled at my old friend, but he didn't respond. I smiled again, but nothing. I was the stranger in town. I was caught in a whirlwind, calling out to my dearest mate but being ignored. No one would rub my shoulders and tell me everything was all right. He pulled on his wig and left for the stage.

WE FINISHED THE play unharmed. The audience's applause echoed like crashing waves across the hall. With spotlights in my eyes, I could only distinguish the first two rows of punters, howling and whistling madly.

I felt as one with the cast through our clenched network of hands. We bowed once more as our new fans turned up the applause. Two more weeks of performing now seemed like an honor rather than a chore. For this brief moment, those little *accidents* seemed trivial, filed in the wastepaper basket. Nothing could spoil this feeling.

We headed out to party, crowding into the Pedestal. Nellie shimmered in a tight-fitting gold dress. Its mirror-ball effect left me spellbound as I headed toward her like a sailor lured by a siren. A siren in disco drag. Her silver suited band revived the hits and the forgotten treasures of the mid-seventies. Synthesized notes quivered through the crowd, urging them to stomp their feet and find their "cool."

Maudi, Samantha, and Warwick took to the dance floor, as a rare favorite of his thumped its domination over the crowd. Disco bunnies of every persuasion invaded the space, some dressed as if they came from a costume party. A few resembled unwanted Christmas decorations.

Some partygoers wore fur bodysuits resembling funky barn animals. They were inviting others into their unique boogie circle. One man sporting a tight Dalmatian-patterned shirt encouraged my belief in puppy love.

Back at the bar, Guy and Pedro sat quietly. I went over to prompt conversation.

"Why don't you celebrate with doggy boy over there, Guy?"

"My wings would be in the way."

"You mean, if you dance?"

"I get carried away and inevitably knock someone over."

I had the impression that this had only happened once.

"How often have you tried?" asked Pedro.

Guy didn't answer. Instead, he focused on the crowd. At this stage, Warwick was on his way back from the dance floor, raising my alarm bells at the thought of enduring the next chapter of his amorous adventure from an A-grade seat.

"Okay, Guy, here is your chance to face your fears and be a man!" said the playwright.

He seized the hand of the angel, leading him gallantly to the dance floor. I was relieved at his sense of timing as Warwick sat himself next to me. They stood an arm's length from the rest of the dancing crowd, Guy's wings nowhere near anyone he could knock down.

"Maybe Pedro's heart's in the right place," I said.

"That's not all that's in the right place." Warwick grinned.

"I thought you said he didn't measure up?"

"There are ways around it."

I did my best not to scream.

"How serious is it between you two? I mean, you seemed pretty pissed off when I mentioned that he may be out to get me."

"Allan, he's no psychopath."

"Regardless, you said you would break up with him after the run of the play."

"Maybe sooner."

"So is it time to end the fling?"

"Just about. Is it the right thing to do before the play has finished its run?"

"It might inspire him to actually act."

Warwick chuckled. He reached around and hugged me from behind. The bristles on his face brushed against my neck, making me want to throw off my clothes and let his unshaven whiskers drag themselves down the base of my spine.

"I miss you, you know," I said in a low tone.

"I know, but I haven't gone anywhere."

"Warwick, you have gone somewhere. I'm just not sure where." He pulled away from me. "Why did you...?"

"Pedro might see us. You know how jealous he gets."

"Oh, right."

I was in limbo again. Toyed with like a yo-yo. Sometimes close, at other times too far to mention.

People flirted and embraced as the retro music broke down their inhibitions. But Cupid had overlooked me and Warwick, and Guy for that matter. He knocked over Mr. Puppy Love, who even on all fours knew how to wag his tail. Guy mimicked the fall next to the dog. Dalmatian boy smooched the angel and got back on hind legs to dance. Guy got up, but didn't accept the invitation.

The angel bowed his head and meandered toward us. I demanded another vodka and cranberry from the barman and rushed over to the wannabe stud. Pouring the concoction down his gullet, I spelt out the rewards one can uncover when feeding an animal. Soon Guy was back on the dance floor.

As I wandered back, the barman served Warwick two vodka and cranberry cocktails.

"You know, I'd love our friends back home to be here at the Pedestal with us," I said.

"I don't think they'd necessarily kill themselves to get here."

"Looks like we'll need to settle for our *new* friends. And I'll have to get used to Pedro."

"Trust me, he's not bad. But I guess when I break up with him, they'll be no reason for you to get to know him."

"Warwick, he's not going to take that well. You know how moody he is."

"Yeah, I know. But there's something odd about that." My friend watched his boyfriend swivel his hips like he was mastering a hula hoop. "In bed, we have a lot of fun. No one says 'I love you.' It's just sex. But when it comes to you, he gets all worked up."

I sipped my drink. Pedro was in a world of his own on that dance floor, which was a relief for me. I had alone time with my dearest pal for the first time in ages. I placed my hand on his shoulder, leaning into him and telling him to observe Maudi. She was like some bizarre mechanical doll that was wound up by a key.

"How innovative," he said. "I guess there are only certain disco moves you can make when wearing a corset."

"Fluidity is not an option."

He turned, nearly bumping noses with me. His face stayed close to mine. I grinned, believing all my Christmases had come at once.

Warwick then moved away to view the dance floor. My heart sunk. I felt like the bachelor no one wanted to be seen with until I realized Pedro was on his way back, followed closely by Samantha and Maudi. Guy stayed, swinging his arms and his wings with Dalmatian boy. They'd found that special bond between master and dog.

"Just good friends, eh?" Pedro said.

How I wished I'd pushed him off that Ferris wheel the day before.

"Of course," I replied. "But we all have to tippy-toe around your fragile ego."

"Is that the vodka talking?"

"Maybe? But you have got a vindictive streak in you."

"I have not!"

"That wasn't a question. Some slippery goo on stage today. The killer stage light yesterday. What are you up to, Pedro?"

"You're blaming me for a few minor mishaps?"

"Yes, Allan," said Samantha. "You are drawing a long bow."

"I agree," added Warwick. "That fortune-teller got it wrong."

"What fortune-teller?" asked Maudi.

"At the Carnival of Lost Souls, I saw a fortune-teller. She told me that the falling stage light was no accident and that some lovers were behind it."

"Pedro and I are the only lovers," said Warwick. He stared at me without expression. "I know you and Pedro have your differences, but you're implicating me in your argument."

"I'm not. For goodness sake, we've been through a lot together. I'd never think for a minute that you're behind anything that would hurt me."

"I know, Allan, I know. But think about it. It's Pedro's play. He's hardly going to ruin his own show. Yet you believe the lovers, which can only mean him and me, are out to destroy the play and take you down with it."

"But there *was* something on stage that made Guy slip," said Maudi.

"Something the stage manager spilled," added Samantha. "Isn't it obvious?"

"Still, I am the director. I'm concerned over such things. I mean, what type of goo would the stage manager need to use between acts?"

"A glue of some kind?"

"We wiped the stage ourselves after our scene," I said. "It wasn't sticky like glue. We couldn't work out what it was. And besides, if the stage manager spilled it, why didn't he mop it up?"

"I can't believe we're having this conversation," Warwick stated. "You really believe that someone is out to get you, Allan?"

"Yes, Allan," said Pedro. "You're hardly devoid of blame yourself."

"What do you mean?"

"You tripped me up during the play."

I knew exactly what he was getting at. From Maudi's tales of romance, I had taken a leaf from her rival and forgotten a line. It was an important cue for Pedro, leaving him speechless on stage for what must have felt like eternity.

"It was an honest mistake. Really! What actor would purposely forget his line?"

The director grinned, peering down her nose at me. My rival didn't reply.

"I think we need to go back to your place, Pedro," said Warwick. He stood up and took his lover's hand, leaving his drink at the bar. "I don't like where this conversation is going."

"We're just discussing a few things that need to be brought out in the open."

"Allan, *you're* discussing them. We're just the white noise around you."

"Come on, Warwick..."

But no matter what I tried to say at that point, my old friend and his ill-chosen love interest strode out of the nightclub like a lawyer protecting his client from the meddling press.

SEVEN

I WAS TOO drunk to enjoy the Pedestal and too sober to block out Warwick's resentment of me, so I dragged my sorry ass back home. I fell back into the sofa wanting its plush fabric to wrap around me and protect me from this mad place. Even if it could, the harlequin money box was spying on me, making me naked for the entire world to see. The lounge would take me to a magic place like Alice down her rabbit hole, but the carnival clown would lasso me back up from my safe haven.

I peered at him, not making a sound. His eyes could follow me anywhere in the room. I latched onto the throw cushions and placed them on my sleepy body, protecting myself like the armor worn by a knight.

My lonely notions finally subsided. I drifted wearily, recalling the last days before my demise. Back in Melbourne, Warwick and I were still with Uncle Bryant.

*

Neither Pamela nor my uncle solicited reasons for us not shagging. Their original inquiry had enough impact for the matter to be considered off-limits. In some ways, I yearned for additional prying. Putting the topic out there might have prompted my feelings to be known. After all, Warwick was my best friend, I'm sure he wouldn't have freaked out. Pretending to have that special loving conversation with my buddy had become far too common back then. When no one was around, I rehearsed my script with perfect delivery, using textbook logic to explain the way I felt. Of course when Warwick was around, stage fright set in.

There was something about my uncle's blasé demeanor, blended with smooth scotch, and Pamela's bohemian nature that set the course for wickedness that evening. In short, the poet didn't need social lubricants to get up to mischief. She had a natural talent for bringing out the naughty adolescent in everyone. During what was affectionately known as Recital Hour, Uncle Bryant fetched his piano accordion, while Pamela warmed up her vocal cords with hot chocolate. She groaned as the tempting beverage raised her temperature. Being a lover of chocolate, I knew where she was coming from.

There's no polite way of saying it. My uncle played badly, but after our fourth nip of scotch, we just pretended it was performance art. Two shrill notes, then Pamela delivered.

Many of us dream of where we want to be,
Some of us search for love to set us free.
Others pin their hopes totally on occupation,
Some will simply coast along without anticipation.

A lonely soul considers "What has this to do with me?"
While one with many friendships sees what this soul can't see.
But our dear Allan longs for a life he thinks he missed,
But if he follows his passion, he'll truly see he's blessed!

"That didn't quite rhyme," Warwick whispered. "But I do agree with her."

He gave me a wink, which, in my drunken state of mind, I deduced meant "let's make love." Taking Warwick's hand, I led him to the guest bedroom. With both of us in the honeymoon suite, I shut the door.

"What is it you want to show me, Allan?"

Thinking on my feet, I replied, "Why do you agree with her poem?"

"Because you *are* truly blessed."

Closing my eyes, I digested his words. This had to be an invitation. Ah, what the hell! Nothing ventured, nothing gained! With lips puckered, I leaned forward.

His three-day growth caressed my cheek, so I turned; my goatee beard riding rough against his bristles. Light sweat dampened his thick black hair. I breathed him in as he buried his mouth deep in my neck, rubbing and nibbling. His moist lips tasted my earlobes before biting delicately, making me groan and sigh and lose the world.

I grabbed the back of his head, sliding my fingers through his curls and forcing his lips to mine. He pulled away, wagging his finger, teasing me before clutching my head in both hands and drawing me to his mouth. We kissed. Our tongues slid as we lured each other deeper, exploring, tasting, savoring.

At least that's the way I'd like to remember it. In all honesty, nothing happened. Just like the words I was dying to tell him that explained how I felt, our love scene remained unplayed.

After he told me that I was "blessed," I was speechless. He then asked what we were doing in the bedroom, rather than with our hosts.

I had no answer. He took me by the hand and led me back to my uncle and Pamela, stopping briefly at the bedroom door, tilting his head, and giving me a friendly wink. I was about to hug him, but he tugged at my arm and continued back to the living room.

"WARWICK, WE NEED to talk."

He peered at me, buttoning up Betty's blouse as carefully as a surgeon stitching a patient.

"What about, Allan?"

"Pedro and you. And you and me."

"Oh what is it this time? I'm going to pistol-whip you before Pedro strangles you to your last breath? We're putting a bomb under Mr. Death's chair that goes off during your stage monologue? Or maybe there's poison in that fake decanter of scotch you drink on stage?"

"Warwick, this is the first real argument we've ever had."

"Because you're being neurotic, Allan."

"Come on. There is something going on here. And I need you to help me work out what it is."

He forced on his wig.

"What's going on here is that I'm having a bit of fun and you can't cope without me."

He stomped out of the dressing room. I was about to scream in frustration before I remembered there was a play being performed upstairs, so I shook my fists and grumbled through clenched teeth. Guy popped back to get changed for his next scene.

"You look like a gorilla with constipation," he said.

"I'd rather *be* a gorilla with constipation at this point."

"Warwick's still not talking to you?"

"Oh, he's talking. I just don't like what he's saying."

"Give him time, Allan. He'll soon see your side of things."

"Sooner than later, I hope."

"But make sure you understand his point as well."

"Oh I get it, Guy. He doesn't believe me."

"Allan, you told me you were trying to fall without a parachute. See where destiny takes you. Let Warwick's destiny play out as well. He's still your friend. Just don't push him away."

I was being given advice from an angel. At a time when I was losing a friend, I was gaining another. I felt that warm glow you get when you realize someone else cares.

Guy rummaged around in his trousers. His hand reached deeper than usual as if his prop gun was missing. He made the faces of a comedian in a silent movie, twisting and contorting his body like a ferret had run up his leg.

"It's smaller than usual."

"It is your gun we're talking about?"

He looked surprised as he pulled out a small pistol.

"That's not my gun. I like it, but it's not my gun."

"They must have switched yours with someone else's." I wandered over for a closer look. "It's nice, though." I cradled it in both hands.

Although it was in Guy's pocket, it felt icy against my skin. Its sleek design looked like it would be carried by a spy rather than a gangster. Its handy small purse size made it ready to whip out when that cold war agent was on your tail. The glossy blue-black sheen would impress the enemy before they were wiped out in cold blood.

"So you think you can run this business, Bullet?" I pointed the gun at Guy. "You've got delusions of grandeur."

"I pretty much run this business already, Mr. Death," he replied. I lowered my aim and admired it in my palm. "That pistol suits you."

"Hmm. I'm not a gun person. Never held one. Still, it does give you a sense of power, doesn't it?"

I aimed at the door and pulled the trigger. Bang! Guy hit the ground so fast I was knocked over by his wing. I tumbled backward. The pistol flew out of my hand, then clanged loudly somewhere on the floor. Two eyes stared at me from behind his trembling wings. I gasped like a fish out of water. I rose to my feet, clumsily. My angel chum gazed past me as if some horrific news story was being reported on a TV behind me. I turned.

Splintered wood framed the edges of a huge hole in the door. Brittle ash drifted around the room like light snow. A crisp scent burnt my nose as I brushed the grayish residue from my jacket.

"What just happened?" asked Guy.

"The lovers have a score to settle."

Maudi's head appeared, framed by the jagged outline in the door.

"What in heaven's name is this all about?" She let herself in, studying the damage with the door halfway open. "Are you taking your roles a tad too seriously?"

"I'm really concerned for Allan's safety. There was a real gun in my pocket."

"And in the next act, we shoot each other," I added.

"I know, dears, I know," she said. "Something is rotten in Denmark. But who? Why?"

"It's got to be Pedro. He's got it in for me."

"Sweetheart, like Warwick said, this is Pedro's pride and joy. He wouldn't sabotage his own creation, beyond writing a mediocre script."

"It's about the role change. He's getting back at me for playing Mr. Death."

"He's not taking any prisoners, is he?" said Guy.

We all examined the hole, chipping off the loose pieces. Soon the other cast members came scurrying down the stairs. It was intermission.

"Well, gentlemen," said Samantha, "what kinky games have you been up to?"

"There was a real gun in my pocket," said the angel.

"And it was loaded," I added.

Warwick huddled near me, placing his hand on my shoulder.

"Are you okay, Allan?" he asked.

I wanted him to take me in his arms and whisk me back to my uncle and his girlfriend.

"I've been better," I replied.

Maudi clapped her hands three times to grab our attention.

"Now my darling cast, we have a serious problem."

"Not these 'accidents' again," said Pedro. "If the cat had kittens, I'd get the blame."

"No one's blaming anyone, or at least as long as I'm the director around here. Tonight will be our last run of the play. I don't want to be responsible for one of my cast getting hurt."

"But Maudi, the show must go on," I said. "Don't end the run just for my sake."

"Allan's right," declared Samantha. "It's all just circumstantial evidence at this point. Pedro's play needs to shine like any great work."

No one spoke. The bombshell's eyes darted around, giving us all a blank stare. Our theatrical dame broke the silence.

"Regardless of the merit of Pedro's work, at the end of the third act we'll retire our run."

"We should do at least one more performance," I said. "I don't want to be the one responsible for our run being cut short."

"Besides, who believes in fortune-tellers anyway?" asked Samantha. Her eyes darted around once more. "We can't go by a loose stage light and some goo on stage."

"But what about the gun?" asked Guy. "In the next act, I shoot Allan. You saw what it did to the door. He'll be doubled over in pain like a wounded animal." He shook his head. "No, Maudi's right. The play ends tonight!"

"I agree," said Warwick. "I don't believe any of us are responsible for this, but there is something fishy going on here. I need to protect my best friend."

I boldly took his hand from my shoulder and held it. I didn't worry about what that thing he called a boyfriend would think. He was mine, and he cared. I wanted to bury my head in his chest and bathe in his comfort for all time. And more than anything else, I wanted that monster who believed he was in love with my man to disappear back to the 1920s.

"Can we at least do my play one more time, like Allan suggested?" Pedro whined. "Geez, I've worked hard on Mr. Death, Mr. Money, Bullet, and the rest, and I feel like I'm being punished for things that have nothing to do with me."

I met eyes with our tireless director. "One more time, Maudi. For Pedro's sake."

She sighed.

"Okay. One more time. Tomorrow is our final night." The murmur of the audience could be heard. "Sounds like act two is about to begin. Now I want nothing fishy to happen for the rest of the tonight's performance. And that goes double for tomorrow night!"

"But what about my gun?" asked Guy.

"Improvise!"

*

"I'm the brains," I said once again as Mr. Death. "You're the brawn. It's that simple."

"I can be both," Guy replied as Bullet.

"You ain't got the smarts. My empire would collapse in your hands."

"I guess there's only one way to find out!"

I charged over and pulled my friend up by the collar of his shirt. He drew his pistol, but instead of aiming at my forehead, he pointed it to the floor.

"Are you farsighted, Bullet?"

"I'm too scared to point this thing," whispered the angel.

"Didn't you empty it?"

"Of course I did! But I still don't want to fire it."

I let go of his shirt.

"Like I said, my empire would collapse in your hands." Guy stared at me, frozen like a TV dinner. "But there is a way we can figure this thing out."

"And how's that, Mr. Death?" Guy asked.

"A game of Snakes and Ladders."

"And where will we find a game of Snakes and Ladders?" My fellow actor paced aimlessly on stage. "What about a fist fight?"

"Don't want to wreck my costume," I replied. "I mean my jacket." Confused mumbles came from the audience. "What about a dancing competition?"

"I could be your Ginger Rogers."

"We could take on Broadway!"

"Much more civilized than taking over your empire."

"I agree. Why are we fighting anyway? You're my henchman. It doesn't make sense."

"True. Let's talk about it over dinner."

The angel headed stage left. I followed.

"Good idea, Bullet. You've heard of Parke's Diner. Let's eat there. They do the best prime ribs."

"Their mashed potatoes are to die for, Mr. Death. You can't stop at one helping."

*

We left the stage, passing Pedro in the wings.

"Who the hell is Ginger Rogers?" he asked.

"Someone after your time," I replied. "When movies discovered sound."

"Allan, Guy, you've just made my play into a joke. You sounded like a lady's bridge club!"

"I didn't want to fire my pistol," said my onstage henchman.

"First you take my role, and then you send it up. The goo, the light, the gun. They're all you, aren't they, Allan?"

Warwick's footsteps came striding up the stairs for the next scene.

"Pedro, I know my friend," he said. "Don't accuse him of sabotaging your play. He doesn't think like that."

"Thank you," I said. I wanted to throw my arms around my old friend and never let him go.

"And Allan. Pedro's not to blame either. Seriously, think about his circumstances."

Ouch. I was yesterday's news again.

"Yes, Allan," the ill-chosen lover sniped, "you're just fighting for attention."

"Now, now, darling, Allan's not fighting for anything."

"Warwick, sweetheart, we have to go on stage. The lights are up."

"In a minute." My old friend gazed into my eyes and rubbed my chin with his thumb. I was melting. "Tonight you need a friend. I'm coming straight home after the play." I melted on the spot.

EIGHT

"HAVE YOU EVER seen an animal here?" I asked Warwick.

He sat next to me on the sofa, pondering my question with a glass of merlot against his lips.

"No, Allan, I've never seen a *live* animal here. I've seen roasted pork at the Carnival of Lost Souls, but not a live animal. For that matter, I've only ever seen human beings. No Martians, Saturn-folk, or Plutonians."

"Interesting observation. I must be in a coma. I wouldn't have animals or aliens wandering around in my imagination."

He leaned over and tenderly blew a whiff of air on my face.

"Awake yet?"

I smiled. The mellow piano playing on the turntable brought a touch of class to the moment, as if we were on a date. He sipped his wine with the sophistication of a well-traveled man, knowing the subtlety of flavor as if he'd tasted the champagnes of France and the crisp white wines of New Zealand. I wanted to be that lover on the side. The one he longed for when he made love to that failed playwright he supported, but his sense of duty wouldn't let him leave.

"That's a bold act, Warwick. Wistfully blowing air on my face like that. What am I to think?"

"We are friends, Allan, gay friends at that. We can get away with little flirtations."

"I know gay friends kiss each other when they say hello, but that warm wisp of air was a bit different than a gracious peck on the lips."

"Why is it different?"

I leaned over and blew lightly. He closed his eyes, letting out a long sigh. When I stopped, he sighed again. He savored his wine before opening one eye and grinning like a Cheshire cat.

"That's why it's different," I replied. "Warwick, you're a bad tease."

"I thought I was good at it."

"But why do you do it?"

"For fun."

"But why here? Why now?"

"Allan, I'm just trying to cheer you up. You've been stressed lately."

"Warwick, just talking to me will cheer me up, unless you want to take our friendship to a new level?"

"Why do you ask?"

His beautiful brown eyes studied me like a psychiatrist analyzing my secrets.

"Your gentle shoulder rubs and your expertise at exhaling," I replied.

"So?"

I placed my hand on his knee. It didn't faze him.

"How much do you remember of our former lives?"

"Less and less each day. Why?"

"Were we ever in love?"

He laughed briefly, then put down his glass. He gazed at my hand before placing his palm on my fingers.

"Maybe. We might have been." He looked up. "Nah, we couldn't have been."

"How can you be sure?"

"Allan, I don't remember any romance, but then..."

"But then it could have all been forgotten."

"And maybe we were something in between, just bonk-buddies."

"Uncle Bryant and Pamela did ask. Maybe more was going on than we remember, Warwick. Now and again I recall snippets. Sometimes I look through the photo album and rediscover that hospital-emergency-themed party. Sometimes I just remember things from our past out of the blue."

He moved his hand from mine.

"Allan, I don't think we were lovers, or even bumping uglies on the side. What have you remembered?"

"The escape from our jobs. Our time with my relatives. A role I was about to be cast in."

"Mainly things to do with you and me, right, Allan?"

"Yes, mainly things to do with us."

"That's because we have a very special friendship."

"Have or had a special friendship, Warwick?"

"What do you mean?"

I took his hand and cradled it between both of mine. The soothing notes of the piano eased my sadness. It understood my emotions, letting me know it was okay to feel the way I did.

"While we've been here, you haven't been around."

"Allan, come on. I'm having a bit fun. A short affair. If you were in the same boat, I'd understand."

"True, you would. But I've been targeted by someone involved with the play. I don't mind you having some fun, but I've needed you."

"I understand, but I really don't believe anyone's targeting you. The gun thing was a bit disconcerting, but I'm sure there's an explanation. None of us bothered to find out what it was. Plus, you blaming Pedro was over the top. He's hypersensitive. You took his role."

"Is he really that special, Warwick?"

"He's a nice guy. Although I know he's more into me than I'm into him, at least I think."

"Are you still breaking up with him?"

"He talks about our future together..."

"That's not what I asked."

"Yes, Allan, after tomorrow night's run, it's time to move on."

I wanted to smirk like the evil queen who knew Snow White was doomed. I bit my lip. He leaned over and kissed me.

"What was that for?"

"For being my friend."

I moved forward to kiss him back. Before I reached his mouth, the tip of his nose touched mine then tenderly made a path up to my forehead. He gave my brow a loving peck, then continued giving me tiny kisses in a trail back to my mouth. The piano swooned, urging me to let myself go. I slid my lips gently over his as we kept our mouths closed. His maroon lips moistly rubbed mine until eventually we broke apart.

"Well, Allan, I guess that makes us very special friends."

MIXED SENTIMENTS ALWAYS accompany a final night. Usually there's that fine line between the relief of never having to utter those same words on stage again, and a sense of loss in disbanding that short-term family known as your fellow players. Somehow in that last recital, you give it your all, making every line and nuance count, carried along with the electric anticipation of every thespian's favorite pastime—the after-show party!

The white seats were filled with acquaintances and newcomers, dressed in their finest festive attire. Maudi had placed herself in the second row, sporting a turquoise ruffled-sleeve dress with matching fan even though the temperature was mild. Her middle-aged friends positioned on either side wore similar apparel, one dressed in scarlet, the other in pale blue. They sat chitchatting, looking as if they were about to watch the latest play by Oscar Wilde.

All sorts of creative misfits were there dressed to the nines. Samantha's friends, Wilma and Peter, sat together. Wilma called out and waved to various members of the audience as they took their seats. Peter seemed to be trying to work out who her associates were.

As much as I loved theater, I was looking forward to tonight being the last time I had to endure the importance of being Pedro! Warwick's teasing nature the night before was driving me on, like an athlete with his mind on first prize. I stood backstage reflecting on his affection. For some reason, another memory of our former life returned in glorious Technicolor.

*

Warwick had visited me with a collection of vintage Stevie Wonder records that belonged to his older brother. He was convinced to shake me out of my love of synthesized melodies by bringing over music with heart.

There was some sort of spirit involved with us that night, although I couldn't remember if it was vodka or scotch—at the time, the two most likely candidates. I shifted myself off the couch and casually made my way to the record player as he suggested I play a track called "As." Before I could reach for the control that raised the tonearm, he tackled me to the ground by lunging at my feet. It was a soft landing as we play-wrestled on the carpet.

It didn't take long for me to be pinned down, struggling against my physically stronger buddy. I bent my knees, lifting Warwick from his triumphant seated position just below my navel. But it only resulted in him being able to place more force to my wrists, while bringing his face closer to mine. We seemed transfixed in that position for ages: me gazing into his eyes praying he would kiss me.

"I'll get you next time," I said.

I turned, rolling him off me.

"You'll have to learn to take me by surprise," he replied.

*

I shook myself from this memory, glad that my trousers were baggy. Soon the stage manager gave me my five-minute call as I channeled the spirit of Mr. Death.

The theatrics were slightly overstated on everyone's behalf, as we played up to our audience. My favorite part had Warwick shimmy in stage left in his fluffy pink stole and overstated high heels. Betty had entered my headquarters.

"You know, Poopsie," said my friend as his alter ego, "I always loved the way your eyes twinkle when there's a full moon." Although I'd never done it before, I clutched my heart with both hands to complement his line. "I always look forward to the tiger within you, holding me down and making me a woman!"

I was counting down to the end of the play. I wanted to kiss as special friends, the way we had the previous night. I wanted to see where it would take us.

"I have a confession to make, Doll," I announced. "I've been seeing someone else."

"Oh, baby, don't kid me."

"No darling. I'm not kidding. I'm a cad. A hopeless Casanova. An unfaithful brute. An incredible lover! But darlin', you're good for me. You stay by my side. You support me. You're there when I need you. I know what you see in me." So I paraphrased a little. There was no harm is sharing my true feelings even in the guise of a gangster.

"I see a man who needs love. More than anything else in this world, I see a man who needs love."

So true! I knew there was more in Warwick's meaning. This was the night for switching his affections.

"What good is a man who might be in jail, or worse still, dead?"

"Poopsie, even dead I don't think I would ever leave you!"

For the first time, I blew Betty a kiss as she meandered off stage, even though it was the wrong subtext for the scene.

*

As Warwick played Betty with zeal and Samantha took top marks for her alluring portrayal, it was Guy relishing in his part as Bullet that really surprised us all. With Bronx accent to the hilt, it complemented the menacing character, which seemed unsettling coming from an angel. Soon, an awkward scene between me and Pedro was upon us.

*

"You knew I was the man of this town. I had this city in the palm of my hand!" Pedro, as Mr. Money, makes these accusations as Mr. Death sits in his den. "Then you just march in and take it all as if you had a right to!"

It was spooky how close this dialogue was to the truth. I played with the idea of changing my lines to "Mr. Cash, don't be so damn stupid. You lost your grip on this town through no fault of mine!" I stared at the people in the first three rows before my thoughts returned to the task at hand.

"Mr. Cash, what makes you even think I give a damn?"

"I know you don't give a damn. I'm nobody to you. I never was, and I never will be."

"Get over it!" That line was never written in his play; it just sprung out uninvited. Pedro gave me a stare that could turn lost sailors to stone. Before continuing, I glanced at Maudi with an evil smirk. "Mr. Cash, Finance, Money, whatever your name is, give me one good reason why I should care."

His voice lowered. "Because unlike you, Mr. Death, I am an honorable man."

I wish I had turned to stone. This line was the most motivated I'd ever heard from Pedro during our run. Here I was, planning to take away his lover. What honor did I have?

*

"That was a good scene, Allan."

Warwick caught me backstage briefly after my confrontation with Mr. Money. His striking brown eyes seemed full of admiration under his bad wig.

"You've inspired me today," I said. "In fact, I'm remembering just how inspiring you've always been."

"I'm glad I put a spring in your step. Promise me you'll always think of me in that way."

"Warwick, how could I think of you in any other…"

Before I could finish, he fondly kissed my cheek and stepped on stage.

*

Another half hour of passions gone wrong, allies confirming their suspicions, and hamming it up to record highs ensued before the stage manager summoned us for our curtain call. Pedro and Guy entered the stage first, since they played the smaller roles, followed by our two gals, Samantha and Warwick. I made my way to an adoring public. Grinning like a maniacal clown, I clutched hands with the mistress and the girlfriend and bowed in unison.

Finally I was out of costume and joined the party. The crowd was like any other theater crowd. Champagne-guzzling bachelors swanned between ex-lovers and lovers-to-be; directors desperately searched for their next charismatic lead; the wannabe glamour-pusses found self-esteem by association; while the levelheaded, like Maudi, were far too wise to dip more than just a toe in the water with *these* sharks. The writer and try-hard actor was surrounded by fans, five well-groomed men who sat together. Pedro clutched his champagne like the belle of the ball, sharing seductive glances with each of his newfound posse. I gripped my own champagne as if it was an extension of my arm, studying this mutual appreciation society with Guy.

"It looks like Pedro might find someone else to keep him warm tonight," I said.

The angel ruffled his wings.

"Allan, the Warwick thing. You can't let someone else be the custodian of your own happiness. Besides, friendships often last longer than romantic liaisons."

"Guy, he's giving me signs that he's interested. I just need to stoke that fire."

"Just be careful. I don't want to see you get hurt."

Near the catering, Warwick was getting to know Samantha over martinis. Maudi and company seemed intrigued by their conversation. The director and her girls were stylishly posed, fans across their bosom, taking in champagne in chic little sips.

"Maudi has to be one of my favorite people here," I said. "Classy, wise, and overdramatic. A gay man's dream gal pal."

"Interesting," replied Guy. "I would have thought Samantha was more a gay man's gal pal."

"On the first day I met her, definitely. After watching her perform, I'm not so sure."

"Why do you say that?"

Samantha laughed out loud as the others followed suit. Some of Maudi's friends even fanned themselves as they giggled wickedly.

"Now she's natural, sharing a joke with Warwick and the others. But she's usually not like that."

"That's probably because of the martinis. I still don't get what you mean, Allan."

"She could have been really good in her role as the devoted street worker, but something kept holding her back until tonight. For some reason, she finally let her guard down and enjoyed herself, like she's doing at the moment. Usually she struts around the theater like it's her birthright, yet you can tell it's something she's only convincing herself of, as well as others."

"You seem pretty certain, Dr. Freud."

"Guy, I've been involved with the theater for a while. I know acting when I see it."

Maudi headed toward us, arms open like a grand dame making an entrance. She left her friends with Samantha and Warwick and began looking down her nose at me like an accusing headmistress.

"Your wicked streak came out again, Allan."

"You mean about the line change?"

"More than that. Don't think anyone didn't notice the way you flirted with Warwick on stage."

"Whatever do you mean, Miss Maudi?" I acted coy.

"There seems to be a hidden competitive trait in your nature after all. It's time to get serious and broadcast your intensions."

Guy fluttered his wings. Maudi gestured with her fan in Warwick's direction. I matched her intent by striding toward him like an eagle swooping to claim his prey. Midway I stopped, glanced back at my comrades, nodded, then continued to take my prize. I could hear Guy's wings ruffling again as the events that followed dragged out in slow motion.

A shrill flick of a fingernail on the stem of Pedro's glass took everyone's interest in his direction. I halted once again in limbo, halfway between the open space that separated Maudi and Guy and the writer's party. His posse seemed as excited as he was in the news he was about to share. Warwick made his way to the little gathering, leaving me to just totter aimlessly toward Maudi's fan-wielding friends, all of whom I hadn't met.

"My dear colleagues," began Pedro. "Let me cut to the chase. The glamour-puss that played Betty with such a sultry edge has decided after several deep and meaningful chats to cohabit in my modest abode."

His team of confirmed bachelors raised their glasses, as the rest of the room followed suit. I wanted to glimpse at Warwick, but just couldn't. I closed my eyes and listened to the cheers, the laughter, and the clinking glasses. I could feel myself blushing with embarrassment. I turned to face my angel and my dame. Gradually, I opened my eyes. In what now was becoming a catchphrase, Guy gently mouthed the word "ouch."

NINE

NELLIE WAS CROONING again at the Pedestal. I stared at the bottom of my glass, which a minute ago had been filled with vodka and cranberry juice.

"Doesn't that singer ever go home?"

"Allan, you're slurring," said Guy. "You need to talk to your best friend."

"Darling," Maudi said, "if your friend has found something fascinating about that lackluster writer, he must be using a microscope."

She sipped her gin and tonic.

"Precisely, darling," I garbled. "Warwick is looking more radiant than he has a right to!"

"Rubbish!" declared the angelic one. "Everyone is important. Everyone has their talents."

"Yes, my dear, you're so right," replied Maudi. "Pedro's talent is reminding us how not to write plays." Guy fluttered his wings as Maudi caught the barman's attention. "Dear, would you pour our feathered friend here a drink? Something with orange liqueur, lime, and soda. And make it a double. We all know he needs it!"

"At some point, Warwick has to know how you feel, Allan," encouraged Guy. "It won't mean he'll come back, but it will give you closure."

"I'm a coward. I admit it. I'm a coward. I've left it too long, and now Warwick's shacking up with that lover and his poisonous personality."

"My dears," interrupted Maudi, "it wasn't pussyfooting around that scored me my most ardent associate. Lord Edward Thorne was betrothed to another when I decided that this man was to be mine. I had small affections for him at the beginning, but it wasn't until he pronounced his engagement that I came to know my true feelings."

"How did you win him over?" At this stage, I needed all the advice I could get.

"Let's just say that I used all the feminine charms I could muster."

A three-piece band accompanied Nellie. One member, a willowy man in a pastel suit jacket, white T-shirt, and faded jeans, caught my attention. His hair had a punk aesthetic, but the music was far from reckless. His double bass sent me dreamily to another place. Where his bristly hair would arouse my nipples. Where my goatee would tickle his chin. Where I'd be far from the pain Warwick caused.

"You're in your happy place, aren't you, Allan?" asked Maudi.

As the barman placed our sober angel's drink on the table, Maudi ordered another round for each of us.

"I don't think that's wise," said Guy. "Look how drunk Allan is."

"My dear friend, alcohol is God's nectar. It helped Lord Edward Thorne see the errors of his ways and realize that my womanly talents far outweighed that of his betrothed."

"Just how did you make love in the 1800s?" I asked. "I mean, you can't just rip off all those layers of clothes for a quickie."

"Maybe that's when the art of striptease was invented," replied Guy. "That slow dance would have heightened passion."

"You're right," I said. "By the time they got their clothes off, who needed foreplay?"

Maudi looked smug. She waved her fan over Guy's face, then over mine.

"A lady never tells."

The music had become upbeat since we entered. Nellie gently swung her hips while one hand snapped in rhythm to the beatnik-like tune. The drummer and the guitarist played it hip in dark sunglasses, as if posing for a fashion shoot. The spiky-haired bass player soulfully strummed his instrument like it was an extension of himself. I wanted to be his groupie ready to take on his deep throbbing melody.

Around us, groovy patrons found their swing. With arms waving and bodies gyrating, they crowded the floor.

"Does this jazz feel too cool for you, Guy?" I asked.

He propped his chin on both hands, staring at us through blurry eyes and gesturing more gracelessly as the orange liqueur took hold.

"In this state," he mumbled without moving his jaw, "I could even listen to Barry Manilow."

He downed his drink as if it was water waiting for a marathon runner.

"Come on, guys," I said. "There's a party in full swing. Why aren't we dancing?"

I shuffled my feet into the crowd, holding hands with my drinking companions. We oozed into the jumbled rhythmic pulse of the bodies twisting and spinning around us. There was no Warwick or Pedro here to make me sad, just a group of friendly strangers sharing the beat.

Guy created his own tempo as his hands clapped out of synch. Even his wings got into the act, making him look like a seagull caught in a fishing net. Maudi's upper half gyrated back and forth, yet still poised like the cultivated lass she was.

I danced with them but somehow in my own space, wanting to shed my skin and take the joy of this party home with me, albeit with just the bass player. The primal pulse of his talents would inject the same life into me as he was to his instrument. We'd come alive, sweaty, breathless, ecstatic!

"Allan, darling," said Maudi. She leaned over to my ear like Mata Hari about to share a password. "That bass player is sober. You are drunk."

"So?"

"So if you approach him, you'll look like a sleazy rogue."

"How did you know I was interested in him?"

"Sweetheart, nobody here can miss your unsavory curiosity. You're slobbering over him like he's a juicy peach."

"And how I'd love to nibble on that peach. And that banana as well."

"Dear, take the matter in your own hand. No one will get hurt."

"What about friction rash?"

She shook her head. As she pulled away, Guy gazed at me, clawing his hand and purring like a tiger. Was he sending me up or saying he was horny as well? I considered it. My sex life was on life support, but would I go to hell for sleeping with an angel?

From that moment on, the rest of the soirée was a bit of a blur. I recall being chatted up by a sexy bald-headed gent in a white safari suit, or at least I'd like to think he was chatting me up. Guy danced on one of the tables to a jazz version of "Shaft." Hearing Nellie croon "Shaft" was equally bizarre. A dreamy guy was sung "Happy Birthday" while blowing out candles on a cake. Some poor elder tripped backward onto the cake. I think a group of girls helped him scrape the baked delights from his shirt, but they seemed a little anorexic so perhaps they were just hungry. I believe a man was dancing in white boxers, or maybe he was a stripper?

"Here, try this."

While my head was filled with delightfully twisted fantasies of me and the bass player, the birthday boy sidled up and shoved his finger in my mouth. Rich gooey white-chocolate cake melted down my throat.

"Is that the sample pack?"

"If you play your cards right. Besides, I have a mad desire to show off my birthday suit."

"Do I get to blow out the candle?"

He grabbed the back of my head and pulled my mouth to his moist lips. Our tongues swam, locking us to each other. An addiction I didn't want to break. I could hear the bass urging me to take this man home. Its sensual strum wouldn't lead me astray. But this man would, with all the right moves.

"Allan," Guy garbled, "if you don't take this man home with you, I will."

"You should listen to this angel," the man replied.

"What's your name?" I asked.

"Tarquin."

He leisurely glided his index finger from the bend in my arm up to my palm. A thousand nerves began to tingle. His fingers slid between mine, lifting my hand. His other hand wrapped around my waist. We were waltzing, jazz style.

"My name is Allan."

"I know. The angel already said."

I pressed my cheek to his, tracing my nose up to his temple. His dark hair was slightly damp, sweetly smelling of perspiration. My lips were moistened by the taste. He moved his mouth to meet mine. We kissed again. I was caught in the eye of a whirlwind where inside, it was safe. Nellie, my friends, and everything that I loved about the Pedestal stood outside, checking in on us, making sure all was well. Soon I'd break the trance and take Tarquin home where romance could get dirty.

TEN

TARQUIN PEELED UP my T-shirt, stopping at my chest. He crouched slowly and began licking my navel. I pulled at my top, flinging it onto the sofa as his moist mouth explored my stomach, causing me to shiver and chuckle at the tickling sensation.

"I'm feeling so sensitive," I gasped.

He raised his arm and placed his finger to my lips. I didn't say another word. I licked his finger, taking it into my mouth. With eyes closed, I imagined it was his boner resting on my tongue. My head moved from side to side until eventually Tarquin gently pulled it out.

With both hands, he undid the top button of my jeans. His tongue slithered from my tummy to the tip of my pubic hair. He burrowed like an animal looking for food, but without the strength to dig. I unbuttoned the next stud on my jeans as his face buried itself deeper into the denim.

I knelt, casually easing him to the floor. I undid his jeans, worked the zip down steadily, and reached inside. He was half-erect. I could feel it pressing at his underwear, knocking against the cotton, dying to be let out. I kissed him on the lips while clutching him downstairs.

As I moved my head forward, he rubbed his chin into my hair in small circular motions. Finally I nestled my face to his chest, groaning tenderly. He laid his head back as I traveled downward to his cock. Its warm rosy glow peeked at me. I licked it. The moist salty tang spread across my tongue like butter.

I pulled his jeans to his knees, giving his dick some breathing space. It rose in my mouth, becoming hotter and wetter with each stroke of my tongue. Its sweaty odor urged me to savor every bit of this tasty delicacy. I worked my way down the shaft steadily, craving to gulp down its rewards.

This was my escape. It might not have been love, but it was the next best thing. The sweetener to the bitter pill I was trying to recover from. Not too saccharine. More like honey. Enough to sugarcoat my heart ache.

*

"You're pacing around like your wife is giving birth."

Tarquin was right. I was digging a hole in the carpet with my footsteps.

"I feel like I've been unfaithful."

"You never told me you had a boyfriend."

"I don't."

My one-night stand sat up. We had spent the night on the floor of the living room.

"Allan, if you don't have a boyfriend, how can you feel unfaithful?"

I stopped in my tracks.

"Long story. There's someone in my life who I wish was my boyfriend, but he's not so I'm just being silly."

Tarquin patted the ground next to him. His blue eyes gazed at me like an old friend. I sat down.

"Does this man know how you feel?"

"I'm not sure. I thought he might have picked up on it by now. I haven't said anything, but I'm sure he knows. I've given him enough hints."

He started rubbing my back.

"So which is it, Allan? He *may* have picked up on it by now, or he knows?"

"Tarquin, it's complicated."

"Complicated is my specialty."

He gave me a concerned look.

"I think we may have been lovers already, before we were here in the Afterlife."

"And you're not sure because you can't remember."

"Correct."

"What does he think?"

"He doesn't believe we were anything but friends."

"It's a hard one. You get here and you can't remember bits of your past, and you go madly searching for the lost puzzle. I know how that feels."

He stopped rubbing my back, so I sat back against the couch and encouraged him to nuzzle into me. He did. I wrapped my arms lightly around his chest as he rested his temple against my cheek.

"What's your story, Tarquin?"

"I lost my life in an accident, but it took me a long while to remember. At the time, I was with my fiancé, Kent, for five years, and we were about to get married. Everyone in our church was looking forward to our wedding, but I never got to the ceremony."

"I'm sorry to hear that."

"Don't be. It's ancient history now. I've processed it all a million times, and I'm okay with it."

"You were getting married in a church?"

"Yeah, that's where most people get married, Allan."

"Some sort of special gay church?"

"No. Is there such a thing as a gay church?"

"Back where I came from there was. The Metropolitan Community Church." I moved my lips to his ear. "Tarquin, what year did you have that accident?"

"Twenty sixty-four. Why?"

"You're from my future."

"I'm used to that. I've hardly met anyone here from my time. I'm that strange future-boy everyone wants to question."

"And you were religious?"

"I was Christian, and Kent was interfaith. His religion was common in our time."

"Then this version of the Afterlife must seem strange to you. No God. No Jesus."

"But there is an angel."

"Tarquin, you know what I mean."

He turned and nodded.

"I'm used to it now. It all makes sense. In a spiritual world, why do we need figureheads? We have our own spirituality. We find it through a deeper understanding of ourselves."

"That doesn't sound very Christian."

"Kent's interfaith beliefs rubbed off on me a bit. He used to say 'Religion is for people who don't ask questions.' You're asking those questions, Allan. That's a good thing."

"But I'm not coming up with answers."

"You'll find them. After all, aren't you friends with that angel who crashed here last night?"

I broke away from our cuddle and stood up. I scanned the room as if I were looking for a burglar.

"Where is he?"

"Here," called Guy from my bedroom. "Don't you remember I came home with you?"

"Why did you do that? You're not some kind of voyeur?"

"Allan, you insisted he come home with us," replied Tarquin.

"Yes, Allan. I wanted to go home, but you insisted your place was closer. You wouldn't take no for an answer. Don't worry, I passed out straight away. Didn't hear a thing."

"Where's Maudi?"

"She went home," said my one-night stand. "She insisted."

Guy's scruffy hair and wings entered the living room, before collapsing on the couch.

"Allan," said the angel, "you just made love to this beautiful man. Why are you still obsessing over Warwick?"

"Because I love him. Sorry, that's the only answer I can come up with. I love him."

"Sounds like you've got it bad," said Tarquin.

"He haunts me constantly. I think about him most of the day when I try so hard not to. Then at night I find it hard to sleep no matter what I try to think about. Warwick crashes into my thoughts before I've even realized." I shook my fist to emphasize my point. "There's something incomplete here, I know it. What I didn't do with my life, I'm failing to do in the hereafter."

"But how can you be sure, Allan?" Guy sounded frustrated. "Pedro might be who Warwick needs to be with for his own sake. You've begun to move on by your actions last night. Don't stop now."

"But you've just said 'Pedro *might be* who Warwick needs.' Maybe he isn't?"

"I said more than that. Didn't you hear?"

"I heard the most important part."

Guy stared blankly into space.

"Monique," he said.

I nodded. "That's a really good idea."

"Who's Monique?" asked Tarquin.

"A fortune-teller. One I actually believe in."

Three sharp knocks rattled the front door.

"Who is it?" I called.

"Your oldest and dearest friend," replied Warwick. "The one you might not want to talk to."

"That's him, isn't it?" whispered my one-night stand.

Before I could answer, Guy leaped out of his seat like an abducted earthling speared by an anal probe. He grabbed Tarquin by the wrist and raced to my bedroom. As casually as I could, I opened the door.

"Before you say anything, Allan, I *was* going to leave him."

"But turtle dick has won your heart." I kept the deadpan expression of a youngster who'd opened his only Christmas gift and found a pair of socks.

"He knows how to use it. Besides, he's not that bad when you get to know him."

"So are you in love?"

"I think so. Over time we've become closer, and I've come to appreciate his little oddities."

"Like his dick."

"Like his fragrances. His colognes are terrific. One in particular called 'Trench coat' encapsulates him beautifully."

"Sordid and musty?"

"Masculine and brutish." He peered over my shoulder. "Can I come in?"

"Oh, sorry, of course you can."

He strolled in with the blissful air of a youngster who'd opened his only Christmas gift and found remote-controlled parents.

"I've actually come to pick up my stuff." I opened my mouth to speak, but Warwick interrupted. "Yes, I know I said I was going to leave Pedro, and I told him I was going to before the play, but he convinced me to stay."

"Yeah, more than stay. You're moving in with him!"

"You're upset because I've disrupted our long-running flatmate relationship. Why don't you ask Guy to move in? You guys are close. Keep him drunk, and he'll be fun!"

It wasn't a bad suggestion. Stay drunk.

"Warwick, you mean more to me than you realize."

"Can we continue this conversation in my bedroom? I need to pack."

"Um, right now?" I hid my panic, knowing his bed would look slept in.

"Yes, now. What's wrong with now?"

"Wouldn't you like to have a cup of peppermint tea or something?"

"Allan, I know you want me to stay longer, but I really must go."

"A biscuit, perhaps?"

"Allan!"

"Ginger sponge cake?"

"What's with you?"

"Chocolate éclair?"

He headed to his room. To my surprise, his bed was made. The red crocheted blanket had been thrown on shoddily, and the pillows looked like they were tossed on top at the last minute, but it was passable.

He pulled out a modest sports bag and began folding his clothes. I perched myself on the edge of his bed, letting its soft bedspread cushion my sadness. It was a unique shade of red. It reminded me of the color of the toy car ridden by the giggling child. I remembered his reckless abandon and decided to take off my parachute, risking all. It was time to let my friend know that I loved him.

"Warwick, I'm in..."

Behind him, in the corner of the doorway was the tip of Guy's wing. I clasped my friend by the hand so he couldn't turn back to the closet and see our angel friend eavesdropping.

"Allan, you're in what?"

"I'm in a lot of confusion."

"About what?"

"About what to do next."

"You can start by letting go of my hand."

"Good suggestion. We wouldn't want anything to stop us having this important conversation."

As my tone grew louder with each word, Guy's wing disappeared from view.

"I'm all ears, Allan, but you're acting a bit weird."

"Let me get back to you on this."

With the subtly of an elephant, I headed for the doorway and shuffled Guy and Tarquin back to my bedroom. I gestured to the front door before giving last night's treat a slow kiss, then headed back to Warwick. I sat on his bed again.

"As I was trying to say, you mean so much to me that..."

"That what? Allan, you're becoming the master of the pregnant pause."

While my friend was staring at me, Guy was tiptoeing past the doorway. Again I grabbed Warwick's arm so he wouldn't turn around.

"I'm trying to say…"

Tarquin now stood at the door, looking my unrequited love up and down. Warwick noticed what had to be the look of horror on my face and turned around. Guy had yanked the curious man out of view just in time, but the sound of clumsy feet couldn't go unnoticed.

"Who else is here?"

"No one."

"Allan, what was that noise?"

"What noise?"

My friend threw his hands in the air and went to investigate. I followed like a nervous Chihuahua. There was no one in the lounge room. Well, no one we could see. I looked out the sliding glass door to our balcony.

"There are people in the hallway outside. Maybe you heard one of them."

"Allan, the sound came from just outside my bedroom."

"Warwick, we're in the Afterlife. Who knows what that sound was? This whole place is one big mystery." I turned to him, noticing Guy and Tarquin huddled in the galley kitchen to my left. "Go and pack, Warwick. Go and pack."

"You're really acting strange."

My friend headed back to his bedroom. I pointed frantically to the front door as Guy nodded. Tarquin sported a mischievous grin. I blew him a kiss and left them.

Warwick shoved the last shirt he could fit into the over-packed bag, before he swung it over his back. He stood still for a moment, smiling at me.

"I'll pop back later to see how you are."

He gave me a hug, but I held on. I breathed in the manly scent at the back of his neck and felt his strong arms protect me.

"Hey, this is really bothering you, isn't it?"

I gulped back the tears and convinced myself this wasn't the end.

"Warwick, in some ways, you are more special to me than you realize."

"In what ways?"

"For a long time now, I've been…"

Slam! My household guests shut the front door with the gracefulness of a train wreck. Warwick bolted to the living room.

"Allan, who was here?"

"A ghost?"

"Allan!"

He returned to the bedroom, picked up his bag, and headed for the front door. I followed.

"Okay. Guy was here. He didn't want to disturb our conversation."

"Well, it's a conversation we'll have to return to later. Pedro is waiting for me."

"Is it love, Warwick?"

"It's something. I just don't want to define it." I felt like an abandoned pet. "Hey, don't take it so hard. I'm still your friend, your best friend. Just give me some time to play with Pedro. You never know; I might be in love."

"And you're in love with someone who hates me."

"Don't freak out about him. He's just projecting his unhappiness on to you. He'll come around. Hey, maybe you should come round for dinner? See Pedro in his comfort zone. Get to know him."

"I'll see." I did my best not to appear too lost. "Your idea about Guy moving in isn't a bad one, if he's up for it. Or I might just enjoy the space to myself. Luxuriate in my bachelorism to the hilt."

Warwick kissed me on the forehead and embraced me again. I didn't clutch him this time like my happiness depended on it. I held him tight for a moment or two to show my love for his friendship. As I pulled away, he winked at me.

"Allan, I'll arrange dinner soon."

We gave each other a quick peck on the lips before he left. He wandered down the stairs outside my front door, and even when he was out of view, I stood at the doorway pining. Eventually I closed the door, leaning back with my hand still on the doorknob, waiting for him to come back to pick up something he'd forgotten.

*

My mind reeled back to the day he whisked past me at the office, out into the corridor while I clutched the doorknob wondering who he was.

Halfway down the stairs, he turned back. He had forgotten something, although nowadays I couldn't recall what it was. As he looked up at me limply holding the door open, he introduced himself.

"I'm Warwick, the new guy."

I was under his spell. An instant bond, which I didn't realize would have potent repercussions in the future.

"Allan, not quite the new guy."

"Are you in Fiona's office?"

"I wish. No, I have that adorable black hole of need as my boss."

"Oh yes, I've heard about Mr. Beasley. He has quite a reputation."

"I have a talent for ending up with clueless managers."

I felt totally myself with this stranger. He stood framed amongst the dreary white cement walls and floor-to-ceiling glass panels, giving a spark of interest to my mind-numbing day. Another staff member, whom I took no notice in, ambled between us as we continued our conversation.

"So, Warwick, whose office are you working in?"

"Steven's. He hired me a couple of weeks ago. I was sure I wasn't going to get the job, but he told me that the aftershave I splashed on for the interview clenched the deal!"

"It pays to have the right accessories when being interviewed by the lavender mafia."

Fiona strolled past us, so we both came back inside and continued our chat near the doorway.

"Have you given Pat your five dollars for the sweep, Allan?" she called out, looking back in our direction. I didn't break my mutual gaze with Warwick as I answered.

"Yes, Fiona, but I didn't get a good horse."

Warwick chuckled as I took note of his alluring features. He was handsome. His cute Maori nose highlighted his Aboriginal characteristics. A gorgeous indigenous mix. His eyes spoke confidence, ready to guide me into his web of friendship.

"Allan, I'd better get back to Steven. *I'm* the typing pool."

"I'll come with you. I want to see how you've set up your office."

Those idiotic words just fell out. I liked this guy. I wanted us to be close from the start.

"Follow me," he said.

I didn't know why, but for the first time in ages, I had a spring in my step. I felt like I was courting, even though I had a boyfriend at home.

"Where do you live, Warwick?"

"I just moved into Balmain. Nice terrace house with three other friends. You?"

"Uptown Dulwich Hill. Balmain, huh, expensive?"

"A bit. I think I made the wrong decision, but I'm trapped there for at least six months. Who do you live with?"

"Oh, a friend," I said. It wasn't a complete fib. My boyfriend and I were acting more like friends at that point in time.

We entered his office. A sturdy stapler and hole punch sat to the right of his desk in an era when most people had embraced a paperless office. To his credit, there was only one binder on a shelf behind his chair. Everything else was placed in neat little groups. A bronze cup and saucer with a teaspoon sat diagonally left of the in-tray. Post-it notes in small, medium, and large were piled on top of each other next to his phone.

Warwick was either a neat freak or a serial killer. Death by staple! Nametags for his victims made of yellow Post-its. Who's who and where in the compactus you will find their bodies, all printed out on A4 in his binder. The boys would be cataloged behind the blue divider, and the girls behind the pink. The yellow was for those no one's sure about.

"So what do you think of the place?" I asked.

"I think we should catch up so you can fill me in on the office gossip."

"Warwick, it's a definite date."

"Allan, is it short notice to have you over for dinner tonight? I'm making nachos for my housemates. Why don't you join us? Just come home with me after work."

Although I was afraid I'd been putting on weight, the offer sounded too good. Mary, the trolley girl, often showed off her wares around morning teatime. I was powerless against her raspberry danish. Having that delicate pastry and custard melt in my mouth reminded me of the sex I was missing. I was one desperate puppy. Grated cheese and sour cream just might have had the same effect. I accepted Warwick's invitation.

I called my boyfriend and told him that I was working late, although I didn't think he believed me. I wasn't sure if he actually cared. That morning, he'd been glued to the television when I left for work. He didn't even bother offering me a goodbye kiss.

Warwick's house was one of those Balmain terraces, a little rundown but perfect for renters. There was about a meter of space between the decorative rusted iron fence and the building. Between the two, the cement was covered with blue tiles and a couple of huge pot plants. It was the perfect low-maintenance garden for city dwellers in this suburb.

Inside, the home was like any other share house. Slapdash furniture with a decent-sized television for entertainment and old worn carpet ready to be replaced if the landlord ever decided to move in. A gleaming silver mini hi-fi provided the soundtrack for the evening.

"Do you like Lou Rawls?" he asked.

"I'm not sure I know who he is."

"Allan, wash your mouth out with soap. Aren't you into soul?"

"If the mood's right."

He played me a few tracks. He was a bit pedestrian for my tastes back then, but I didn't say anything. When he dug out some vintage Soul II Soul, I felt more in the groove.

Warwick's housemates were nice, two girls and a guy. They were all staff at a local restaurant, where they had met and decided to move in together. Warwick was the latest addition, his share of the rent helping finance the extra channels they decided to add to their pay-TV bill. They probed me with a hundred questions, as if they were checking my credentials in the husband stakes. Once I explained that I was already attached, I was off the hook.

After dinner, his friends cleaned up as we sat chatting at the dining table.

"Won't your boyfriend be worried about you, Allan?"

"Let's not go there today, Warwick. You can meet him later. For now, I'm getting an impression of what makes you tick."

"That's easy: people. I love meeting new people. That's why I'm trying to find out what makes *you* tick."

To me, this sounded like a come-on. Maybe in hindsight it was.

"You've put me on the spot, Warwick."

"Well, I know you like music, Allan."

"Yes. I'm suspicious of people with just one CD in their collection, or people that tell you they love Elvis but can't recall 'The Edge of Reality.'"

"I know what you mean. My last partner was like that."

"What? An Elvis fan?" I had visions of Warwick making love to a man in a jumpsuit.

"No! He only owned one CD. One of those recent hits collections, which he'd throw on for parties to prove he was cool."

"Long relationship?"

"No, just a fling. We'd run out of things to talk about."

"Opposites attract," I said.

"Yes, but rarely ever stay together," Warwick replied.

We shared a merlot, a Western Australian favorite from his wine club. We continued discussing music, then switched to movies. He mentioned how he made extra money at nights and on weekends.

"I'm an extra."

"You're an extra?" I repeated.

"Yeah, in commercials and movies."

"Were you in that weird sci-fi flick they shot last year, *The Attack of the Fembots*?"

"Yes, Allan. That was one of the more fun jobs I did. The money they poured into that thing! It was an international coproduction."

"It was like manga meets B-grade. Bikini-clad women shooting laser beams from their eyes while missiles would shoot from their arms. It went straight to video here, but it found a cult audience in the US and Japan."

Warwick shook his head as he filled our glasses. "Are you a fan of the genre? You seem to know a lot about that film."

"I was in it." My new friend tilted his head and glared at me like a cat about to become roadkill. "Just in one scene, but it was a two-day shoot. Now and again, I get invites to sci-fi conventions, but I can't afford the flights overseas."

"How did you get the time off work?" he asked.

"Oh, I was in between jobs. Well, sort of. I didn't really have one. The office gig has been a financial relief after three years of doing odd jobs to pay the bills in between little acting roles. Well, more like extra roles in commercials."

"Do you still act?"

"Only in community theater from time to time. Although, there is talk now and again of a Fembot sequel."

"Who were you in the film?"

"Remember that nerdy professor who hid in the cellar from one of the vixens? He ended up making love to her, helping her realize that humans can be good for something."

"Allan, I didn't see the film. I just hid myself in the background."

"Lucky you. Anyway, once she finally turns good, she decides to march right into the army barracks, thinking she could have some more fun. They kill her in a spray of bullets."

Warwick nearly choked on his wine, spilling a little on his jeans. He wiped his mouth with his wrist and looked up at me.

"Why didn't she just laser-beam the army to death?"

"Warwick, it's a B-film. It's not supposed to make sense. Maybe my lovemaking brought down her defenses?"

We ended up quite drunk that night, and to this day, I still believe his housemates were leaving us alone to see if there were any sparks. That was about a year ago, and even though there was a connection, it was as friends. It was some time later that I admitted to myself how I actually felt. And here I was, twelve months after we'd met, realizing that I'd missed the boat.

ELEVEN

"NO ONE BELIEVED you, did they?" Monique asked.

"Some did. Others, definitely not."

I sat shuffling her tarot deck. She gazed at me like a counselor planning the best way to broach a difficult subject.

"Not everyone wants to face up to what's going on around them."

"By everyone, you mean Warwick?"

"Is that who didn't believe you the most?"

"Samantha thought it was all rubbish as well. Oh, and of course, Pedro, the guilty party."

"I can tell you there will be no more falling stage lights or attempts to hurt you. The lovers are trying a different tact."

"You know all of this without looking at the cards?"

She shrugged.

"I know a lot of things, Allan. I know that you'll be offered a role in another play. I know that you've been thinking of leaving the Limelight Quarter and joining us here at the Carnival of Lost Souls. Don't! You need to take to the stage again."

"Why? I've already lost Warwick. Maybe Guy's been right all along. I need some 'me' time."

"Have you finished shuffling the cards?"

I looked at the deck in my hand. I'd been shuffling for so long that the corners were wearing down. Monique raised an eyebrow as I handed them to her. She began to lay them out.

I noticed the murmur of locals outside her tent. The distinct traits of various voices soon lent itself to a streamlined babble. I closed my eyes to deal with this murmur, which got louder and eventually echoed in my head. I opened my eyes, but as it had the last time my cards were read, everything disappeared. No Monique. No tent. There was just a fuzzy white haze that soon morphed into a giant Monopoly board.

I looked at my hands. They had aged. Wrinkled like the hands of a farmer after years of pulling at his crops. The murmur in my head was now the hum of a chorus, church-like, gothic almost. It soothed me as did my weightlessness. I was floating as I watched my mud-stained work pants and bare feet touch down on Baltic Avenue. I slid on the white cardboard, slamming down on my ass. As I groaned in pain, a pair of hands reached around me. It was Warwick, also in soiled work clothes. I clutched his hands and pulled them tighter around me.

On the square marked "Go," a tall charismatic man in top hat and tails began to read a poem from a crumpled piece of paper. Although he looked nothing like me, it was my voice I could hear read the poem over the gothic choir.

In another life, we were paupers
I fell ill
You held me tight
I died too soon

Warwick was now wearing a starched white shirt. I felt myself being dragged away so I held onto him. We were on Illinois Avenue.

In another life, we were lovers
You yearned for respect
You yearned for affection
I seldom listened

I could feel him crying in my arms. His body jerking with the outpouring of each tear. My own sadness choked me before Warwick leaned back and reached out to me again, looking proud in a purple robe.

In another life, we were royalty
Our world was our own
I held you tight
We kissed, we slept

I was locking lips with my man on the outskirts of Community Chest. Soon we were dragged away to St James Place where a little person was waiting for us.

In another life, we had a child
Sandcastle building
Insect collecting
We had a child

I was overjoyed. Our youngster was running around us in a circle, giggling as if she was chasing a never-ending stream of friends. But then she vanished.

In this life, we missed the boat
We shared our lives
Held back on love
But never sailed

We were slumming in secondhand clothes on Vermont Avenue.

In one more life, we'll know it all
Tales of triumph
Wisdom collated
Journey completed

For a moment, I found Warwick and me sitting on the "Go" square, but soon he wasn't there, as Monique and her tent returned to view.

"Welcome back." She took her glasses off and blew on the lenses before wiping them with a lilac cloth. "I think you've had quite a trip."

"You're understating it just a little. What the hell happened?"

"Your lives happened."

She placed her glasses back on her face, sliding the frames up her nose with her index finger. Her cavalier attitude did not match my sense of bewilderment. My brain felt as twisted as a strip of licorice. Another trip like that and I would have considered hiding under my duvet and never venturing out of my apartment.

"I was with Warwick, over and over again."

"And you've been with Warwick, over and over again. You and your soul mate have lived, laughed, and loved, but somewhere in there, you lost your way."

"Somewhere between having a child and our last life as friends."

"You're catching on quick."

"So why was I shown all this?"

"You need to get back on the right path to complete your journey."

"But it's not as easy as you think."

"Allan, nothing ventured, nothing gained."

I could sense a huge rope pulling away in my hands. I looked up and saw Warwick tied to the other end, floating away like a helium balloon. I let go of the rope and let uncertainty spread like an illness through my upper chest and up to my face, making me feel numb. The vision disappeared.

"He's slipping away, isn't he?" I asked.

"You both are, from each other."

"Like Guy said, maybe I need to let him go?"

"Don't! Once you lose each other, you'll lose yourselves. You'll drift aimlessly here, without purpose, without goals."

"Then I should tell him. Problem solved. He wouldn't want his soul to drift aimlessly, so he'll agree to be my boyfriend."

"That would be fake," she warned me. "You need to win his heart, not play with his head."

"Warwick's my destiny."

I sat sipping a cup of tea with Guy and Maudi at her place, soon after my visit to Monique.

"And that's definitely what she said?" asked Guy.

"We've had many past lives together. We've been a couple, but this time we've drifted apart."

"Boy meets boy, boy loses boy," said Maudi. "Boy meets boy again, but boy runs off with the most boorish man this side of the theater."

"That pretty much sums it up," I replied.

I placed another sugar cube in my tea with an elegant set of tongs before I sank into her lounge. Its fabric depicted small wrens framed in tree branches, delicately outlined in fern-green and gold. I was in the realm of old-world charm, where being a guest would bring the home comforts of grandma with a slightly biting edge.

The opulent grandfather clock struck three, unnerving me, making me spill a little of my tea. As Maudi took out her handkerchief to wipe clean the Chinese-influenced design on my saucer, I gazed through her lace curtains to the classic garden outside.

"You're daydreaming about him, aren't you?" asked Maudi. She promptly took the tea-stained hankie to the laundry and returned to the couch. "Allan, you will never win his heart by simply daydreaming."

"I know."

"Need I remind you about my courtship with Lord Edward Thorne? We were like royalty. I, the queen of his world, and he, my debonair prince."

"We get the picture," said Guy.

"I promise to go after Warwick and win his heart."

"But not with your own heart on your sleeve," the angel counseled. "Allan, my advice is the same as when I was telling you to let Warwick go. Stay in control. Tread carefully or you may lose him."

"I get your point, Guy, but at this stage, I have no idea how I'll get him back."

"My dear," said Maudi, "this is where we come in."

"Yes, queen of the world, how do I snare my debonair prince?"

"Did you read that play I left with you a couple of days ago?"

"Yeah, I loved it. It was like reading an updated version of a García Lorca play."

"And what did you love about it, Allan?"

She peered at me like an English teacher, conducting a verbal revision test. I responded like the teacher's pet.

"It was so surreal. A witch, a warlock, and the man in the moon casting love spells on mortals. What's there not to love?"

"Go on."

"Yes, go on, Allan," said Guy. "Samantha's been going on and on about this play, but I haven't read it yet."

"Fabien is an Irish master of magic, who casts a spell of sexual tension between a happily married couple and a younger man, who are yet to meet. They are introduced at a party that has been thrown in the couple's honor to celebrate their twentieth anniversary."

"And it gets a tad more sordid," said Maudi.

"Yes, yes," I replied. I clasped my hands together as if I were telling a tale I had written myself. "As the three mortals are awakened by their sexual desires, Fabien starts to brag. His colleagues become intrigued with the social experiment and add their own spells into the mix. A friendship develops between the couple and the young man, but Ipan, the man in the moon, doesn't like what's happening and keeps watch on them, moralizing constantly. But this is the best bit. The couple talk about their feelings regarding a possible ménage à trois, as the younger man grapples between his duty not to come between them and his desire to share *cum* between them.”

“You obviously like this play,” said Guy.

“I love it. They keep analyzing the situation on all sides. Should they go there? Should they leave their desires alone? It’s delicious!”

“Well, congratulations are in order, Allan,” announced Maudi. “You and Guy are taking the stage again. And Warwick is in the cast as well.”

“And Pedro?”

She screwed up her bottom lip. “Unfortunately, yes.”

“You cast Pedro in the play?”

“Oh, it wasn’t my doing, dear. I’m not involved with this one. Samantha is directing the play, and she insisted you be in it.”

“How spooky. It’s just as Monique predicted.” I sipped my tea. “Pedro didn’t write this one, did he?”

“Written it! I doubt he’ll understand it.”

“Allan, it was written by a teenager whose mother goes to Samantha’s gem collector’s club,” said Guy.

“Samantha collects gems?”

“Yes.” The angel stood up, pushing out his chest the way Samantha often did to accentuate her undersized breasts, before strolling around the room with a vaguely innocent look. “We all met each other at a club for people who collect gemstones, and after months of admiring each other’s clothes, we had a makeshift fashion show. Just ourselves! We felt like stars.” He flicked his imaginary long hair. “We just used what was in our wardrobes. Then we all talked about how different we all looked in certain outfits. Gloria looked like Marlene Dietrich in her husband’s suit. I looked like a little fairy in one of Paul’s transvestite outfits.”

“There’s a transvestite in their club?” I asked.

“Well, it is a gem collector’s club,” Guy replied as himself. “He probably makes his stones into jewelry.”

“Makes sense.”

“Suddenly, like magic, we were overcome by the spirit of theater! We became motivated to put on a play, so our next gem night was a play reading night, and we all presented our own scripts.”

“So what do you know about the playwright?”

Guy broke out of character again.

"All we know is that it's written by the nineteen-year-old son of someone named Gloria."

"I think at his age, Gloria's son is privileged to far too much sexual experience."

"You realize the gem meetings are a front for a swingers club," reported Maudi. "They look at gems before becoming amorous."

"It's official. My time here is getting weirder and weirder." I put down my cup. "Does Samantha know that you know her gemstone-collecting club is a front for swingers?"

"No, dear. I have friends that have been."

"As far-fetched as that sounds," said Guy, "it's sort of believable."

"That is part of the reason I wanted to discuss this with you, Allan. And in light of your little visit to your fortune-teller, my timing could not be more immaculate." She leaned over in her seat, lowering her voice like a nurse coercing someone to use a chamber pot. "It's time to take a leaf from this play. Make this about the three of you, not just about the two of *them*. Become Warwick's mistress!"

"Maudi, I don't need more complications in my life."

"My dear, threesomes are the new black, or so I've been told."

"By whom?"

"My other friends at the gem club."

"Maudi, can't Allan just lure Warwick away from Pedro?" asked Guy. "I'm not sure how he'd go about it, but it would cause the least pain."

"My dear angel chum, the mistress is the one with the least commitment and all the rewards." Our friend's wings drooped. "Now listen. When I was the star of the stage, a little tramp named Claire was affianced to a simple chap whom I loved deeply."

"Yes, Maudi, we know," I said. "You've mentioned him over and over. Lord Edward Thorne."

"Precisely! I can tell you that it wasn't my complacency that won his heart. Alluring perfumes and tempting offers handwritten in private notes, all helped my Eddy see the error of his ways."

"And *you* called Claire the tramp!"

"Allan dear, the difference between good sex and bad sex is the level of guilt you feel afterward. In your day, it may have been about a shared level of bliss, but in my day, the bliss was measured by how important it was to keep it discreet."

"You naughty girl."

I looked at Guy, who was rolling his eyes.

"As I always say, guilt is a wasted emotion. Besides, you shouldn't concern yourself about tomorrow. You can't guess how someone will respond. Just go and snare your man!"

"So how do I set a trap for Warwick?"

"You're halfway there already. You have history. Now make a future."

TWELVE

I FROLICKED INTO the theater like Red Riding Hood on her way to Grandma's, inspired to make this first rehearsal a fresh start. Guy was there to greet me, as were Samantha and a few cast members I had yet to meet. Samantha asked me what I thought of my role.

"What a beautiful old gentleman Ipan is. He's warm and loving, and moralistic in a *good* way."

"I'm glad you like the role. I think you'll do wonders with it. I have a special moon costume for you."

"Huh?"

A moon costume wasn't quite the plan I had for Ipan, but for the moment, I put blind faith in my director. Samantha looked the part with round brassy glasses and a dark gray suit, almost like a naughty librarian. With her bag full of stationery, she passed for the type of schoolboy fantasy that could answer all his prayers and then help him with his homework.

As we waited for Warwick and Pedro to arrive, Guy and I talked to Janice, the actress who would play the wife. She seemed an assured thirty-something. Her sloppy green jumper highlighted her wavy red hair and strong cheekbones. A pencil with an eraser on the end was poised in one hand, while her script was marked with endless acting notes.

"You're our conscience," she said.

"Yes, I do my best to keep you in line," I replied.

"Are you that moralistic in real life?"

"I like to pride myself that I'm not, but at the end of the day, I don't take the chances I should."

"We're all guilty of that, sometimes."

"Some more than others," added Guy.

I glanced down at the rows of white seating and saw Warwick and that lover of his enter the theater.

"Ah, there's my husband," said Janice. "And the love interest."

"Oh. Which one's your husband?"

"The elegant dark one."

Warwick romped ahead of his mate to greet me. He asked how I was, so I told him I enjoyed living alone. It wasn't exactly true, but I wanted to appear upbeat.

"That's great, Allan. You've been in my thoughts." I looked at Samantha to see if she wanted to begin rehearsal. Warwick did the same. She returned our gaze. "I'd like to catch up this week if that's okay. How about a line run?"

"Tomorrow night's best for me," I replied.

"It's a date."

"Hi, Allan," said Pedro. He didn't make eye contact.

"Hi, Pedro, have you lost something on the floor?"

He looked up. "Sorry, just going over lines in my head."

"Hello, everyone," said Samantha. "Welcome to what will be a season of lust, loyalty, and magic, all in three acts!"

I gazed at Warwick, wishing the director's words encapsulated *my* life. He looked handsome in his simple short-sleeved shirt, black with scarlet stitching. As the director spoke, my psyche drifted to a rocket on the moon. There we were, weightless inside our craft, trying to catch one another, bouncing ourselves from various fixtures into each other's arms. Our astronaut suits would casually drift away as, naked, we would attempt re-entry.

My lunar thoughts were crudely disrupted by a fate worse than puberty. Resembling a giant pimple waiting to be squeezed was Ipan's moon suit. Samantha unzipped its protective covering and unveiled this crime of a costume. It had a dinner jacket and bow tie sewn onto it, and a separate elasticized hood. I put it on and glared at the mirror, looking like a cross between a panda bear and a bloated gingerbread man.

"Beautiful!" Samantha exclaimed.

Everyone watched me stumble around in this roly-poly nightmare. She told us that this was her touch of genius and made me apply white grease paint to complete the look.

At first tea break, Guy tried to console me.

"It's not that bad. Hey, look at what I'm wearing." He picked at the shiny metal stars on his black tunic. "Could I be more stereotyped?"

"At least you look like you've walked off the set of *Bewitched*. I look like a giant beach ball! It's a wonder there's not a huge sandcastle on stage."

"This is going to be a long rehearsal period."

"How did Samantha come up with these revolting outfits?"

"Apparently, she sketched them herself."

"That woman should never be let near a pencil again! I'm hardly going to win Warwick over in this padded pantomime disaster."

"Play the sympathy card. It might work."

I looked down at my stretchy white gloves. "At least I'm seeing him tomorrow night, away from Samantha's disturbed imagination."

"How will you win his heart?"

"Guy, I have absolutely no idea. Dumb luck? Answer the door naked? Get him stoned? No idea." A wicked smirk appeared on the angel's face. "You think I should get him stoned?" He nodded. "Let me get this straight. A celestial being is telling me that I should get shitfaced with Warwick to get him into bed?"

"I wouldn't put it that bluntly, but yes, that's the general idea. Leave it to me, Allan. Just make yourself available before rehearsal tomorrow. We have a visit to make."

Our break was over, and I was asked to step on stage.

Warwick as James and Janice as Simone dried dishes in their kitchen, stage right. Pedro as the forbidden fruit was in front of his stereo wearing headphones, stage left. I was center stage struggling not only with my costume, but with the spell of sexual energy that Fabien had cast. I glanced to either side before presenting my monologue.

*

"This is just not right. A loving couple supports each other. They've shared their adventures and their dreams. Then there's the young idealist, searching for affection at an age when passion flows. There are more kisses to share, more fantasies to fulfill, more love to desire, but not together. Fabien, this is not a game without consequence. It's not for your entertainment. Real respect could be lost. Special memories could fade."

"But new memories could be made," replied Guy as Fabien, walking in from backstage. "Special moments to lose themselves in. A test of love that's already there. Why not share it?"

"There's more than enough love between James and Simone. Why cause disruption?"

"Because sometimes intimacy bonds people like no other encounter can."

"But look at this young man. His future is bright, and our couple couldn't be more in love. They'll fall apart, and he'll be burnt by the incident. Fabien, why play with lives?"

"Ipan, why let life pass them by? Let the emotional become the physical. Let them share this special gift with one another."

At this point in the play, the lights would fade on us, as James and Simone take over the scene. Samantha stopped us from continuing, firmly shaking her head.

"I don't think so," she uttered. "You're a warlock, and you're the man in the moon. You're not real-life characters. You're playing it all too seriously."

"But this is a serious part of the text," I replied. I waddled to the front of the stage. "It's conversational and tells a lot about our points of view."

"Yeah, but that's boring," said the director with a dismissive hand gesture. "Swirl around the stage, Allan. You're the moon. And Guy, add in a few evil laughs. Let the audience know you're the bad guy."

"But Samantha, maybe *I'm* the antagonist. Maybe they *should* make love."

"The antaga-what?"

"The character against the theme of the play," interrupted Warwick.

"Oh, nonsense. You're the good guy, and Guy's the bad guy. Simple as that!" Samantha browsed through her script as if feigning authority. She directed us to begin the scene again, this time as a farce. Quick sideway glances were shared by Guy, Warwick, and I before we murdered our roles with disregard for the play's poetic text.

THIRTEEN

"So you're the man who wrote that wonderful play." I shook hands with the young adult. "Apparently you also can help with some marijuana."

"Yes, I can," he replied. "But I think Guy had something else in mind."

I stared at the angel who had walked ahead of me through the front door. He smirked.

"Advice is what he means," my winged friend replied.

"Advice?"

"Yes, Allan, advice. Before swimming in uncharted territory, you have to do your research. What better advice is there than from the person who wrote the play?"

I shook my head, feeling like my unrequited love was front-page news.

"He's right, you know," said our host. "But your situation is different, Allan. Mine was mutual; yours needs work."

He ushered us into the lounge room.

"Okay, mine's not about a blissful threesome, but there is intensity there."

"And there's still passion to be had. Why should you miss out on that, no matter the consequences? The fallout can't all be bad."

"Now you're sounding like your own play," said Guy. "But it's the fallout that worries me most. You don't want tears before bedtime."

"Just the thing Ipan would say," I commented.

We shared Brady Bunch smiles. Our host sank back into his worn terracotta-colored armchair. The coffee table wobbled as he placed his feet on it. Stale cigarette butts in an ashtray on the balcony and the three-quarter-empty bourbon bottle in the kitchen blended in a scent that shrieked bachelorism.

"Sorry about the state of this place," he said. "My flatmate smokes."

"Boys will be boys," I replied. "Where is he?"

"Out. No idea where. Probably at the Pedestal."

"Like I said, boys will be boys."

I gazed at the orange typewriter on their smoky-glass-topped dining table. A box of carbon paper and a pile of clean foolscap sheets sat near the writing machine, as did several bottles of liquid paper.

"Let me guess. You're from the seventies."

He nodded.

I wandered over to the typewriter and admired its slightly curved edges. It was a testament to what was once considered modern styling at a time when mission-brown and burnt-citrus shades were considered futuristic. The clattering of keys would pulse in rhythm under the writer's fingers, only stopping when the clunk of two letters slammed into each other as they raced to make their mark.

"I'm impressed," I said. "Wait a second. I only know you as Gloria's son."

"And that's all you'll ever know me as." He gestured for me to sit down. "Some of my friends call me Glory for short."

"Eek! I don't think I could call you Glory. Too weird!"

"Weirder than Gloria's son?"

"No, I can live with Gloria's son. Is it a case of an embarrassing first name, or do you have some creative artistic reason?"

"A bit of both. I think Mum named me something embarrassing for artistic reasons." Guy and I chuckled. "How's the play going?"

"We've only had one rehearsal. There's still a lot of work to do." I tried to sound as positive as I could. "How deep did you and the couple get in your relationship?"

"I didn't lay all my cards on the table, so that's why the sex is unresolved in my play."

"I'm not sure that answers my question."

Gloria's son winked at me before leaning forward.

"Allow me some discretion, Allan. But you came here for advice on your love life, not hear the ins and outs of mine." Now I leaned forward. "Does he flirt with you?"

"Lately he has. Or at least he did before he moved in with Pedro."

"That's not a bad thing. This way you know he's interested. Now steal a kiss backstage."

"But what if he pulls away?"

"Then at least he knows you're ready to take it further."

"Hold on," said Guy. "It's not Warwick that will get hurt if Allan puts himself on the line."

"Thank goodness I wasn't around in the twenty-first century. Allan, you and Warwick sound so uptight!"

"Correction. I'm really the one that's uptight," I replied. "Everyone around me had friends with benefits. Even Warwick had little liaisons from time to time."

"So take a leaf out of his book. Just let love flow. If he doesn't kiss you back, at least he'll go away and consider it."

"But I'll feel like a total goose."

"Not if you think of it as just sex. It's merely an extension of the love you guys already have."

"So I should just aim for a bit of fun and not romance?"

"Bingo!" Gloria's son rubbed his hands. "My work here is done."

The cautious angel flapped his wings several times. "Isn't it better to kiss him tonight, when he visits you at home, Allan?"

Our young advisor nodded. "Guy has a point. If he's coming around without Pedro, you can take it further then and there."

"I'm still scared," I admitted. "I don't want to wager too much emotional baggage on the roulette wheel."

"Allan, if you don't place the bet, you'll never win," advised Gloria's son. He reached below the coffee table and pulled out a box made of woven bamboo. "Besides, I've got something that will help you in your quest."

Inside was a clear container of marijuana, surrounded by its associated implements. With the expertise of a watchmaker, he rolled a generous joint for me to share with Warwick. By the odor of the dried weed, I could tell we'd be having a fun time even without sex.

"Do you want one as well, Guy?"

"Yes, please. I think I'll need it after rehearsal."

AFTER ANOTHER UNINSPIRED afternoon under Samantha's direction, Guy escorted me home so we could lick our wounds. Warwick went to Pedro's, but promised to visit later and run lines. I was desperate for a shower to rinse my clammy self, after sweating all day inside that ludicrous moon suit.

Cassandra Wilson's slick vocals played on the stereo. The soft patter of bongos and the rich throb of the bass cushioned my stress, making me yearn to share my soul. In time, the transition would be complete. Calm would reign after the play's chaos, and my love and I would stand together, serene in each other's arms.

I cleansed myself back to normality with each drop from the showerhead, reflecting on how water, whether observed or experienced, never failed to console. The silky bath towel massaged my scalp as I inhaled an alluring scent coming from the living room. Guy was enjoying his gift from this morning's visit, spread out on the sofa like a rag doll.

"I couldn't wait," he said. "It's hot in that tunic, and I need to forget about today."

"There's a fresh towel in the bathroom. Take a shower. You'll feel better."

"Anything to wash away today's melodrama."

He took another puff and handed me his joint.

"Don't forget, tonight is about me and Warwick. I don't need you hanging around too long after he gets here."

My friend headed for salvation as I clouded my senses in front of my wardrobe. Should I wear a red T-shirt or a black short-sleeved top? It was such a dilemma.

As I felt the smoothness of a well-worn pair of jeans swallow my thighs, the music filtered through my thought patterns. I wished that my winged music student would be seduced by this type of jazz, as it normally appealed only to diehard fans. If not, there were Vince Jones and Kurt Elling CDs on hand to make the transition smoother or Marlena Shaw to ease him with a camp aesthetic.

I took another puff, aware I was overanalyzing. I considered how Ipan could've been such a beautifully vulnerable character, instead of his portrayal being marred by a confused director. Perhaps I was being paranoid, but whenever anyone was hitting their stride, Samantha would direct them off course. Pedro seemed to do whatever he wanted with minimal direction. His portrayal of the open-minded love interest was as believable as a naive pool cleaner in a porn flick.

The shower was running, and I knew Guy was rebooting his soul. As I drifted in front of my mirror, I stood upright as Ipan should, as suggested by the text. He was meant to be a proud man, full of wisdom and old-fashioned values. A kindhearted chap, out to do the right thing. Not a pantomime fool.

Guy peeked into the bedroom. He mouthed "he's here" and ruffled his wings in slow motion. I passed the joint back to my friend so it could be offered to my visitor. I was already dressed, so all I needed to do was make my way to the living room. I summoned my feet to walk in the general direction, and on second request, they responded.

"I love it when you're in this state," said Warwick. He studied my eyes. "They're as red as raspberries. How many puffs have you had?"

"Just a few. Guy's clutching onto it now."

"This is so cool!" remarked our winged companion.

His eyes were closed as he swayed to Cassandra's crooning.

"Warwick, you might as well finish the joint," I said. "We don't need any more puffs."

I took it from Guy's fingers. With a deep breath, my friend inhaled what was left of the wacky weed.

"Hmm," he remarked.

I glanced back at Guy, who was giving me a look I couldn't comprehend. Was it supposed to be a look of seduction? If so, he needed practice.

I was reminded that before this whole experience, his kind was only something mentioned in religious texts and popular novels. I now took his gray wings for granted, like a friend with a scar or bad acne. The reality of where we were was a little easier to digest in this ethereal state of mind.

"Guy, I have a question for you," I said.

"Yes?"

"How does an angel have sex? I mean, don't the wings get in the way?" I stepped closer to examine them. "Are they an erogenous zone? It can't be comfortable lying on your back, can it? Can you lie on your back?" I stroked them, feeling their fleecy texture. "If you could fly, would it take a lot of effort to remain airborne and still make love? Could it technically be called the mile-high club?"

"That's more than one question, Allan."

"I think I'm over Pedro." This admission from Warwick took a while to sink in, simply because it had nothing to do with the current conversation. "I shouldn't have moved in with him."

I gradually turned, jaw wide open, no doubt resembling one of those fairground clown heads you place balls into.

"How does Pedro feel about it?" asked Guy.

"I haven't told him yet."

"Are you going to?"

"Hmm."

"You're being a coward," I said. "Are you sure you're just not over the honeymoon stage?"

"Hmm."

Warwick was more contemplative than conversational.

Guy turned to us, fluttering and raising his feet several centimeters off the carpet.

"Guy, do you know what you just did?" I said.

The angel looked at the distance he traveled. A goofy laugh followed as he pointed back to where his feet first left the ground. He fluttered again, this time flying back to the stereo in an attempt to change the CD. Cassandra's vocals ended on impact. The disc tray flung open as the sound system tumbled backward with Guy.

Sprawled out over the music machine, his dopey laugh returned. I was relieved that no first aid had to be administered as, in my subdued state, he could have bled to death before I noticed the red stain on the carpet.

Our angel pal leisurely crawled over to us, staggered to his feet, and encased us with his wings. His intention was clear. Fortunately I had enough social additive under my belt not to freak out. After all this time trying to know Warwick in the biblical sense, I was about to get the "steak knives" thrown in for free.

Guy took one hand from us each and placed them on his butt cheeks. Our hands were snared under his jeans, exploring the supple textures of his underwear. That feel of well-laundered cotton—was there anything more intense? Judging the package from the front of his jeans, it was easy to tell that this angel was the Master's favorite.

Warwick turned to my horny comrade, opened his mouth, and waited for a response. He got his answer. How I felt about this was all still ambiguous. The weed had buffered my emotions, killing any hint of jealousy while letting a sense of longing take over. If this is what it took to sleep with Warwick, so be it. Now Guy's lips beckoned me. The moist embrace sent me to another zone. Warwick who?

Guy shot a quick glance side to side at us both, before moseying to my bedroom with our hands still captive to his cotton-clad cheeks. He led us to the waiting bed. All of us lay humbly facedown. My hand journeyed upward to explore the contour of his back, where the base of his wings met. Warwick's hand took the excursion south, but Guy's jeans halted any further investigation.

Our angelic love doctor eased his way to a kneeling position, instinctively making us turn on our backs. He gestured for us to sit up. As we did, he placed his hands behind our necks and brought us to his mouth. Our tongues reached out, touching at the tips before sliding in all directions.

Guy smelled fresh and clean, like talcum powder, while Warwick's musky fragrance made me want to melt with these men into one heaving, throbbing beast. I too clutched the back of their necks, bringing this three-way kiss to an intensely liberating encounter.

Our celestial friend broke away, pushing Warwick and I together. We kissed madly. Our tongues sliding and exploring. My world spinning, blissfully waiting to lose control.

Guy moved his hands from our necks, gently running his index finger from my navel to my crotch. I peeked and saw Warwick getting the same treatment, both of us stiffening as he rubbed. My kissing partner groaned. I joined him in cries of ecstasy.

The angel unbuttoned our jeans, exposing us to his whim. Warwick and I glanced down as Guy tasted what my friend had to offer. With both hands, I forced Warwick to my mouth, kissing him as he moaned in synch with Guy's rhythm.

Then I sighed as I felt our buddy lick my shaft. His warm mouth taking me in, making my body wilt like a flower long before I was spent. Two sets of tender lips were using me for their pleasure, and I for theirs.

Guy's moist tongue swirled around my knob as I whined. Warwick kissed me harder. The angel swallowed me whole and drew back before pushing down again. His tempo made me quiver.

I reached around and caressed Warwick's back, lightly weaving my fingernails around his shoulder blades. He moved his mouth to my nipple and bit gently. He reached down to my balls and caressed them. Guy's expert mouth moved away as Warwick gripped my cock and held tight.

I kissed the top of his head, burying my face in his thick black curls. His lovely scent refreshing me. Here was the man I was in love with, making me feel special. Making me feel that this was a new beginning in our relationship. From here on, we could never just be friends.

Our angelic instigator watched from the side of the bed, curled up with his hands around his knees. Soon we made love. My goatee beard rubbed my lover in all his private places, before my tongue took over. The starlight peeked through the curtains like a voyeur, casting a soft glow to this overdue ritual.

*

"Guy left at some stage last night, and we didn't notice."

I looked up, peering around the room. Warwick was right. Our angel friend had exited discreetly when we were too caught up to realize.

"How amazingly selfless of him."

"Well, he is an angel," my lover replied. "It's probably his role here."

"He's one of the best friends anyone could ask for."

"He knew what we wanted and made sure we got it."

I tilted my head.

"He knew what *we* wanted?"

Warwick stared at me.

"You didn't know?"

"I had no idea."

"Really?"

"Yes, really." I sat up. "How come I never knew?"

"I have no idea, Allan."

"I don't remember you saying anything."

"Well, that's because I haven't actually said anything. I've been trying to give you these looks."

"What looks?" Warwick demonstrated one. It was reminiscent of Rudolph Valentino giving his look of love, all facial expression but without the charisma. "No. What you should have done is more like this." With bedroom eyes, I did my best Humphrey Bogart.

"Allan, it looks like your sleeping pill is kicking in!"

Warwick tried another look.

"Now you look like a drag queen after she's realized she's wearing the wrong shade of lipstick."

We laughed.

"Do you remember this conversation before?"

"What, about tragic looks of love?"

"No, Allan, I mean between us. We've had this conversation before. The details are sketchy, but we've talked about romance already."

Something vaguely rang a bell.

"Warwick, a lot of our former life has faded. Did we actually kiss?"

"I'm not sure."

"That's your problem," called a voice from outside the bedroom. "Lack of communication."

Guy swanned into my room with a breakfast tray. Sizzling bacon and softly poached eggs on three plates made my mouth water.

"You're a cheeky devil for someone who's an angel," I said. "Getting our motors running, and then leaving when yours was still idling."

"This was never about me, Allan."

"Thank you, Guy."

"But there's something I want to know." He poked his finger repeatedly into Warwick's collarbone. "If you were in love with Allan, why did you run off with Pedro?"

"Like you said, lack of communication."

"Oh come on, Warwick, that's just scratching the surface."

"Yes," I said. "Guy's right. You're avoiding the question."

"Allan, you were involved with someone else back in Sydney. So what's the big deal about me running off with Pedro?"

"Oh please. You were the one who kept asking me if my relationship ever really started. You knew the vultures were circling."

"Still, I didn't want to be the home-wrecker."

"Huh? You were the one who took me out all the time. You socialized with me while my boyfriend did other things."

"Other things?" Guy asked.

"Yes, other things. I don't know what he did. He just did other things."

Our angelic pal let out a frustrated sigh. "Warwick, to go back to my original question, why did you run off with Pedro when you were in love with Allan?"

"To be honest, I'm not sure I know why myself."

I discreetly put my finger over my mouth, signaling to Guy to stop inquiring. I didn't want to pressure Warwick if he didn't want to talk, as I was scared of pushing him away. I would dig for the answer myself once we were alone.

I took my breakfast plate and reminded our angel that he had, for the second time since I'd known him, briefly flown. He showed us the bruise on his thigh from the collision with the stereo. I assured him that regardless of the battle scars, this was a good start. He begrudgingly agreed, and after a little more chitchat, he left Warwick and I to our own devices.

My mouth was hungry but not for the remaining fragments of breakfast on my plate. My lover put his meal aside and jumped on top of me. His silky chest hairs tickled my knob as he slithered his way up my body until his face met mine.

"This should have happened long ago," I said. "Long before we met Pedro."

"Don't trouble yourself about him, Allan. He's my problem."

Warwick began to kiss my neck.

"Not quite," I gasped. "We both have to face him tonight at the theater."

"Let's enjoy this calm before the storm," he replied in between each small delicious peck.

"How can we?" I exhaled in delight. "It's opening night." I groaned. "What if he does something rash?"

My man looked up and gave me a cheeky wink.

"Then it will make that dog of a production a thousand times more interesting."

FOURTEEN

I BLEW WARWICK a kiss. This in itself was no great dilemma, but the moment I chose to do it caused turmoil.

It was opening night, and act one was going as well as could be expected under Samantha's direction. Guy was on stage as Fabien, summing up the body language of James, Simone, and their love interest during a tranquil picnic. Warwick, Janice, and Pedro relaxed on the picnic blanket as Guy delivered his lines.

"Ipan is such a moralist. Look at them, all too scared to share each other."

He waved his wand and spoke some gobbledygook to bring on a spell, instructions not originally in the text. Pedro, playing the young man, did his best to suddenly appear drunk. He reclined with his head on Janice's lap as Warwick took off his shoes to massage his feet.

"Thanks, James," said Pedro. "Make sure you rub between my toes, please."

As my friend-cum-lover placed the footwear to his side, he caught a glimpse of me waiting in the wings. I blew him a kiss. I could almost see this sign of affection be carried through the air and burst into a thousand small stars on his cheek. He gave me a knowing grin, making me want to waltz in as Ipan and tell the audience I was in love, all in song.

Pedro jumped up and glared at me, causing the audience to gasp. Guy, Warwick, and Janice watched the disorderly actor like they were hostages to a crazed gunman. The angel soon noticed it was me that he was scowling at, and began to ad-lib.

"What a strange reaction. I'll have to double-check my spells." He waved his wand, staring at the actor like a disapproving cop. "Sniggity fidgety foo, calm down, boy, love will ensue."

Pedro slowly lay back down. Janice rubbed his head as Warwick massaged his feet once more.

"I don't know what made me jump up like that," said Pedro.

"Ants," replied Janice.

*

Samantha rushed backstage to offer encouragement and to have a private word with Pedro. Gloria's son also popped backstage, greeting Guy, Warwick, and I, and looking as if he'd seen a ghost.

"What has she done to my play? You should have said something."

"She may have massacred your play," I replied, "but I'm the one who has to spend the next few weeks looking like a scoop of ice cream in a penguin suit."

"Don't even begin on the costumes. They're nothing like I imagined."

"That's the curse of being a writer," said Guy. "You have to let your work go and be reinterpreted as the director sees fit. It's not what you'd like to hear, I know, but it's the truth."

The playwright shook his head. I looked at Warwick, wondering if they'd met.

"Do you know...?"

"Yes, I've met Gloria's son briefly through Samantha and Pedro."

"So you don't know his real name either?"

"Allan, don't fish," the nineteen-year-old said. "Just enjoy the mystery."

I rolled my eyes.

"I'm also sorry about what we've done with your words," said Warwick. "We were told to throw ambiguity out the window."

"Ambiguity?" questioned the young writer. "Life is about ambiguity!"

I looked to the ceiling and began reciting as if I was a father concerned with his own son's marriage.

"There's more than enough love between James and Simone," I pleaded to Guy. "Why cause disruption?"

My fellow actor replied like a close friend justifying his actions.

"Because sometimes intimacy bonds people like no other encounter can."

"But look at this young man," I said with the tone of a prosecuting lawyer. "His future is bright, and our couple couldn't be more in love. They'll fall apart, and he'll be burnt by the incident. Fabien, why play with lives?"

"Ipan, why let life pass them by?" My angelic actor advised like a wise elder. "Let the emotional become the physical. Let them share this special gift with one another."

Gloria's son applauded.

"That's exactly how I heard Fabien and Ipan in my head when I wrote it."

"Did you have the same debate in your own head when *you* were the love interest?" asked Warwick.

"Allow me some discretion," he replied. He looked coy.

"But they must have called you something during affectionate moments," I asked.

"Nothing that will give you a hint of my real name, and definitely nothing I want to be called by my friends." I shrugged. Warwick had a cheeky smirk. Gloria's son moved his eyes back and forth between us. "Okay, guys, I'll spill the beans about my love life if you tell me about yours. What's happening between you two?"

Guy raised his wings. I glanced down and bashfully rubbed my toes into the floor. Warwick took one breath and responded.

"We've connected."

"I'm glad. It's a better match than you and Pedro."

"Thank you for your blessing," I said. "Now, did you let the emotional become the physical?"

"Unfortunately, no. We came close several times, but at certain stages, one of us would chicken out. Then there were those times it just came down to fate. We'd plan to get together, but weird stuff would happen and stop us from going through with it. Like a phone call or something."

"How clever," said Warwick. "The man in the moon and the warlock represent fate."

"And mortal fears." The end of interval bell sounded. "I'd better take my seat. Break a leg in the second act. Or at least break Pedro's legs, then we can replace him with someone who can act. Bye."

*

In act three, scene four, Ipan waddles on stage left to reason with Fabien, which I was to deliver as the most anally retentive being in the cosmos.

"I know it's unsettling, but a crisis here and there can help bring people together." I rubbed my heavily grease-painted chin. "It brings out the best in people and makes them appreciate what they've got. I recall the time Yvonne and Piers were troubled, but it took a simple dilemma with their—" From the wings, Warwick blew me a kiss with the discretion of a nuclear bomb. Pedro was right behind him. I smirked at the no-talent-actor like a man in love, before finishing my speech. "—simple dilemma with their daughter to see reason."

Pedro attempted a look of death. Even in real life, he couldn't motivate.

"Every situation is different, Ipan," said Guy. "In fact, I don't see how Yvonne and Piers compare to James and Simone. They're different people."

"But don't you see, Fabien? Can't you..." In the wings, Pedro and Warwick were arguing, trying to keep their voices down. "Can't you see the similarities? Some situations make couples closer. Some pull them apart." Pedro and Warwick were now looking at me. "This is sure to, whoa..."

As I stepped forward, I lost my footing. I fell onto my side, trying desperately to rock myself back up on my feet. Guy rushed over to help me as the audience roared with laughter. I waved my arms like a flightless bird as my angel buddy tried to grab my hand. His knee tapped my costume, and before I knew it, my world was spinning. I rolled off the stage and onto the floor, feeling like a bowling ball heading for the pins. I bounced several times before reeling toward the crowd, trying to steer myself into the aisle.

I almost made it. Wilma, the theater critic, felt the full force of my moon outfit knocking her off her perch. She screamed for help as other spectators tried to pull her off the floor. She panicked, taking their hands and hauling them to the ground. I was abandoned, kicking my feet and shaking my arms in some strange dance.

One hand reached out to me. It was Warwick, my knight in shining armor saving his Humpty Dumpty. He carefully led me back on stage where I tried to finish the scene over Wilma's whimpers. As I muddled through my words, I could sense my face turning bright red with embarrassment through the white grease paint.

THE NEXT MORNING, I was summoned to Maudi's quarters. I was expecting an outpouring of sympathy after my mishap on stage. Maybe even a glass of gin and tonic to cheer me up. Instead, the grand dame had something else in mind. She stared out at the world from behind her crème lace curtains. The grandfather clock made its 11:00 a.m. call as I sat eager to discover what she had to say.

"How do you think you and Warwick are going?"

"Splendidly. Maudi darling, I'm in love!"

"That's nice to hear."

She gestured to her favorite journal on the coffee table. The cover of this edition of *The Stage Door* had the posed ensemble of an upcoming production of *Who's Afraid of Virginia Woolf?*, all seated on a mustard sofa. I knew this wasn't what she wanted me to admire. I reluctantly turned to the gossip pages.

*

Is the husband in the flight of fancy directed by our own Samantha making more than just a lunar landing? Is the man in the moon sharing more than just his rocket? Sources say that an unsuspecting writer/actor isn't privy to the antics on the dark side of this satellite, but should be wary that he may be party to an aborted mission. Watch this space with telescopes in hand.

*

"It's all about discretion," said Maudi. She turned from the outdoor scene.

"That was in your day. Besides, after last night, discretion went out the window."

"Allan dear, either way, you don't want to be in the gossip pages. It will ruin your career."

"But this could be the break I've been waiting for. Warwick obviously didn't tell Pedro, and now Pedro knows for certain, so all is for the better."

"When my Eddy left Claire it was ended with honor. There were no gossip pages spelling out what had happened. There was class in my affair, not scandal!"

"Hold on a second, Maudi, I'm supposed to be the *mistress*, remember. They were your words. 'Become Warwick's mistress.' They were your exact words."

"And your point is?"

"Mistresses are about scandal. You don't become one and expect the fallout to be sweet."

Maudi didn't reply. She again looked out her window before making her way to the kitchen.

"A cup of tea, Allan?"

"Definitely. I need to calm myself before I see Pedro."

"In one way, this might help your performance. Give you more of a reason to keep the couple and the young man apart."

"It might help Pedro act too. Motivate him not to give in to Ipan's concerns."

Maudi popped her head from the kitchen.

"Allan darling, Pedro couldn't motivate himself to pen a decent play, let alone use his true feelings to inspire his character on stage."

"Well, we all saw that yesterday. That idiot broke out of character to scowl at me. I've never known anyone to be so jealous."

"Allan, where did Warwick stay last night?"

"With me."

"I see."

I was on a winning streak. Maybe we were butchering Gloria's son's play, but at least stealing Warwick away from Mr. Teensy Dick was giving me a wicked sense of pleasure. Pedro's broken heart might encourage him to write about something real. Surely I was doing this budding artiste a favor!

My host returned with a tray holding a fine bone china tea set, before resting in an armchair. Her casual olive dress fanned out around her feet, elegantly clashing with the burgundy rug.

"The point I'm trying to make, Allan, is that when Lord Edward Thorne left Claire, it was of his own intention. I had lured him from under Claire's nose. No dramas. No scandals. No tears. Well, no tears that I was aware of. All was perfect in the world of Maudi and Eddy. You have several more weeks of performance and already the cat's out of the bag. Until you're in a position to claim your prize, the mistress should be cautious."

I sipped my tea but could hardly concentrate on her advice. All I could think of was finally making this strained love triangle into a fitting double act.

FIFTEEN

"WE'RE HERE IN the Afterlife, and we still observe weekends," I said. "Go figure?"

"Didn't God make the earth in six days?" replied Pedro. "That's why we're having Sunday lunch."

"But Allan's got a point," said Warwick. "There's no reason for it to be Sunday. There's no earth revolving around the sun, so there's no reason to keep track of days."

"Hmm. I never looked at it like that before."

I had entered the dragon's den. For some reason, my rival invited me for a feed, even though Warwick was cooking. Both claimed that it was to console me after my humiliating collision with Wilma several days before. I was unnerved at the prospect of dining with my lover's boyfriend, but he insisted that he wanted to wipe the slate clean, seeing that he was dating my closest mate.

Pedro's décor was New York chic, 1920s style. A mini female statuette held a spherical frosted globe, which shed light to the contents of his bulky desk. A sturdy typewriter took pride of place on its surface. Its sleek black sheen and raised gold logo could seduce any writer. The capital letters on the round black keys would need strong fingers rather than a gentle touch to make their mark on the crisp white page. This machine was probably dying to create a masterpiece.

Those little *accidents* during Pedro's gangster farce made me wonder if he would send it crashing to the back of my skull during lunch. He'd struggle to pick it up while I was in the kitchen helping Warwick plate up. As I walked out holding the salad bowl, he'd strike me repeatedly, screaming something about his unfaithful spouse and my misplaced affections.

"You like my typewriter, don't you?"

"It's the second one I've seen since I've been here. The other was a 1970s model."

"I write all my plays on it."

"Nice."

Warwick left us at the dining table while he summoned the spirit of Nigella Lawson in the kitchen. The fragrances coming from the cooktop had my salivary glands working overtime, but I was determined not to know what was on the menu until it arrived on the dining table.

"Pedro, my Bronx accent wasn't that far off the mark, surely?" I asked.

"Well, let's just say you got better at it." I peered down my nose at him. "Allan, let's face it. I'm sure it would take me time to acquire an Australian accent if I had to."

I sipped merlot while he drank Riesling. His cheerful manner made me feel guilty about bonking his boyfriend.

"Lunch smells good," I said.

"Yes, but I'm sure you already know what a good cook Warwick is."

I nodded. Another moment of silence followed. I admired a painting of a fiery damsel driving a dark green sports car.

"You like that one, Allan?"

"I think it's gorgeous."

More silence.

"Lunch is ready," called Warwick from the kitchen.

"Do you need help serving?" Pedro said.

"Just sit! Let me spoil my two favorite men."

Forward as this statement was, I wasn't sure if Pedro knew of my mistress status. He may have assumed during opening night, but I had the feeling that Warwick smoothed things over somehow. With a soy-style substitute for minced meat, we dined on bolognaise rice slice and a side dish of baked celeriac and celery salad.

"What is celeriac?" I asked.

"It's the vegetable that looks like it's grown in outer space," said our cook.

"It reminds me of baked potato."

"I helped Warwick cut it up beforehand," said the playwright.

I was glad to stop this tedious conversation with the first mouthful of the rice slice. I smiled graciously at Pedro several times, and he returned the gesture.

"So are you writing anything at the moment?" I asked.

"I'm toying with the idea of a pantomime. Something for the kids."

"Clowns? A wicked witch? A few fairies?"

"A tale set in the Garden of Eden. A horse wants to become a unicorn for the magic powers."

"I didn't know unicorns had magic powers?"

"It's a pantomime, Allan. Someone has to have magic powers."

I bit my bottom lip.

"How do you make someone look like a horse?"

"Two people play the horse in a costume with a back and a front half."

"That can't be comfortable for a whole play."

"And they're on roller skates!"

He smirked wickedly. I chuckled.

"Pedro, what do Adam and Eve do in the play?"

"Not quite sure yet. Just frolic, I suppose. I'm still jotting down my writer's notes." I sat silent. "Allan, I'm kidding."

We laughed and toasted to the beginning of a new friendship. Now I was certain my host knew nothing of my frequent rendezvous with his lover. More idle chitchat followed before Pedro asked his boyfriend where he was several nights before.

"We were running lines," replied Warwick.

"Running lines with whom?"

"With me," I said. "I've taken up some writing of my own, and I asked Warwick around for a reading."

Pedro's fork dived like a spear into something he was trying to kill on his plate.

"I always thought you would make a good writer, Allan. What's your play about?"

"Love," I replied.

"You're probably more of an expert than I realized."

I didn't reply. I believed it was best to leave the conversation there. Unfortunately, Warwick couldn't read my mind.

"Yes, Allan's play is about love that's not felt by siblings."

"By siblings?"

In unison, Warwick explained that they didn't feel love from their parents, while I said they didn't feel love for each other.

"So which is it?"

"Well, because their parents were hardline—" I began.

"—they don't love each other," Warwick added.

"Do the parents love each other?" Pedro asked.

"No," said Warwick.

"Yes," I replied, "Well, maybe. I haven't got that far into the play yet. Only the first few scenes are done. I don't know where to take it from there."

"Maybe I should come and read it. I can give you a few ideas."

"No!" Warwick and I both screeched in unity.

"It's just that I don't like anyone reading my work until it's done. Too many opinions take it away from what I'm trying to say."

My host smirked like a fox in a chook pen. He glanced down at our empty plates, then stood and gathered them.

"Well, I'm satisfied," he said as if he was referring to the meal.

"Delicious, Warwick," I added.

"I'm sure he is."

Nothing more was said. Warwick and I collected the used cutlery and serving dishes from the table and made our way to the kitchen with Pedro. Warwick filled the sink with water and detergent as I began washing the dishes. Pedro excused himself to fetch another bottle of merlot from his makeshift cellar in the laundry.

"I don't think I should stay around and drink that merlot," I whispered. "Will you be all right here with that trivial man?"

"He's putty in my hands, Allan. Nothing my lips can't fix."

"Is it worth it, Warwick? He's not a pleasant guy."

"You don't know him like I do."

"Eek! What an unsavory thought. Life would be much simpler if you just moved back in with me. I'd see more of you, and you'd see less of Pedro."

"Allan, I know this is hard for you to understand but I'm enjoying my life the way it is at the moment. He makes me laugh."

"Yes, in a laugh *at* him instead of *with* him way."

"Allan!"

"Okay, I admit it. I'm jealous. I feel like the second fiddle."

"You're not. In some ways, you're my original number one. My first fiddle."

He wrapped his arms around my waist and kissed me. I swooned, letting myself be elevated beyond the concerns of the daily grind. I caressed the back of his neck, pushing my tongue deeper into his mouth and groaning like a man who'd been starved of love.

"Let me top you up," called Pedro from the dining room.

He walked into the kitchen with my glass in one hand, and a bottle of merlot in the other. Warwick and I pushed away from each other as I stared at Pedro like a schoolboy who just got sprung cutting off Heidi's plats. He filled my glass as if nothing happened.

"This is a different drop, Allan. I'm told it's smoother than the other wine I gave you."

"Thank you, Pedro."

I took it and gulped down half the glass. I waited for a sly comment.

"Why don't you both sit down? I'll clean up later. I want to get to know you more, Allan. You're a special talent."

Was he being sarcastic? He didn't elaborate, and I was too scared to ask. We all reclined and finished another few bottles of wine, and for whatever reason, my snog with his boyfriend was never brought up.

Instead, we talked about our former lives. When it was time to go, Pedro insisted that Warwick walk me home.

*

"He never acted like Jessica Fletcher, confirming his doubts," I said. I opened my front door.

"Should he have?"

"Yes! The smallest sexual innuendo is enough to bring out his green-eyed monster every other time, but when exhibit A is on full display in his own kitchen, he didn't bat an eyelid."

"Maybe we got away with it?"

"Hmm?"

I kicked off my shoes near the coffee table as Warwick noticed a full bottle of scotch above the pantry. Without prompting, he poured two drinks over ice as I joined him in the kitchen.

"A nightcap," I said. "What an excellent idea. It will get us in the mood."

He paused before putting down the bottle.

"Allan, you know you mean the world to me." He handed me my glass. "We've had so many good times together."

"Why does this sound like a conversation I don't want to be part of?" I knocked down more of my scotch than I intended. He paused again. "Warwick, what are you saying?"

"I don't want to be unfaithful anymore."

"And by unfaithful…" I choked on my words, gulped down the rest of my drink, and stared blankly ahead. "And by unfaithful, you mean to Pedro?"

My friend and lover-no-longer avoided eye contact as he nodded. This moment in time was frozen as the world hushed. An incident with such clarity it would burn into my consciousness and not disappear no matter how much I prayed it would. He reached to hug me, but I shrugged to stop him. He tried again.

"No, Warwick, I mean it." He froze. "Warwick, just leave."

"I can't leave you in this state."

"Darling, just leave." He tried to hug me again. "I mean it!"

"Allan, I really want to be your friend and look after you."

"And you believe that out of everyone I know, you're the person I need comfort from at this time?"

"Surely I can try. We've been friends longer than we've been lovers."

"And how does that make a difference? You know how I've felt about you. Whether it's been one year or one minute, it's all the same!"

"I didn't want it to end like this."

"Warwick, that's such a cliché. They're the type of words Pedro would write." Warwick placed his scotch gently on the kitchen bench. "You're off the hook. Now please, for my sake, just go. I'll be fine."

He kissed my forehead and let himself out. I clutched my glass and gradually slid to the floor. I shut my eyes to drown out my feelings. It didn't work. Inside, I was screaming, crying, and shaking Warwick with my bare hands until he understood how I felt. I questioned him a thousand times on why he was doing this. Why he was giving me signs but running away like a coward? I shook him harder until he knew every emotion I had been through since we met. Every time I thanked the gods he was in my life. Every time I felt lonely. Every time I feared rejection.

There was a knock on the door. Guy let himself in.

"He left me," I mumbled. "He cooked me lunch and then dumped me!"

"I know. He sent me. Perhaps he fed you to ease the blow?" The angel crouched beside me. "He *does* love you."

"At this point in time, I couldn't care less."

"He has to follow his heart, Allan."

"And I'm never following mine again."

Guy held me. I finally broke down.

SIXTEEN

MY PERFORMANCE AS Ipan took on a whole new subtext. The couple and the young man sleeping together? Never! That husband played by Warwick experimenting with bisexuality? Latent homo! That wife played by Janice? She can do better! As for that young fellow struggling to be played convincingly by Pedro? Home-wrecker! That warlock portrayed by Guy? He just likes to watch!

Guy played along with my changed persona and interpreted Fabien as an old sleaze who liked getting people together to satisfy his voyeuristic needs. Samantha relished the tweaking of our characters, patting herself on the back and claiming that we finally understood her direction. That was until the night we went too far.

*

Guy, as Fabien, lowered his voice and caressed his chest as he espoused that "the love is already there. Why not share it?"

"There's more than enough lust between James and Simone," I replied as Ipan. "I know you want to join in. Why cause disruption?"

More anally retentive than an accountant, I outstretched my arm to Fabien's chest and pushed him back to dissuade him.

"Because sometimes intimacy bonds people like no other encounter can," he replied. His tongue caressed his bottom lip.

"But look at this young man. He's a better option for *your* desires. Besides, he needs the experience."

*

Pedro shot me the look of death. Warwick and Janice were sniggering. Maudi shrieked in wicked approval from the audience. Gloria's son told us during the interval that he was relieved to see his words given life, even with the wrong intent. As for Samantha, we didn't wait around for her feedback after the performance. We escaped to the Pedestal, which had become our regular after-show haunt since my breakup.

THAT NIGHT, NELLIE was upbeat, chugging along with a seven-piece swing band. Even Guy was grooving.

"It don't mean a thing—" I began to sing in time with the vocalist.

"—under Samantha's direction," responded Guy.

He slurped his chocolate-honey cocktail while I ordered a cranberry and vodka from the barman.

"Are we being too bitchy?" I asked.

"I've spent too much time with Samantha greeting newcomers to care about her anymore."

"Ouch! What are you getting at?"

"Um. Hmm. The more I know her, the more I distrust her."

"Why?"

"I really can't put my finger on it, but I don't think she's the airhead diva she tries to be."

"That's a big call. Why do you think that?"

"I don't know," he replied. He shook his fist in comic frustration. "It's a gut feeling."

"But there must be something that makes you believe that?"

"Allan, I think we need to watch who's pulling whose strings."

"It's all in the subtext, I guess." I tasted my drink and then stared at the remainder in my glass. "I'm never letting Warwick pull my strings again."

Guy reached up to my cheek and wiped a tear I didn't know I'd shed.

"Maybe there's more subtext there than either of us realize?" he said.

Nellie snapped her fingers in rhythm, while the tuba and drums competed to become the alpha male. Examining her audience, it was clear that some of the women were superior contenders for that position. Nellie flirtatiously winked at a dark-haired lady with crimson lipstick, who was salaciously lit by the flame of a candle. As the instruments continued their fight for dominance, Nellie strolled to the woman and planted the most exquisite open-mouthed kiss I had seen in a while.

"So what do you think of Nellie's music today?" I asked.

Guy's foot was tapping to the beat.

"I think I'm hooked on jazz."

"What changed your mind?"

"I started listening with my heart, and not my ears."

He closed his eyes and moved in rhythm. I considered other genres that I could introduce him to. Nu soul perhaps? A dose of Kofy Brown possibly? Or maybe just play it safe and blend acid jazz into his education?

Different musicians entered my head as I recalled how Warwick and I loved introducing each other to our favorite artists, when we were getting to know each other. The first time he visited me, electro-synth played from my modest stereo. He was a rhythm-and-blues type of guy, so couldn't make heads or tails out of the strange group we were listening to. He studied the cover and simply asked who the Nine were. I told him they were a 1990s band with a 1980s sound. He replied by saying I needed a music overhaul.

Guy started clapping in time and singing "doo—wop" between lyrics. Even his wings got into the act, jutting out separately in turn to the pulse of the music. After a while, he opened his eyes to sip his cocktail, breaking out of his jazz trance.

"You need a one-night stand, Allan. Tarquin was nice. You should see him again."

"Sex doesn't mend a broken heart."

"No, it's a bit more like aspirin. It soothes it for a while, making it easier to deal with later."

I picked up my drink. "So does this." Guy shook his head. "In fact, I've got a great idea." I signaled to the barman. "Eight shots of schnapps, please. Mix up the flavors."

"Why, Allan, why?"

"Why not?"

Two lemon, two peppermint, two vanilla, and two butterscotch shots were served. With one finger, I pushed a lemon drink toward my angel. He shrugged and drank it back in one mouthful.

"Wow, a few more of those and I'll join Nellie on stage."

I drank mine. It went down like a drop of heaven. We followed it with the all-time favorite, butterscotch, a taste reminiscent of hard-boiled lollies, which I advised Guy to smear around his mouth with his tongue. The peppermint was a take-it-or-leave-it experience, but we agreed that vanilla was our favorite.

I hadn't had a schnapps overload since Warwick and I moved in together in Sydney. With all our belongings still in their boxes, we toasted our roommate status with a bottle of butterscotch schnapps. The alcohol had been a present to me from my inane ex-boyfriend, which due to my lack of affection for most things he'd bought for me, stayed untouched until I left him behind.

Sometime that night, I looked at my close friend in a romantic way. It was the first time I'd thought of him like that. The twilight sky cast a blue hue against his dark skin. His black hair turned indigo in this strange light. Like Krishna, his joyous nature was my saving grace. I was no longer that obscure little gay man. I had someone to share my fabulous adventures with.

Guy and I ordered another round of drinks, and then another. I swung my hips to the music as best as I could while balanced on my stool. Guy picked out men in the bar for me to chat up, but while I wallowed in self-pity, my friend stood up and beckoned me to take his hand. We started waltzing, although how we did it to the jazz soundtrack was anyone's guess.

As we danced, Guy popped up four fingers on my back. The barman knew that he wanted four more drinks of no particular flavor. It was like taking part in a lottery. He wandered onto the dance floor with petite glasses on a tray, half-full of orange liquid. Peach was never a favorite essence of mine, but at this stage, who cared? We downed each glass before the barman left us.

"That open-shirt guy swaying in front of the stage," said Guy. "He's very *you*."

I lowered my mouth to my friend's ear. "The one with the textured white shirt?"

"Yes, Allan. The *only* guy with his shirt open, swaying in front of the stage."

My forehead rested on Guy's cheek as I whispered into his neck, "I'm not ready."

He tilted his head and kissed me on the forehead, before stumbling toward his prey. Midway, he stopped, glanced back, and extended his arm in one sweeping gesture. I took Guy's hand and attempted to rumba toward our sensual target. My angel blew him a kiss as we danced on either side of him. He replied with a devilish grin. As I practiced my best disco moves, I lost balance but saved myself from an embarrassing fall.

My friend began to laugh. Any sophistication I thought I had up until this moment disappeared.

Our mystery man had the cutest dimples and the thickest black hair I'd ever seen. His man-of-the-world manner made me want him to take control. To make me lose myself in escalating passion and throw away the hold that Warwick had on me.

He grabbed my hand and placed it under his open shirt, then did the same with Guy. We both explored his manly chest. His muscles made me tremble with delight, yearning to taste their sweaty outline. His deep green eyes beckoned me to kiss him. I slid my mouth over his. Our moist tongues glided over one another in their own sinful dance.

I felt detached. My desire wrenched out of me like the life of an animal at an abattoir. I was no longer trembling in delight, but with shame. I was being unfaithful yet there was no good reason to feel that way. I kissed harder, but he moved away. He gave me a peck on the cheek before slipping away, causing our hands to exit his shirt. My angel buddy and I turned to him as he blew a kiss and left the dance floor.

"He knew I wasn't into him," I said.

"Even I knew you weren't into him." We went back to the bar and sat down. "Allan, I know what Monique said about you and Warwick, but for the sake of your own sanity, you need to reassess if you want to win him back."

"I've been reassessing all day and all night."

"And you needed a break from that assessment." He pointed at our lost object of desire. "He was the perfect break!"

"I was almost on the same page, Guy, I really was. But when push came to shove, I just couldn't go through with it."

The combined sound of the crowd and the band reverberated in the background. The barman presented us with four more glasses of schnapps, which I cherished like a lost camper finding water. My angel buddy blurred into the crowd as I felt self-aware and a little nauseous.

"We're going to visit Warwick so you can share how you feel."

"Huh," I said without moving my lips. "But I'm happy being delusional."

"No, I mean it, Allan. It's time to put a stop to this. He needs to know how you feel regardless of the consequences. After all, I'm an angel. Soul-saving missions are my specialty." Guy rose. "Plus you look like you need the fresh air."

With that, he seized my hand and dragged me off my seat. I took one last glance at our mystery man who was unaware we were leaving. I listened to Nellie's soulful voice to regain focus before staggering out of the Pedestal.

"ALLAN, WHAT'S THE one thing you need to say to Warwick?"

"I just need to tell him that I love him."

"He knows that, Allan. Think harder."

Guy was still dragging me along the streets of the Limelight Quarter. The crisp night air was reviving my spirits, albeit through my drunken stupor. Many colorful folk whisked past, some briefly staring at us as they made their way.

"You realize Pedro will be there," I said.

"That's why we're going to call Warwick to come downstairs. You need to talk privately."

We arrived outside of their balcony. I rubbed my arms to keep warm as Guy placed his hand on my shoulder.

"Warwick!" I yelled. "Are you there?"

There was no answer. A couple adorned in bohemian black, stopped in their tracks the moment I shouted to my ex-lover.

"Broken heart," whispered Guy to the interested onlookers.

"I understand," replied the woman. She looked up to her man. "Poor thing."

"Go on, Allan, call out again."

"Warwick! Warwick! I love you." My voice echoed from the building as I looked to my angel friend. He nodded and caressed my shoulder. The couple nodded as well. "Warwick, are you home? I need to talk to you. Will you come down, please?"

"Keep going, Allan."

"I really need to talk to you. I have so much more to say to you. I should never have let you walk out of my door the other night. I've wanted to talk to you so many times during the last few days, but there's nowhere private at the theater. Plus I'd probably break down, which is not a good look when you're wearing white grease paint."

A few onlookers came out from their balconies. I glanced at Guy who was joined by a small audience. Some parents had let their kids stay up well after bedtime, and their freckled little girl was giggling at me. Her mother shushed her so she sat on the ground, sulking.

"Don't worry about it, Allan. Just go on."

"Yes, we're right behind you," said an elderly lady with bad teeth. "You make him listen."

"Warwick, I love you, and I know you love me. You told me so. You said you've been waiting all year for me to make a move, and as you know, I've been waiting for you to make that move too."

"You tell him, love!" interrupted the old woman.

My support team began to chant Warwick's name. I was empowered. I encouraged them to clap their hands in time. They did. There was about ten of them now, and their support gave me a warm glow in that frosty breeze. However, Guy looked worried.

"Allan, shouldn't you wait until he comes downstairs?"

"My dear friend, Warwick is a coward. I know he's up there, but he's too scared to come down because he doesn't want to hurt that imbecile's feelings. The very imbecile who tried to hurt me physically during his dumb-arsed play!"

"Allan..."

"No one should ever break your heart," alleged a handsome older gent behind me.

"Thank you." I turned back to address my ex-lover. "Now listen here, Warwick! You told me that you'd been waiting for me to make a move. I did. We made love over and over under that so-called playwright's nose. And what happens when the going gets good? You freak out. What the hell for? Was the sex that bad that you preferred old teensy-dick instead? Was it all getting too intense for you? Is that the reason?" The crowd became quiet as I felt the bitter cold again. "Were you too scared of being in love? Too much intimacy for your murky heart to deal with? Too much real emotion for your juvenile soul to cope with? Too much effort to be in love with someone who's madly, deeply in love with you? Too much..." I shuddered. "Too much..."

Guy grabbed me from behind as I felt my legs give way. He eased me to the footpath and shielded me with his wings. I howled, before tears streamed down my face.

"It's okay, Allan," said the angel. "This is a big step for you."

"He doesn't love me, Guy. He doesn't love me the way I love him."

"I don't think that's true."

I began whimpering like a child being punished.

"He's not home." This female voice came from somewhere above. I peered through Guy's wings and saw a short woman in a loose jumper on their neighboring balcony. "I think Pedro is in, but Warwick has gone out."

At that point, she called out to that dreary fool next door. He approached his balcony cautiously, spying on us like Anthony Perkins summing up his victim in *Psycho*.

"Yes, Annabelle, Warwick's not home."

My breath became choked.

"Guy, what...what if he is home and...and doesn't want...to face me?"

"If he heard what you said, he'll face you in his own good time." The angel kissed the top of my head. "But don't make assumptions."

I gently pulled his wings to cover me fully.

"If he's not home, there'll be one hell of a gleeful storyteller to convey what happened."

"That's not a bad thing, Allan. That's not a bad thing."

Guy huddled closer to me as we sat in public view for what seemed an eternity.

SEVENTEEN

"MY DARLING, YOU'VE embarrassed yourself in front of your main competition." Maudi peered down her nose at me as Guy and I walked beside her. "As they said in the twentieth century, 'not a good look.'"

"I thought we were here to cheer me up," I replied.

"Yes, Allan's been through hell and back. We need to lift his spirits before the performance tonight."

"First things first, my dears. When you both get together, you share an addiction for misconduct. That, my friends, has got to stop."

"I'm not proud of myself, Maudi, but at least the cat's out of the bag as far as my feelings go."

"Yes, but those thoughts should have been a private monologue, not a soliloquy."

"Point taken. Enough already."

The fallen leaves crunched under our feet as we strolled to a clearing near the outdoor stage of Limelight Park. Our thespian elder positioned a parasol above our heads to shade us from the hot sun. This reserve was a popular spot for open-air theater, but today only us three and a family flying a kite were benefiting from nature.

I laid out a picnic blanket as Guy poured homemade lemonade into crystal wine glasses. Maudi insisted that just because we were staying sober didn't mean we couldn't dine in style. She had made cucumber sandwiches with the crusts cut off for our light lunch, which she delicately placed on small china plates before showing me the latest copy of *The Stage Door*.

"Allan, my dear, according to the theatrical bible, your offstage antics have been duly noted. Page five, top right-hand corner, gossip section."

Samantha dominated the cover, surrounded by old-world artwork of the moon and a warlock placing a repulsive toad into a cauldron. I followed her instructions and flipped the pages. Screaming at me in black and white was a recap of my inebriated night.

*

Pedro, the shining star of pen and stage, was interrupted during a refreshing late snack of goat's cheese and bread salad by a less than civil commotion from outside his spacious apartment. He likened it to a high school musical—too many extras not knowing what to do around the main cast. The former Mr. Death was playing his own swan song, lamenting for his lost love while comforted by his costar. Has the sky fallen on what was regarded a promising career, or do all his answers lie in the bottle? Watch this space.

*

"Ouch" was my only reply.

"My darling, I give you the break you deserve and look what you do with it."

She sounded like a disapproving headmistress as she wagged her finger.

"Maudi, we're here to cheer Allan up, not berate him."

"True, but I'm just making sure the poor fellow doesn't lose his standing in both love and theater."

"This isn't going to be another lecture about Lord What's-his-name and his little hussy?" I asked.

"No, Allan. It's a genuine sliver of concern."

"I appreciate it, but I'm trying to forget about it. After all, you're supposed to be consoling me before I face Warwick and Pedro again."

I sipped some lemonade as the dame nestled a cucumber sandwich against her thumb and pointer, taking petite bites. Guy sat quietly with his glass clutched in his hands.

Auburn leaves spread scarcely on the dozen or so trees, as if they were to be used as a backdrop for anorexic models in a gothic photo shoot. For the first time, I wondered if seasons had any significance here. Today the sun was beating down, yet last night I was freezing in the night air making a fool of myself in front of my rival.

"Pedro's a bit of a dark horse," I said.

"I thought Warwick and his tawdry attachment were off-limits as far as conversation is concerned," Maudi stressed.

"They were until I started thinking about last night, and the days before, and Pedro in particular."

"Dear, that man is the personification of cottage cheese. No taste and no texture."

She finally took a big chomp out of her sandwich.

"Allan," said Guy, "maybe we *need* to talk about it to cheer you up? Why do you think Pedro's a dark horse?"

I tucked my knees close to my chest and gently rocked.

"The obvious 'mishaps' during his silly gangster play, for one. Plus something odd happened the other day when I visited for lunch."

"Do tell," said Maudi.

"You know how he gets jealous at the drop of a hat." My friends nodded. "He didn't flutter an eyelid when he walked in on me and Warwick smooching in his kitchen."

"He didn't see you," our angel surmised.

"I don't believe that. He'd have to be blind not to have seen us. I think Maudi's theater gossip rag may have been right the other day, just like its right today about an event that happened only last night. He *did* know about me and Warwick, and he's known for some time, but he didn't care. Well, not quite. Sometimes he did care, but on the whole, he didn't."

Maudi raised her eyes to the sky. "My dear, you're clutching at straws long after you've lost your rose-colored glasses," she replied.

My hand clutched my mouth. "Oh, dear."

"What's the matter?" my friends asked in unison.

"The lovers? What if Warwick was in on it? What if my best friend and his petty boyfriend are out to get me?"

"Allan, I wouldn't believe that about Warwick for a second," said Guy. "I'm a good judge of character, or so I've been told. I know love when I see it. There's something else at play here."

"But Pedro was on stage with me when the light fell. Where was Warwick? He didn't take me seriously when I talked about Monique's warning about the lovers. And he definitely wasn't around when that slippery stuff was on stage or when you found a gun in your pocket. Then the second reading I had from Monique told me that the lovers would try a different tact. I was the mistress Pedro knew about. They were in it together. We enjoyed a nice lunch before Warwick walked me home to stab me in the back. That's definitely a 'different tactic.'"

"I'll have to agree with Guy on this one, Allan. Even I recognize love when I see it, even if that love is misguided. Remember, I had to put my Eddy straight."

"But Maudi, I can't remember the last days of my life. Even if I'm certain we were good friends, how do I know I'm remembering the whole story? Maybe we fell out?"

"Good friends don't fall out for long," replied Guy. "Remember what Monique told you. You're soul mates. You've lived and loved many times. Last time, you just 'missed the boat.' Regardless of how Warwick feels about that fortune-teller, I've never known her to be wrong."

I buried my face in my hands. Maudi tapped me on the shoulder.

"Darling, what can we do to cheer you up?" she asked.

I looked toward the kite that the child was flying. It was bird shaped and blue with a rainbow tail made of streamers. The kid was no more than five years of age, with twisted orange locks and freckles on his cheeks. His youthful chuckle brought out my inner nanny. I had this mad urge to go and help him blow his nose or something. Teach him that a spoon full of sugar helps the medicine go down. It's so easy to be clucky when you're gay. For most of us, children were like library books. You always know you'll return them.

"Did you hear me, Allan?" asked Maudi. "What can we do to cheer you up?"

"I want to see Guy fly."

"Well, that came from nowhere," said the angel.

"The kid with the kite, that's where the idea came from. You've almost flown a couple of times. Why not try again?"

"Come on," said Maudi. "It's about time you soared like a bird. Have another sandwich for sustenance and take to the air. It is your birthright!"

He gave us a coy smile. I watched the airborne kite as if it would give me an insight into aeronautical science.

"Why do you think your friend Joshua failed in teaching you to fly?" I asked candidly. "Wrong place, wrong time perhaps?"

"I was too much in love to communicate effectively," confessed Guy. I raised my glass and proposed a toast.

"Here's to lost love." We all drank a decent mouthful. "So what's stopping you from trying to fly again?"

"Nothing, I guess."

Maudi gestured to the sky. Guy wandered to the outdoor stage and used it as the start to his imaginary runway. Like a sprinter, he gathered speed while flapping his wings with the grace of a chicken being chased by Colonel Sanders. He didn't take flight, but he did provide a refreshing breeze.

"It's a shame he never learnt to fly, being an orphan and all that," I said.

"My dear," whispered Maudi, "have you ever wondered how an angel can be an orphan?"

"What do you mean?"

"He's an angel. If he had parents, then they'd have been of *this* world."

"*This* world?"

"Yes, Allan, this world."

Guy was desperately trying to leave the ground when her meaning hit me.

"You're right. Technically, his parents can't die. They would have been angels."

"We're on the same page, my dear. It never occurred to you before?"

I tried my best not to change my facial expression as we watched our angel, even though he wasn't looking in our direction. He stood, vocally mulling over what he might have been doing wrong.

"Maudi, I guess I've been too caught up in my own affairs to even realize it. What a bad friend I must be."

"Allan, remember, guilt is a wasted emotion. Besides, I've never asked him myself. I thought it best to wait until he's ready to talk about whatever he's trying to hide."

Guy looked back in our direction, smirking as if he'd worked out the mechanics of flight. Maudi and I shared glances in that awkward way people do when they fear they've been caught sharing malicious gossip, even though there was little chance he heard any of our conversation.

"Now, dear, getting back to you."

"Do we have to?"

"Let's face it, you're not going to get any closure in a hurry. If it wasn't for your soul mates conundrum, you could leave the Limelight Quarter and make your own adventures. As it stands, you need to woo a man who presently has a tawdry attachment. Like a boil or an unsightly monobrow."

"Maudi, can't we just watch Guy try to fly?"

"Allan, you're in limbo at the moment. This drama has worn you down, yet you still have to find the strength to make your fortunes change, and I think I have the answer."

She drank her lemonade and watched the kite weave through the air, pulling the child like a dog taking its master for a walk.

"Well, don't keep me in the dark. What's your idea?"

"Bury yourself in creativity. It will revitalize your soul."

"What? Paint? Write? Nail Pedro to a cross and call it modern art?"

"Good idea but not what I had in mind." She put her hand to her chest. "Reinterpret Gloria's son's play."

"Reinterpret Gloria's son's play?"

"Yes, Allan, reinterpret Gloria's son's play. Cast Warwick and show up those theatrical wannabes he's been hanging around. You have the dramatic insight. Why else would I give you the lead role in that idiot play? You took my direction and made that part your own. Now go and show the Limelight Quarter what else you can do." She leaned toward me. "It may not win him back straightaway, but it will put the wheels in motion."

I couldn't control the smile that spread across my face. I loved this idea. I took Maudi's hand and kissed it. At this point, Guy was striding back in our direction. Before I could ask why he was giving up, he crouched on our picnic blanket, taking a sprinter's starting stance. He darted past the outdoor stage, raising himself a couple of meters before slightly stumbling on his landing. Both Maudi and I stood up to applaud.

"Bravo!" I yelled.

"Get used to that word, Allan. That's what your audience will be shouting."

EIGHTEEN

THE MAKEOVER HAD begun. I'd spent several afternoons grilling Gloria's son, who enlightened me about his well-lived amorous life, as well as giving me a clear sense of what his play was about.

"Samantha missed the point of the fabled characters," he complained. "Fabien and Ipan represent the internal dialogue of the main protagonists."

"Yes, you've mentioned that before," I replied. I jotted wildly in my notepad. "The more background details I have, the better."

"Are you worried about what Samantha will think about your version?"

I opened a bottle of merlot and poured two glasses.

"I'm sure she won't get it, but what she thinks has nothing to do with why I'm doing it." I lounged back in my armchair and tasted my wine. It was mellow with a slightly sharp aftertaste. "By the way, Guy and Janice want to be in my version."

"Who else is in it?"

"Warwick, hopefully. Maudi, definitely. Oh, and she has a friend to play Ipan. His name is Frederick. Apparently, they've shared the stage together before. Now all I need is the love interest. Someone young enough to play him. Not someone who's nowhere near the right age, like Pedro."

Gloria's son sniffed his wine and shrugged in a devil-may-care attitude. He took a huge mouthful.

"Nice wine, Allan."

"Um, I said 'someone *young* enough to play him.'" He stared at me like a post-lobotomy patient. "I was thinking that art should imitate life." He grinned. "Would you like to play him?"

"I thought you'd never ask. How many performances are we doing?"

"Only one."

"Just one?"

"I'm going to shoot it as a movie on my video camera. I've always wanted to make a film, and as I've got nothing better to do, why not? No time like the present."

"That's a terrific idea, Allan. I've never seen a film in the Afterlife, not even television." He paused, took a sip, and then put his glass down. "Anyway, about your movie, I'm going to help as much as I can with sets and models and stuff. I want to see my play done right."

"Which still gives me the problem of your name. I can't put 'Gloria's son' in the credits."

"Use GS."

"That sounds like a sports car. Come check out the new GS! Smooth, refined, and a pleasure to ride."

"It's the closest you'll get to a name."

I shook my head.

"Mr. GS, you still haven't let me know if you'll play the part."

"Allan, you realize I'll have to pine over Warwick, *if* he takes the part." I slumped.

"Oh yeah, you're right." I took a small sip and swirled the wine around my tongue. It gently warmed my throat with its rich flavor. Gloria's son tilted his head, staring at me like a Mormon wife wanting to know if it was her turn in the master's bedroom. "GS, I really would love it if you'd take the part."

"Then I'll take it."

*

The main challenge was the portrayal of the fantasy elements. On stage, it was easy. The audience fills in the details of how and where Ipan and Fabien live. But through the lens, all had to be revealed.

At one stage, I had this odd idea about the magical folk appearing out of nowhere in the homes of our earthbound characters. Like ghosts in the background mingling where the action is. This would have saved us looking for extra locations to shoot in. Gloria's son argued that this was too 1960s supernatural sitcom, and tackier than anything Samantha would have dreamt up. He was right.

So we decided to let them inhabit the sky. Gloria's son knew a friend of a friend who had a warehouse. On inspection, it was evident we had a perfect rehearsal space, and somewhere to create a cosmic feel for Fabien and a new character he wanted to introduce named Farah, a love interest for the man in the moon. The young playwright hung fabric on a curved rail, on which we projected images of the night sky. Fabien and Farah would stand in front of this illusion, wearing vivid flowing gowns that would subtly waft for effect, thanks to small electric fans.

For Ipan's establishing shots, we made a cobalt-blue papier-mâché moon, which could be lit to portray its different phases. Maudi let us use her apartment to represent his dwelling under the moon's surface. We added a telescope so he could keep watch over our main protagonists and replaced that stupid moon suit with a dark red military coat. Frederick looked like the conductor of a brass band, eccentric but with an air of authority. I directed him to be a widower who still pined for his lost love. His sense of duty toward the couple took on a new meaning, as he both cared for them as a parent and saw himself as one of them. This led to some truly tender rehearsals with this veteran actor.

Gloria's son also rewrote the dialogue to honestly reflect his true experiences. I began mining my laptop for suitable music. With everything coming together, I just had Warwick to convince. I took him aside before our performance one night and put on the hard sell.

*

"Do you think it's fair not to ask Pedro?" he asked.

"Absolutely. He might say yes." Warwick didn't answer. "See, even you think it's a bad idea for me to ask him."

"You can read me like a book, Allan."

"So will you do it?"

"I really want a break after this show. Get to know Pedro better, away from the spotlights."

"But it's a video shoot. We should wrap it up in two weeks. I've already started rehearsals."

"That's not what's bothering me."

"Ten-minute call," yelled a stagehand from the wings.

While the others were putting on their final touches, I stood with Warwick on stage behind the rich red curtains. The audience chatted eagerly on the other side, fueling my fear of rolling down the aisle again.

"Warwick, what can I say to get you to do my film?"

"It's not that I don't want to do it. It's just that I have a life with Pedro now, and doing your film will take me away from that."

"But it's only two weeks. Hasn't he got another half-baked idea of a play to write?"

"He's got a few ideas."

"So give him some space while you act in my film."

"Guys, you'll need to go backstage soon." The stagehand was laying out props for the first scene. "And Warwick, act in Allan's film. It's got to be a hundred times better than this circus."

"See, even the stagehand agrees with me." I gave him my best puppy-dog-eyed expression. "And you'll get to play James as Gloria's son wrote him, intelligent but questioning his manhood. Come on, pretty please."

My friend looked earnest, like he had lost something valuable.

"Maybe, but I'll have to think about it. I really would love a break..."

I kissed him on the cheek, being careful not to smear my white face paint on him, and waddled to the green room dragging him by the hand.

"Thanks, Warwick. You'll be great in the role."

*

We played out our purgatory on stage at night and kept rehearsing during the day. Maudi was our new sassy witch, Farah, while her friend, Frederick, portrayed Ipan with a kind heart and a wealth of stagecraft.

For Guy and Janice, it was troublesome not to bring the new direction into their nighttime performance. Little nuances spilled through, but Samantha didn't seem to notice. We planned to start shooting several days after the final-night party.

Gloria's son guided us during rehearsals, adding little touches of business for my earthbound characters from his own reminiscences. A small caress of a shoulder, the ease of holding hands in public without thinking about those who might gossip, or a playful slap on the bum all helped differentiate the real characters from the mythical.

We rehearsed all our scenes at the warehouse. There was makeshift furniture scattered around that we positioned as Ipan's home, in line with how we would rearrange Maudi's apartment when we were ready to shoot his scenes. In another area, we recreated my flat, as that would be the setting for James and Simone's house. I'd often shoot the rehearsals for later study, but as I was still without someone to play James, I would sit in place with script in hand and direct from within the scene.

"You're not in love with him, are you?" my character asked.

Janice as Simone dried the dishes.

"Oh, god no! I can't do the younger man thing. At no stage have I thought of running off with him. In my mind, it's always the three of us."

"Why are you so keen, though? Has my husband developed a taste for bisexuality?"

"No, but somehow I don't think of him as…" I looked at my fellow actor with uncertainty. "I just don't understand why. It's like our minds keep moralizing, yet our souls are telling us it's natural."

"This isn't a new take on a midlife crisis, James?"

"Babe, like you, I can't be the older married one, no matter what sex the bit of fluff is. I'm still passionate about you. Besides, I can't see myself in a canary-yellow sports car just yet." I held my pose. "Okay, well done, Janice."

"Maybe *you* should play the part, Allan?"

"Then who'd shoot it?"

"We could all take turns."

"Thanks, Janice, but no thanks. There'll be too much variation in shooting styles."

"Any word from Warwick?"

"Not yet, and I don't hold much hope. It's final night tonight, so I think our chances of convincing him are slipping away."

"SO HOW IS your version going?" asked Samantha.

She clutched a glass of chilled pinot noir as if her life depended on it. I sipped my merlot and considered my answer carefully. Warwick stood with us, guzzling champagne like the rest of the cast and their friends at the final-night party.

I was ecstatic that I'd never wear that corny moon costume again. There was a residue of grease paint on my face, because as soon as Guy stuck the glass of wine in my palm, I stopped washing it off and symbolically left this horrific ordeal behind.

Frederick came to watch the final performance, but was warned not to take his characterization from what he witnessed on stage. He and Maudi, along with Janice, huddled around Gloria's son, animated in conversation.

"I asked how your version of the play is going?" repeated Samantha.

"Brilliantly." I didn't mean to gloat, but it was hard to conceal my excitement. "We couldn't have made it without members of the original cast, though. Your direction has helped them immensely."

Warwick shot me a blank stare.

"You can have any of the costumes," she suggested. "It will save you time."

"Thanks, but no thanks. We're reinventing the outfits."

"Oh, you're not keen to use my most inspired work?"

Warwick nudged me.

"Allan, the play wouldn't be the same without your moon suit," he said. Now I gave him the blank stare.

"I know, but it's a stage versus screen type of thing. On stage, you need big costumes so the back row can appreciate them. On video, you need to be restrained as the camera magnifies everything, even performance."

I gulped down my merlot and scanned the room for Guy. He was suitably sozzled, chatting up a friend of Gloria's son's. The love interest leaned against the stage, observing the other patrons.

"I thought the idea was to take the stage version to the screen," said Samantha.

"Well, it's Gloria's son's rendition of the play. He's done some rewriting." The blonde pursed her lips. "I was never out to make the same version. What would be the point of that?"

"I just thought that since the play was already directed."

Warwick came to my rescue.

"Samantha, if Allan was going to shoot *your* version, he'd simply set up his camera on a tripod in the aisle. It's his baby now. Let him nurture it his way."

"Okay," she vaguely replied. "Oh, there's Pedro. I've got to go and tell him how pleased I was with his performance tonight."

She abruptly left. Gloria's son watched her leave and dashed over with a bottle of wine and a bottle of champagne.

"You didn't need to pop over," I said. "We could have come to you."

"I was looking for a reason to leave that conversation," he replied. "Too much negative critique." He refilled our glasses. "You both looked bored talking to Samantha."

"And your friend looks bored talking to Guy," Warwick said. "He needs your company more than we need it. He's either looking for a better option, or he needs his glass topped up."

Guy's left wing was around the man's shoulder.

"My friend is just playing hard to get. It's his style."

"He's in for a good time," I said.

Warwick gave me a devilish grin. I returned the gesture.

"What's that look all about?" I wiped the expression off my face. "Did you guys have a threesome?" We didn't reply. "Come on, Allan. You've grilled me at length about my sex life, and you haven't even told me that you guys did it with an angel."

"Guilty as charged."

"It's what brought us together as a couple originally," added Warwick.

I felt a wrenching in my guts. As brave faced as I acted in front of my friends, I couldn't trick myself. A thief had stolen my lover's heart and with it, some sense of closeness. I'd been lapping up my time with him at this party, short as it was, and praying that Pedro would fade into oblivion now that the run was over. But I was the fool, taking my camera in hand, filming my friends, and going down a different path without my mate.

"Are you okay, Allan?" asked Gloria's son.

"I'm sorry," said Warwick. "I should have thought before I opened my mouth."

"It's okay. I have no right to..." I looked toward Janice, Maudi, and Frederick. The older thespians were holding hands, listening to their costar in between sharing tender smiles with each other. "I'm happy for you, Warwick. Just like I'm happy for Maudi."

She was sixteen again, wistful and prized. Her loving gentleman also had a youthful step. Janice seemed to know that she didn't have their full attention, eventually trailing off midsentence and instead just gazing at the lovebirds. There could have been a major earthquake or a deadly fire around them, but they seemed untouchable. As if a romantic shield would protect them against the pain of daily life. I'd have given my right arm for a small slither of that magic shield.

"Maudi's definitely smitten," said Gloria's son.

I took a breath to bring me back to the moment. "Yes. I'm looking forward to learning a lot from her friend," I said. "His acting knowledge is well worth tapping into."

"Yes, Frederick's summary of the stage version was spot-on, 'the theater of the bewildered, both cast and direction.'"

"That's why I've decided to do your film," announced Warwick. He winked at me before sipping his champagne. "Allan, why have you gone quiet?"

"You could have knocked me over with a feather. What changed your mind?"

"Pedro has some new play in mind, so he needs the space. Plus Samantha's attitude just now convinced me to do it."

"What do you mean?" asked our young playwright.

"She was giving Allan the third degree about his version of your play, as if it was a crime to change her direction."

"True. I felt like I was in confession, and I'm not even Catholic."

"What is she, twelve years old?" exclaimed Gloria's son.

"It feels like it sometimes," said Warwick. "I've hung around her too much lately. She fools herself into thinking she's some great director, and she's smart enough to be; she just doesn't know anything about the craft."

"Oh, come on now! She had Allan dressed like a beach ball. It's a wonder there wasn't a beach scene on stage. A giant sandcastle and bucket against a summer sky. And what she did with my words has made me turn in my grave, literally."

"That's part of the reason I want to do this," Warwick added.

"What's the other part?" I asked.

"I want to do this for you, Allan. I think it's the least I can do, considering how I've treated you."

I felt vulnerable. Part of me was screaming for joy at the chance to repair our long-lost connection. We'd team up and show the Limelight Quarter what acting was all about. Warwick and Allan together again! A force to be reckoned with.

But was history repeating? I'd share part of him, but when the game was over, I'd be left holding the last fragments of a friendship I deemed too special to end.

"You've gone quiet again," said Gloria's son.

"I'm just seeing Warwick in my mind, in the part of the husband."

NINETEEN

I DEVELOPED AN eerie curiosity in how Nellie would reinvent herself each time we visited the Pedestal. Her soft tones embraced the songs of the Beatles in a medley. To her right sat a dark-haired blue-eyed young lady with pasty white skin. Her jade dress fitted like snakeskin, clutching her waif frame like a lover who'd never leave. She stroked her lustrous white harp with a depth of feeling beyond her years. Nellie watched over her like a potential suitor. Her pale salmon coat enhanced her crisp white shirt and sophisticated houndstooth trousers. The weaving pattern of rising smoke from a pipe would not have looked out of place nestled in her hand.

"Her interpretation of 'Dear Prudence' is creepily inspiring," I said. "Like the Cure meets Aretha Franklin."

"You're in the artist zone, Allan," said Guy. "When you're busy creating, you respond more intensely to the art forms around you. You're in touch with your soul."

"I didn't realize this was an evening for ethereal conversation. What a shame we're sober."

We sprawled out on opposite sides of an available booth, sipping soda water with a twist of lime. I was keeping away from alcohol as we had a long shoot the following day, but my brain was too active to go to bed. This was my way of winding down.

"Maybe I should have invited the rest of the cast," I said.

"You should have at least invited Warwick. In fact, you should've invited Warwick instead of me."

"I wanted to, but his actions this afternoon changed my mind."

"You mean his dalliance with Gloria's son?"

I shuddered. "It did catch me off guard."

We had come from our last rehearsal where we spoke about what our characters would be doing in ten years' time. Frederick said that as a decade had passed, Ipan and Farah's relationship would have blossomed, and he would have developed an open mind. So Maudi, as

Farah, conjured up the spell of open discussion. I picked up my camera and started recording as Warwick, Janice, and Gloria's son improvised. Mild shoulder rubs and honest communication brought the scene to life, until Warwick took a bold step and kissed the back of Gloria's son's neck.

I gulped so hard, Guy, Maudi, and Frederick noticed. The others were too caught up in their role-play. I took a deep breath and focused back on the task at hand.

"Doesn't he realize how it makes you feel?" Guy swirled his drink with a swizzle stick before meeting my eyes. "I mean, method acting or not, it's still a sensitive issue."

"He has to bring the part to life."

"Yes, but what's wrong with kissing Gloria's son on the back of his head? Going for the neck is a bit forward."

"What can I do? He's not in my life, but at least he's in my film. That's a start."

"Anyhow, it's not like that scene is in the script."

"But that's just it. I think it should be. It ties everything up and provides the perfect end to my film."

Guy fluttered his wings thrice.

"It's your call, but just make sure you know what you're doing."

Nellie now stood to the front of the stage, tenderly humming a tune while the harp wistfully echoed her sentiment. In a statue-like pose, she embraced the microphone stand, rocking gently, lulling it to a place of inner peace. With eyes closed, she lowered one arm by her side and lightly waved the sound of the celestial strings through the crowd.

My angel friend shut his eyes and rocked gently. I did the same. Before long, Warwick's wayward affections drifted from my mind. Instead, I was back in Sydney shortly after we'd met.

*

My failed love life had become the unnoticed backdrop to my life, so Warwick tried to instill a go-with-the-flow mantra. He bought me a ticket to a gay dance party, citing I needed to rediscover my inner vamp.

We left that person previously referred to as my boyfriend at the entrance. He had a special rendezvous planned at the front gate. I was relieved we left him behind. Our misplaced spark had fallen behind the couch while I was vacuuming, months ago. Some empty pasta packet and a tin can probably found it and were making whoopee in the back of a garbage truck. We didn't officially end our relationship. We just drifted apart under the same roof.

Warwick took my hand and carefully led me through the turnstiles. I was greeted by the gracious elders of our ageless culture. Cute indie-music types, sporting fashionable glasses and leather vests, conversed with the elders who told them what to expect. One drag queen in a pink polystyrene dress battled with her high heels. A high school student wearing a T-shirt with black lettering wandered wide-eyed with his group of friends. His top read "What if it's not just a phase?" I once knew how he felt.

Inside, we were in wonderland. We floated past the Mad Hatter under the gargantuan mirror ball, before frolicking with Little Boy Blue who enticed us to blow his horn. So many smiles, hugs, and kisses. So many greetings of "Happy Mardi Gras!" We were all on the same planet. Our arms raised to the laser gods above, as our feet stomped below. Soulful melodic voices transformed into heavy-handed beats. From here on in, the rhythms merged, as they unified *us* with the horde. The seduction was complete. We were a revolution of similar passions, all cheeky, tender, and safe.

*

I quickly peeked at Guy to see if he too was still in his own nirvana. He was. Nellie snapped her fingers as she launched into the first line of "Come Together." Her harpist stopped strumming and clapped in time. Soon she was accompanied by the patrons, as a chorus of sensible shoes and errant heels rapped the beat. The singer growled the song like a waking woman, ready to spring to life at any moment. I closed my eyes to feel the power of her voice.

Abruptly, I was pressed against the wall with my head forced toward the floor. With the general ambience still serene, Guy had bolted to my side of the booth and distorted my body in ways that would make my old yoga master proud.

"What the hell are you...!"

"Shh! Samantha and Pedro are here."

"And Warwick?"

"No."

He carefully allowed me to sit up. I examined the room but couldn't see them.

"Where are they?"

"In that booth at the front."

There were the partners in crime, facing Nellie with their backs to us. Pedro got up to go to the bar, so we crouched again. Oddly, I noticed how worn my sneakers were.

"I guess our bedtime call has come early," said Guy. "Am I wrong in trying to hide us?"

"No," I replied. "The last thing I need is another debate over dramatic interpretation." I tried hard to meet eyes with my angel friend. "Are you sure they didn't see us?"

"Definitely! I watched them walk in, but their attention was on Nellie, the harpist, and a detour to the empty booth at the front."

After several minutes, the cramp in my neck made me sit up. Pedro was no longer at the bar. I studied the layout in an effort to work out why they didn't see us. It didn't make sense. They had to walk straight past us from the front door. Even though there were booths on opposite walls, they were on the same side of the Pedestal as we were, only several booths in front.

"Guy, you have to be wrong. They would have seen us."

"Allan, the cloak room." He pointed to an area near the opposite side of the stage.

"I get it. They zigzagged straight to the cloak room from the front door. Then they walked past the stage to the front booth. I guess if they saw us, they would have come over and shared their toxic temperament."

"That's why I pinned you down as soon as they handed over their coats." Guy looked back in their direction. "Shall we go?"

"No. I have a better idea."

I guided Guy out of our booth, crouching like deformed monkeys as we crept toward the talent-deluded pair.

"Allan! What are we doing?"

"Trust me."

I gently led him under the table of the booth behind Samantha and Pedro. Nellie's melodic musings drowned the bumpy transition to our hiding place. It would be an understatement to say it was cramped. Guy's wings were pressed up against the bottom of the table, forcing feathers into my face. I huddled into a ball, giving my angel pal as much room as I could.

"It's just not working," said Pedro. He was in the middle of a conversation we had missed the gist of.

"Maybe you should admit that you were never in love with him," added Samantha.

"Then he'd go flying back to Allan, and they'd *never* leave."

I darted a look of horror to Guy. He stared back.

"I'd give it more time," said Samantha. "He'll get tired of bashing his head against the wall and leave the Limelight Quarter. Perhaps move to the Carnival of Lost Souls. He'll be among the freaks."

"He'll be right at home."

I was perturbed by this comment. These two obviously didn't *get* the Lost Souls district. It's where the true artists lived. Guy flapped his wrist to ease my attention back to the conversation.

"Where is he tonight?" asked the blonde one.

"He went out to visit Allan."

"So much for keeping them apart."

"Either way, I think we should go. We don't want to be caught in public together."

They didn't rush. My neck was killing me, and Guy's knee was now pressed against my cheek. I also feared that his wingspan was protruding from under the table. They casually finished their drinks and stood during Nellie's rendition of "Do You Want to Know a Secret." They ambled to the cloak room as I sweated, praying that they hadn't left anything behind. If they had, they'd discover us cowering under a table in their field of vision. We were lucky. They strode out of the place like royalty.

"Pedro's not in love with my Warwick." I lifted myself from under the table. "He never was."

"And they both want you to leave the Limelight Quarter."

"But why?" I reached out to Guy and helped him get up. "I need to tell Warwick."

"Good idea, but not yet. He may not believe you. Remember, love is blind."

"And he went to see me tonight. I should have invited him here, like you suggested. He would have heard it for himself." My nerves were shot, so I gestured to the barman for a bottle of wine. "And what's wrong with the Carnival of Lost Souls?"

"From a Limelight perspective, it's a bit too underground. No glam factor."

"Guy, this jigsaw puzzle is not making sense. If they didn't want Warwick and me to hang around Limelight, why cast us in Pedro's play? We would have wandered around discovering the other sectors of this place, instead of settling into this neighborhood."

"Allan, it wasn't Samantha who cast you in the play. It was Maudi."

"But I didn't know Maudi before I met her as the director."

"Maudi knew about you and Warwick before you got here. As soon as she knew you were coming, she included you in the play."

"Guy, how long did you all know that we'd end up at the Limelight Quarter?"

"Allan, don't think in earthbound time."

I slouched. Nellie's sultry voice sung the last lines of "Nowhere Man" as the harpist waved her magic hands over the strings. The barman arrived with two glasses and a bottle of sauvignon blanc.

"It also explains why Pedro wasn't jealous when I kissed Warwick."

"If their plan was to get you to leave the Limelight Quarter, discovering you were having an affair with Warwick behind their backs must have thrown a spanner in the works."

We stared at each other, mirroring our pose of crossed arms. Nellie began crooning "You've Got to Hide Your Love Away" as the barman topped up our glasses and left.

"Guy, Pedro's little displays of jealousy are just a red herring."

"Hmm. You should tell Warwick."

"Tell the person who broke up with me that his relationship is a sham? Like you said, I have to be careful how I phrase this. He might never believe it coming from me."

"Do you want me to say something on your behalf?"

"He might think I put you up to it and change his mind about being in my film."

We both gulped down our wine.

"Guy, they hate me, and I don't know why."

"Professional jealousy."

"But I never asked for any of this. Suddenly, Warwick and I were in this crazy place and thrust onto the stage. Why take that out on us? Or more to the point, why take it out on me?"

"Allan, remember, not all creative beings conceive for a love of art!"

TWENTY

MAUDI HAD A new look. Her loose emerald-green dress was something Farah would wear rather than a nineteenth-century actress. Her long hair draped on both sides of her shoulders, hassle-free, and smelling of lavender. Somewhere in the Afterlife was an enchanted forest waiting for her to frolic in while playing the flute.

Frederick seemed equally laidback. His gentle smile reminded me of a young lad who'd discovered the fairer sex, leaving years of hanging out with his buddies and smoking to be cool well behind him.

Guy and I were seated in Maudi's lounge room, surrounded by old copies of *The Stage Door* she was about to throw out.

"I have to tell you something, Allan," she said.

"You're in love?"

"Are we?" asked Frederick in a joking manner.

"I believe we are, but that's not what I have to tell you."

"Before you say anything, my love, let me fetch some drinks." He got up. "Gin and tonic all around?" We all nodded.

Even though we were knee-deep in magazines, Maudi fished out the latest edition from her handbag. Pedro was featured on the cover in a swashbuckling outfit so tight Maid Marian would think all her eggs had arrived in one basket. Even Guy had a second look. He was supposed to be Mr. Small Dick according to reports. Maybe they doctored the cover?

"Yes, Maudi, Warwick mentioned that Pedro was writing a play."

"When did you say your screening was?" She thumbed her way to a particular page.

"In a fortnight. The edit is coming together better than expected. With one more shooting day, I'll be finished by the middle of next week."

Frederick came out with our drinks as Maudi handed me the journal. Guy peered over my shoulder.

Pedro's photo filled one page. On a desk in the background sat his old typewriter with a single black ribbon, while he posed in a crisp white shirt and slicked hair. On closer inspection, I was convinced that this picture might have been taken in the moldy tenement he once occupied, before his demise. Maudi's index finger pointed sternly to the opening paragraph.

*

Sharpen your swords, avid theatergoers, for a swashbuckling adventure you'll never forget. Our author of substance has done it again! Pedro has penned a tale of deceit, politics, and mystical treasure. Our star writer again takes the stage in his own production, playing the narrator in the form of a traveling minstrel.

*

"I can play a chord or two on my lute," Pedro reports. "But by opening night, I intend to play a whole tune!"

*

"A man of ever-increasing talents," I declared. "I wish him well. It looks like we both have projects to be proud of."

Maudi didn't speak. She leaned over while her index finger hovered above a date in the second paragraph. There was no mistaking the day. Pedro's sword extravaganza was to open the same night as my screening. I guzzled my cocktail, leaving the glass half-empty.

"What is it, Allan?" asked Guy.

"There must be a mistake in the article. I clearly booked the Limelight Theater on that night. I wrote the date at the top of my script after phoning from home. Gloria's son was with me, viewing the rushes. He wrote down the date as well."

"Sounds like your dramas aren't over yet," replied Frederick. "Maudi noticed the date this morning."

"It's Pedro for sure, and Samantha for some reason. I finally break the bonds of their silly productions, and they're still out to get me."

"Just change your screening to the following week," said Guy.

"The run of the play is four weeks," explained Maudi. "He'll have forever to wait."

"So have your screening after that."

"I could, but I've already invited people. I've even popped up some posters. Maybe I'm just being paranoid? Maybe it's a misprint?"

"Allan, you know it's not a misprint. I've worked greeting new arrivals with her for too long. She's been gloating about Pedro to newcomers, while in the same breath downplaying *your* efforts."

"Why is she talking about me to newcomers?"

"You know how jealous she is. She's fobbing you off as an aimless artiste!"

"The question is," said Frederick, "what are you going to do next?"

"Argh!" I grunted. "The truth is I haven't got a clue."

I put down my glass on one of the piles of magazines, before burying my head in my hands. The others sat in silence. I had one more shoot with Warwick and still hadn't worked out how to woo him. I couldn't tell him that his relationship was a sham, and I was making a film that might never see the light of day. I began to laugh.

"What's so funny?" asked Maudi.

"I don't know. I really don't know, but I can't stop."

"My dear, you're delirious."

"No, he isn't, my darling," replied Frederick. "He's the sanest one here."

"Thank you. I have to see this through fresh eyes. Regardless of what we all believe, we have no real proof that the date isn't just a mix-up."

Guy flapped his wings twice. "Allan, you may not have control of your situation, but you have control over how you react."

"They're sobering words, my dear angel friend."

I picked up my drink from the magazine pile, but the condensation from the glass made it stick to the publication. As I slid my cocktail from it, I noticed a young Maudi on the cover. She was dressed as Eliza Doolittle in *Pygmalion*, and even though she was a couple of decades too old to play this role when she had, her slimmer figure helped achieve a youthful glow.

"Is it coincidence that that particular edition was on the top of the pile?" I asked.

Maudi looked coy as Frederick studied the cover.

"You're more beautiful now than you were then," he said.

Guy and I groaned. He took Maudi's hand and bowed to kiss it. As his lips rested on her fingers, she replied, "You're a card, sweetheart, and you should be dealt with." We groaned louder.

I flipped through the journal and found the feature on *Pygmalion*, glancing at the pictures of the first-night audience. There beaming at me in black and white were the faces of two people I wished I'd never met. I trembled, dropping the magazine in my lap.

"You look like you've seen the Wicked Witch of the West, Allan," said Guy. He reached over and took the journal. "What are we looking at?"

"The picture of the couple, second from the bottom, left-hand page."

Guy's eyes widened, and his wings jutted out. He read the print below the photo out loud.

*

Young love in bloom. They may have strutted the boards a few times, but this ambitious pair have higher aspirations. Pedro (left) fancies himself a writer, while his girlfriend Samantha (right) is keen to direct his work of genius. Keep an eye on this couple!

*

Guy dropped the publication. "She's more than just a gal pal!"

"And he's bisexual," I added.

"But that just proves they *used* to be lovers," said Maudi. "I've met many a man who is charmed by the fairer sex before they realize they are the fairer sex." I stared straight ahead, clutching my gin and tonic so hard it was a miracle the glass didn't shatter. "Oh, dear boy, I think I've just cottoned on to what you're really saying. They're 'the lovers.'"

Frederick looked puzzled. "What lovers?"

"The lovers that are out to get Allan," replied Guy. "It's a psychic thing. It was foretold to him, but now it all makes sense."

I turned to my angel companion. "We sat there, cramped under a booth at the Pedestal listening to them, and it never dawned on either of us that they were 'the lovers' all along."

"And together they'll stop at nothing to hide their romance, create little accidents, plot a love affair with Warwick, and try to keep the talented offstage, or worse still, out of the Limelight Quarter!"

"It's more preposterous than one of Pedro's plotlines," blurted our hostess.

"So preposterous no one would ever believe it," I replied.

"But dear Allan, the feeble playwright first got his nose out of joint the day I made you and him switch roles. Isn't that when this dilemma began?"

"No, my dear Maudi. The feeble playwright and the blonde princess got their noses out of joint before Warwick and I set foot in this ego's playground."

We all sat motionless except for Frederick, whose eyes darted around the room like he was watching a tennis match.

"My dear Allan, I was keen to also meet you and Warwick the day you arrived, but Samantha insisted that the sight of her and an angel would be *ample* for you to take in on first impression."

"And then she insisted on going to the Pedestal," said Guy.

"And that's strange because...?" I asked.

"And that's strange because the Pedestal is the second place we take new arrivals to, after they've settled into their quarters."

"What difference does going to a pub before being shown to your accommodation have in this scheme of events?"

"I was about to ask the same thing," said Frederick.

"Think about it," Guy replied. He rose, wandering with his drink to the window. "Within hours of arriving in this alien place, the man you pine after is taken from you, so that your first night is spent alone. Would the plan work as well if you both settled in first? I'm not sure, but this scenario is sure to knock you off your perch. To Warwick, this was a one-night fling, so Pedro tried harder. For a while, it worked."

"Until I decided to be the other woman, thanks to you, Maudi."

We nodded to each other.

"Precisely!" continued Guy. "So Pedro publicly feigned jealousy the day you blew Warwick a kiss onstage to lay a guilt trip on both of you, or at least tried to as best he could. He even broke out of character, jumping up in a threatening stance. But Allan, you still didn't leave."

Maudi pressed her finger against her lips and shook her head.

"There's no reason for Pedro to feign jealousy to lay a guilt trip on young Warwick," she reasoned. "Warwick was with him anyway."

"But it worked in making Warwick split up with Allan."

"Did it? Feigning jealousy just to lay a guilt trip on someone publicly is too risky. I learnt with my darling Eddy that these chats are better left behind closed doors. You have more control."

"Ah," I said. "But there is a reason to feign jealousy when it's public knowledge that there's a love triangle going on, but you don't want anyone to suspect that the love triangle is actually a love quadrangle!"

"You're right!" exclaimed Guy. "Think back to the day Maudi made Allan and Pedro switch roles. He was a bull in a china shop. He matched that intensity when you blew Warwick that kiss."

"True. I give him credit for actually acting. I felt threatened."

"But it wasn't public knowledge before your indiscretion that there was a love triangle," said Maudi. "Remember? It was in the theater bible the next day."

"The theater bible?" asked Frederick.

Guy and I gestured to the piles of magazines on the floor.

"Oh, of course." The old actor clasped his hands and brought them to his chin. "I think there's something that you're all missing here. I saw Pedro on stage that final night of Samantha's production. The man can't act. There's no way he'd threaten you convincingly, Allan, if he wasn't actually angry."

"My darling has a point," said Maudi. "Pedro has the acting prowess of a tossed salad."

"My dalliance with Warwick is not what made Pedro angry. I spent the night with Warwick the day before he created that drama on stage."

Guy nodded as Maudi and Frederick shared baffled looks.

"That only highlights his jealousy at you and Warwick," alleged the actress.

Guy stepped away from the window and paced around the room as if he found his inner Sherlock.

"What Allan is getting at is that Pedro wasn't reacting to the idea of their romance. It's the fact that their romance was ruining the lovers' plans."

"That's right," I said. "That's why I was invited around for lunch, so Warwick and I could be questioned about the state of our affair. Pedro was pretty moody when he started asking about his boyfriend's whereabouts the night we hooked up, but didn't batter an eyelid when he caught us smooching."

"He dropped the act."

"Yes, my winged detective friend, he did. He had his proof, and as he wasn't in love with Warwick, it didn't matter. Oh wait, hold on a second." I bit my bottom lip before knocking back the rest of my gin and tonic. "Warwick split up with me that afternoon. This throws all our reasoning out the window. Pedro already knew beforehand that we were together and had convinced Warwick to cook me a farewell meal."

"I don't believe that," alleged Maudi. "Young Warwick is a kindhearted soul, my dears. Maybe being caught smooching with Allan was enough for him to question his own ethics."

"But now Warwick is in your film," said Frederick. "The very film Samantha and Pedro want no one to see."

Guy sat down. His wings spread lifeless against the bird pattern on the lounge. Frederick and I sat forward as Maudi lounged back like a queen in charge of proceedings.

"It's truly sad when ambition overshadows romance," she said. "Domination is their veritable passion."

"Maybe it's an indication of true respect?" I replied. "Remember, this is a plan they shared. Pedro had a little extra cake and got to eat it too. After all, they're swingers, so his dalliance on the side is immaterial."

"But their plan backfired," added Guy. "As Bullet said in his awful play—'I don't think I amount to second best in your estimation at controlling this town.' The problem was, and still is, Pedro and Samantha still believe that you and Warwick can control this town, whether you want to or not."

"We don't. We were hardly big stars at home. We did amateur theater as a hobby, and perhaps I was going to make it as a cult celebratory. I never got to find out."

"Oh, yes, that offbeat movie you were going to do."

"You knew about that?"

Instead of answering, he raised his wings and fluttered to remind me of his celestial nature.

"Yes, she never got over not being a star," mused Maudi.

"She's doing okay," I replied. "She was a local directing star with Gloria's son's play."

"Not here, darling, back home in the 1950s. She's a failed movie actress. Didn't you know, Allan?"

"Maudi, I had no idea. But that's still no reason to plot against me. I never made the film. And there are no guarantees that it would have been a success anyway."

"You probably never knew this, Allan," said Guy, "but some serious money was being raised to give your feature a mainstream budget. Samantha, on the other hand, starred in one drive-in movie, which was buried as quickly as it was released."

"It was that bad?"

"No. There were just other blonde bombshells around with better cleavage."

I fell back into the sofa. "She never had the career she wanted, and neither did I. So we were both in the same boat."

"Think about it," replied Guy. "She wasn't a star, but you were well on your way. From what I understand, you weren't a bad director with your small theater projects either, while her skills are still questionable."

"But as far as the Limelight public are concerned, I've only appeared in two plays."

"My exquisite Allan," Maudi said. "You didn't do too badly in your first role here. So, after not succeeding in driving you out of town through those treacherous mishaps during my production, and not killing your career with that lemon of a moon suit, you exhibit your full potential by remaking the very script that was to be her tour de force."

"This is all too much. We still have no concept of how the stage light fell, especially as Pedro could have been hurt in the process. We don't know how that slippery goo got on stage or when Guy's gun was exchanged for a real one."

"And does it matter anymore?" asked Frederick. "Eventually you'll find out, but for the moment, you have Warwick by your side for one more shoot, and a film almost complete that needs a new venue to play at. As for Pedro and Samantha, well, they're shallow people who judge everyone else by their own shallow values. Forget them. You don't need to see them again."

I felt a weight lift from my shoulders. "I hear you. Somehow, somewhere, we'll show the film. But I have only one more chance to win back my misplaced friend and lover."

Maudi piped up with the keenness of a knight who'd broken the princess' chastity belt.

"Oh, be a sport, Allan. You can't let Pedro and Samantha get away with what they've done. Revenge is the game of kings."

"But it's the never-ending playground of fools!"

TWENTY-ONE

AFTER MANY DAYS of superlative performances captured on video, an unfamiliar mood breezed in over our little project. We were struggling to unearth a fresh well of creative juice as everyone's acting switched to autopilot.

"Everyone thinks we're already having this affair," said Janice, playing Simone. She sat with her husband in bed.

"I know," replied James, portrayed by Warwick. "I'm even getting offers from other men."

"This is driving me mad."

Simone's words were supposed to convey frustration, but Janice had the dramatic intensity of a shrub.

"Allan, I'm trying to conjure up my dirtiest fantasies to motivate me. It worked in rehearsal."

"I think you have to move from R-rated to triple-X-rated," I replied.

Frederick wandered over and stood next to me.

"Janice and Warwick, this is not a scene about your collective dirty minds," he said. "It's a scene about your relationship. How much you *still* love each other."

The two actors nodded subtly as I stepped back to my tripod and peered through the lens. "Take two. Rolling."

"Everyone thinks we're already having this affair." Janice tried again, this time with the emotive depth of a thimble.

"I know. I'm even getting offers from other men." Warwick sounded like he'd won the lottery.

"This is driving me mad." I felt her frustration, even if she didn't.

Frederick stepped in again while I kept rolling. "I have a technique. Picture an imaginary circle around both of you." The two thespians shared baffled looks before focusing on the direction. Soon the look was a gaze, and even their body language was more affectionate. "Still rolling, Allan?"

"Yes."

"Action!"

"Everyone thinks we're already having this affair." This statement was measured as she shared her anxiety with James.

"I know. I'm even getting offers from other men." James' response was ambivalent, half-adulation, half-apprehension.

"This is driving me mad." I felt her frustration, and this time, so did she.

"Cut! Print! Brilliant! Guys, you've rediscovered your mojo. Frederick, you're a gem!"

"Not bad," said a voice from behind us.

Turning roughly in unison, we discovered Samantha filing her nails and occupying my canvas director's chair.

"When did you sneak in?" I asked.

"Just a moment ago," she replied. She strode toward us. "A masterful piece of direction from Frederick, I see. I'm impressed."

"This production is a breath of fresh air," alleged my skilled elder. "It's theater you can savor, without the calories."

"Sounds finger-lickin' good."

"Samantha, what brings you here?" I asked.

"Mild curiosity, I suppose. I'm not really sure."

"Did you like what you saw?"

"A bit too realistic for my taste."

"But isn't that the point?" asked Frederick.

"It should be a fun production," she replied.

"Allan's bringing a lot of fun to his film. He understands each character's motivation brilliantly."

"Thank you, Frederick," I said.

Warwick and I shared discreet glances as the others crowded around the actors on set.

"Samantha, Allan knows what he's doing," affirmed Gloria's son.

"And how would you know, dear?"

"I wrote the script. Remember?"

"Oh yes." Her face went deadpan while she shook her hand as if shooing away a bug. "I must talk to Guy. Will you give us a minute, Allan?"

"Of course."

Samantha and the angel snuck off to the corner while the rest of us stayed silent. Frederick caught my eye with a curious expression. I shared his look.

"I must fly," called our blonde visitor.

As we all mumbled our goodbyes, she left hastily. Guy stood rubbing his chin as I walked over to him. Frederick trailed closely behind. The others began talking among themselves.

"What did she say?" I asked.

"She told me that we're expecting a man who will lose his fight with cancer tomorrow."

"So why the blank look?"

"I already knew that. She told me yesterday."

"Maybe she just wanted to make sure you wouldn't forget."

"Allan, you can't bullshit a trained bullshit artist," said Frederick.

I smirked. "Am I that transparent?"

"We both know you don't believe that."

Guy nodded.

"So what's she playing at?"

Frederick paused before clasping his hands. "Whatever her game is, I think she's about to lay her cards on the table. Whether she intends to or not."

LATER THAT DAY, we were at Maudi's place. We had just shot Frederick, Guy, and our gracious hostess' last scene. The telescope was set up, and Ipan had been peering back at our spellbound lovers. It was ten years later, and Farah and Fabien had joined him to share in the mortals' antics, well after all magic charms had been lifted. The man in the moon and the whimsical witch were still in love, and while the earthbound characters guzzled champagne, Ipan didn't mind that there was passion in their hearts.

While I reviewed the shoot in my camera, Guy decorated Maudi's living room, Frederick premixed cocktails, and Maudi heated the delicious delights we had all brought for our wrap party.

I soon fussed around my other cast members in the backyard, sorting out two old pairs of reading glasses that were given to me by Frederick. With only the frames intact, I gave them to Warwick and Janice to signify the decade that had passed. They both applied less makeup than usual, and Warwick wore a diamond-pattern sleeveless pullover to give him that nerdy-but-nice mystique. For the sake of art, I knew I had to deal with watching my lost love give into lustful advances, and the thought was tying knots in my stomach.

Clouds rolled into the afternoon sky, making the sun only peer at proceedings below. Its muted streams gave the garden an auburn hue, holy almost, as if Christ was about to step down using one of the sunrays as a path. This calming glow lit my cast. Their inner souls illuminated in the camera frame. They sat in a circle on the grass with champagne flutes in hand, waiting for direction. I quickly set up my tripod.

"GS, I'm starting with a close-up on your glass before I pull out to a wide shot of all three of you. But please, begin the dialogue as soon as I call action."

"Yes, director," he replied.

"Okay, action."

"You realize I was infatuated by you two when we first met," said the love interest. "Seriously, it was doing my head in. I would fantasize at whim. I wanted to be in the middle of you both in a king-sized bed."

"Did you think it was easy for us?" replied James. "You must have known we were in the same boat."

"I had *some* inkling, but I was also aware of how jealousy worked in your relationship."

"Jealousy?" Simone asked.

"Oh, there was jealousy. Subtle, but it was definitely there." He stared at his glass. "I didn't want to be the one responsible for splitting you up."

"And all that time, your cautiousness was driving us crazy."

"Cut," I said. "I've had a change of heart. I feel too distant from you in this three-shot." I took the camera off the tripod. "Try to ignore me as I shoot handheld."

I crouched near my cast.

"Are you sure you're not too close?" asked Gloria's son. "You might be a bit intrusive."

"Just draw that imaginary circle around the three of you. I'll just seem like a large buzzing insect in the background. Something you'll overlook once you're 'in the scene.'"

I called "action" while beginning the shot on Gloria's son. Their words were repeated with more tenderness than before.

"Let me propose something," said Simone. "Something that will shine a spotlight to our doubts."

"What do you have in mind?" asked James. "Spin the bottle?"

"Almost. We're going to take turns kissing, but after each kiss, we are all going to share, honestly, how we feel." Her suggestion was received with uncertain smiles. "James, you and I will start."

Warwick and Janice shut their eyes and allowed their noses to rub. Their lips met, softly sliding against each other as Gloria's son leisurely crawled behind them and caressed their backs. As they moaned, the younger actor nestled up to them, pecking them playfully on the cheek. Soon the husband and wife team parted lips and willingly shared their mouths with the third player.

As I watched through the camera's monitor, a tear came to my eye. Warwick was no longer mine. His independence from me was now complete. No longer would we compare our musical tastes or comment on the virtue of lush red curtains. There'd be no more fabulous parties that we'd throw to celebrate our friends. Our once close bond had been erased. I wanted to fade with it in this precise moment.

"Are you going to call 'cut'?" asked Warwick.

The three actors burst out laughing.

"You must have enough footage," said Janice. "I'll need to cool down if you need a take two."

"I think I have enough," I replied quietly.

"I'm sure you have plenty," said a voice from behind. I turned to see Samantha perched on a stool. "What kind of film are you making?"

"A film about the nature of love, obviously." I felt as if I was being stalked. I stood up. "Your second visit in one day. My, we are blessed."

"The pleasure is all mine." She raised herself with her manicured fingers and strolled toward us. "It looks like your cast is definitely exploring 'the nature of love' as you say."

"They're a true ensemble. Besides, Gloria's son's play is tender and sweet, so this is..."

"But isn't it a play about magic, Allan?"

"I wouldn't say *magic* is the core," interrupted the young playwright. He too stood up. "Ipan, Fabien, and Farah are just voicing the subtext."

"What are you doing here, Samantha?" called Maudi. She and the others had come outside. "You seem to be nosing around like a meerkat, expecting surprises."

"Not really, you kind dear woman. I'm just learning what a breath of fresh air Allan's production is." She peered down her nose. "How much more is there to shoot?"

"That was it," I replied. "The new final scene that caps it all off. It's the future, and the three are still friends…"

"So your version of the play that I produced has fallen into place?"

"Swimmingly." I trailed away on the last syllable. "But as I said before, you've contributed plenty by your original direction of Janice and Guy."

"Yes, well, desire is my forte. But I guess you've given this play a fresh edge."

"How so?"

"Unrequited love is *your* forte."

The cast and I shared mixed glances.

"Unrequited love was my reason for writing the play," said Gloria's son. "Allan's brought a fresh take to my text." He giggled. "I mean, he took a fresh take because he understands it, not because he knows about unrequited love. No, that wasn't quite what I was trying to say either."

"It's in safe hands with all of us," added Frederick. "We've *all* fallen prey to unrequited love."

"Unrequited love carries many a good drama," declared Maudi.

"True, I guess," Samantha said. She smirked, nearly fracturing her plaster expression. "It's just that Allan's lost the magic of my production. I think the locals will make comparisons."

"I'm sure they will," I replied. "They always do. Some will like mine. Some will like yours. Some might even be a bit weird and like both."

"Samantha, why are you giving Allan a hard time?" asked Warwick. His head tilted. "This is so unlike you."

She froze. Guy huddled next to me, wrapping one wing around my shoulder.

"No, Warwick, this is exactly like her," I replied. "It's the Samantha you don't see. It's the Samantha that hangs around her lover, Pedro. The lover that pretends to love you."

"Don't be stupid," my friend said. "Pedro's gay."

"Yes, Allan, don't be stupid," Samantha added. "That accusation is as believable as your interpretation of the play."

"Then it makes it spot-on!" I replied.

"Allan, your imagination is obviously working overtime. Let's hope we see the fruits of that imagination one day."

"So you *have* taken over the theater the night I booked it."

"Whatever are you talking about?" She extended her finger and placed it on her lips. "On second thought, Allan, don't answer. I'm sure it's just another paranoid delusion. Besides, I have a dress rehearsal to organize." She blew us a kiss and turned on her blue pastel heel. "Ta-ta, fellow actors." No one replied. She stamped her feet as she headed for the garden gate, leaving behind the scent of perfume with a poisonous bouquet.

"I told you not to trust her," said Guy.

"Yes, she's a bit of a Tessie Two-Face," added Frederick. He stared in the direction of her exit. "What is it about the theater that appeals to those seeking self-respect?"

"And there went the perfect example," I said. "Besides, what would that Marilyn wannabe know about art? And did you see how tight her dress was? Just to prop up her failing assets. All Betty but no boop!"

"Allan, I think we need to talk." Warwick stood and strode toward me and Guy. "Why did you say Pedro pretends to be in love with me?"

"It's an act. They, and by 'they' I mean Pedro and Samantha, they want me out of the Limelight Quarter. They're swingers, and they're a couple. They're a swinging couple."

"You are delusional."

"No, he's right," replied Guy. "They're 'the lovers' that Monique talked about."

"Monique?"

"The fortune-teller Allan visited."

"You're just as delusional, Guy. You're supposed to be his friend. Why are you feeding him this crap?"

I pointed to where Samantha exited. "Warwick, you just saw how she treated me. That's not the actions of a rational woman. What kind of spell have they cast on you? Why can't you see what's going on right under your nose?"

"Allan, I'm happy. Okay, I'm not with you, but don't be such a sore loser. I'm with Pedro. I'm not in love with you." He paused, intentionally looking to the ground. "Pedro is..."

"Warwick, what's the matter?" I tried to place my arm around his shoulder, but he shrugged it away. "What have they said to you?"

"Allan, you're playing with my mind. I don't know why, but you've got these crazy ideas in your head, and you won't leave them alone. Pedro's my boyfriend. You're so confused with jealousy you won't accept my happiness." He marched toward the exit, his hands gesturing so frenetically you'd swear he was Italian. "Why are you like this? You were never like this before. Allan, if you can't accept me and Pedro, then you're not my friend!"

The gate slammed.

"Remind me to cast him in a dramatic role," said Maudi.

I began to laugh but soon found it hard to breathe. "No," I gasped. Guy held on to me as I trembled. "No. Get me out of here." Maudi took both my hands and clasped them.

"Breathe, dear!" she commanded.

I tried to answer, but no words came from my mouth. I heard my own short sharp breaths before Janice, Frederick, Maudi, and Guy spun around my field of vision. As I tried to focus on each individual, everything went black.

TWENTY-TWO

IT WAS NIGHT. I stumbled out of bed, not knowing how I got home. The shadows cast in my living room appeared eerie, like every item of furniture had its own soul and it was my privilege to inhabit their space. The light fittings sluggishly writhed with tentacles, waiting to lurch out and grab me when my mind was elsewhere. The coffee table would taunt me, crawling away if I needed to put down a drink. The lounge was ready to swallow me if I dared to sit down. I'd be found with my body shattered into pieces as the sofa chewed my weary bones.

Warwick was right. I was delirious.

Outside, the full moon glared through my curtains, ready to relay every wrong move in my failed love life. What would he know? Who was his lover, the sun? And why did they both exist here in the Afterlife? It made no sense. But nothing here, not even Warwick's unlikely behavior, did.

I sat cautiously on the sofa, almost waiting for a giant pair of hungry teeth to bite hard and crack my spine. The harlequin money box knew I was being silly. The weary nature of my overactive imagination made its face smirk. I wasn't in the mood for its cheeky temperament. I was ready to shove a coin not in its usual slot.

As I stared into the ornament's eyes, my thoughts traveled back to Uncle Bryant. I remembered that we had left him and Pamela with our car as we had decided to visit Tasmania. Warwick and I were entering the elevator of his restored Victorian-era building. Unlike the apartment block, the elevator was added several decades after the building was completed, and had been restored as a stunning art piece. All that was missing was a lift attendant in a navy jacket.

*

"Your uncle's found his second youth," said Warwick.

"I know. There was so much sweet love oozing from them, I needed a shot of insulin."

"It's nice to see, though."

As the doors slid shut, I pressed the G button and waited. Nothing happened. I pressed the button again.

"Looks like it's feeling a bit sluggish," I said.

"It's kind of cozy in here, Allan."

"Spending the afternoon trapped in an elevator doesn't sound like fun."

Two minutes seemed like an eternity. I yelled, pushed buttons, pounded my fists, and yelled some more.

"It's not helping us," said Warwick.

"Well, you're not exactly coming up with any answers."

He leaned against the lift wall and stared at me, deadpan. We were silent. I had no idea what he was up to, so I stared back like Patricia Neal in *The Day the Earth Stood Still*, trying to recall Gort's instructions.

"What are you doing? We have to get out of here and take the stairs."

Out of the blue, he rested his lips on my forehead and kissed me all the way down to my neck.

"Allan, why don't you call Uncle Bryant on your phone?"

"That all depends."

"On what?"

"On whether you're going to kiss me again."

I raised myself on the tips of my toes and shut my eyes. His warm mouth melted into mine, taking me beyond each former fantasy I had about my friend. Soon his hands clutched my cheeks as he slid his lips sideways, licking me with his tongue. I opened my mouth, letting in this welcome intruder, letting mine blissfully taste his.

I pulled away for air. "You don't know how long I've been waiting for you to do that."

"I have some idea. I've seen you give me that look."

"What look?" He demonstrated. "Really, is that what I look like? That's more post-orgasm than pre-orgasm."

"So, are you going to call your uncle?"

I grabbed the back of his neck, lurching him against my mouth. I forced my tongue against his, sliding and tasting as much of this beautiful man as I could. Twelve months of pent-up frustration released in my impassioned embrace. I could have sworn I heard wedding bells. My heart jolted. I lost my footing.

A deafening screech reverberated through our chamber. Our gravity shifted. We were glued to the ceiling with the force of a speeding roller coaster, as the elevator plummeted downward.

Warwick reached out to me, but my hand was pinned against my own Adam's apple. The lift jerked several times as our airborne state came to an abrupt end. There was the sound of something cracking along with two blunt thuds. I stood up and helped my friend dust himself off. As I adjusted my T-shirt, I saw two souls watching us. One was a 1950s goddess in a cherry-red outfit. The other was an angel who set my gaydar beeping.

*

"Why are you crying?" yelled the voice from my spare bedroom.

"Who said I'm crying?"

I held my mouth to stop me yelping. My face was drenched in tears.

"Allan, I know you too well." Guy sauntered into the living area. "It's the middle of the night, and you're upset about something." He wandered into my kitchen and returned with a glass of scotch over ice. "Now drink."

"What are you doing here?"

"I said 'drink.'" I gulped a small mouthful. "Frederick and I carried you home. Then I decided to stay the night just in case you needed me."

"Warwick and I were in love."

"Allan, regardless of what Monique told you about being soul mates, this whole thing is killing you."

I howled. My angel chum took the drink from my hand and wrapped his arms around me.

"Our love has killed me already."

"That's one way of looking at it. Now calm down, my dear friend."

"No, Guy. Love killed us the first time around."

"What in heaven's name are you talking about?"

I didn't answer. I wept a little more as my pal held me against him. I rested my head on his shoulder; my wet cheek becoming as warm as a blanket.

A soft pink light radiated from his body. He told me not to be frightened and to encompass whatever I felt. His aura danced with a thousand tiny feet against me, urging me to cry out in despair. A sleek black fog blew from my mouth, looking back at me, sad and defeated. It split into many pieces as a jigsaw puzzle would if it fell to the ground. But these fragments hovered, staring into my soul and forcing me to shake uncontrollably.

"Let it go, Allan. Let them go."

I kissed the air and bid them farewell. They faded with my fear. I whimpered as the angel's aura spread over me with a gentle caress, before tenderly sinking under my skin. I was adored, and for the first time since birth, the center of my universe.

"Guy, whatever you did, it had to be illegal. It felt too good. Is there any chance we could do that again?"

"One angel love session per customer. But for you, Allan, I'll see what I can arrange."

He loosened his grip as I gathered my thoughts.

"I need you to tell me something." I pulled away and swallowed a little scotch. "From time to time, you've let on to little facts about our previous life. Just how much do you know?"

"Why do you ask?"

"My dear angelic friend, don't answer my question with another question." I took a deep breath. "When we first arrived, you seemed to know that amateur theater was a hobby of ours. You stumped me in knowing about a movie I was going to be in. You even knew it was well financed, something I had no inkling of. Plus you've been supportive of me from the start, even helping me get together with Warwick when you were stoned." I paused. "Hmm, what am I really trying to say?" I took another sip. "Guy, I'm surrounded by a nineteenth-century actress, a creative young playwright from the 1970s, a bitter blonde bombshell from the 1950s, and a creepy Casanova from early last century. And there's you, of course, the all-knowing angel!"

"I know," he replied.

He casually moseyed back to the kitchen.

"No, but Guy, you're my angel!"

"I get it, Allan. I'm an angel."

"And then there's 1930s Nellie, the drag king who's like a portable music player."

"That one's just coincidence."

He returned with a glass of scotch for himself and sat next to me again.

"Guy, are you my guardian angel?" I tried to read his face. "Guy, you've been so kind to me. In a way, you've become my best friend. The way Warwick was before we…" A sinister *d* word was stuck at the back of my throat.

"Allan, here at the Limelight Quarter, I was sent to keep an eye on you both. You were beginning your lives as soul mates before that tragic elevator incident. You were supposed to fall in love, but not all plans go the way we intend them, not even here."

"What happens when they don't go to plan?"

"Then you have to live it all over again in your next life. Every heartache, every argument, and every lost opportunity." He shook his head. "Not the greatest outcome, I know, but I think that's why I started pushing you toward Warwick against my better judgment."

"But Monique said we'd walk aimlessly here if we didn't get together. You were doing the right thing."

"Was I, Allan? Look what happened last night. Everything got too much for you, so you passed out. I should have seen it coming."

We sat in silence and drank our scotch. A pale pink glow lit the apartment, while the harlequin money box greeted me with a sympathetic smile.

"I love you very much, Guy. You and Maudi are my best friends now. But there's something I need to know. You just mentioned the elevator, yet I didn't say anything about it."

"I worked out why you were crying a moment ago."

"So you never watched over us when we were alive?"

"I don't know who your guardian angels were back then, but whoever they were, they should have never let you enter that elevator."

"Why didn't I remember what happened when I first got here?"

"Just as you never remember what happens immediately before birth, you also forget what happens just before death. Otherwise, the Afterlife would be full of trauma counselors."

"I think I need a trauma counselor now. Guy, I'm dead."

"A little before your time, might I add. That's why you've been in denial."

"Hmm. So has Warwick."

"Yes, Allan. He found his own unique way to cope."

For the first time in as long as I could remember, I felt control over my own affairs.

"So how do Pedro and Samantha fit in to everything that's happened to us?"

"My friend, like in life, you're all brought together at this point in time, regardless of when you existed in mortal terms. Some souls are more advanced than others. You're closer to knowing yourself." Guy paused. "You and Warwick also appreciate the importance of other people; others don't. Samantha and Pedro continue to play out the self-centered dramas they didn't reconcile in life. It's called unfinished business."

"And Warwick and I had our unfinished business as well, but we got sidetracked. I guess people are just as confused in death as they are in life. What a sobering thought. Gloria's son wrote his erotic memoirs in a play, and Maudi found new love beyond Lord Edward what's-his-name. And all of us are still trapped in the theater. What a set of drama queens!" I placed my arms around my angel chum and held him tighter than I ever had. "Tell me something. Can soul mates also be friends, apart from lifelong partners?"

"Of course."

"So I've known Maudi and Gloria's son before, maybe even Pedro and Samantha?"

He pulled away from me.

"Allan, I have no idea. Maybe they're important in your next life? I don't know. I only met you when you arrived at the Limelight Quarter. I got my briefing about you both, and was told to keep an eye on you, long before the deceitful duo showed their true colors. I may even watch over you when you return to mortality."

"As long as you continue to keep an eye on me here," I replied.

I held him again.

"I'll be here, Allan. I'll be here. Or I'll be following you to the Grand Sector or the Lost Souls, wherever you decide to settle."

I broke our embrace quicker than a boy losing his cherry.

"How did you know I was considering leaving the Limelight Quarter? I've never mentioned that to anyone."

Guy flapped his wings.

"Allan, for goodness sake, I'm an angel!"

TWENTY-THREE

THREE SHARP KNOCKS awakened me late the next day, as I lay in bed mulling over my conversation with Guy hours before. I was at one with my duvet and didn't fancy leaving this undemanding chum. Gentle chain-saw snores wafted from the spare bedroom. As I tottered to the front door, I saw Guy buried under his wings like a fragile creature protected by its shell. It was a wonder his snores didn't reverberate under his cocoon. I reached for the doorknob, expecting Maudi and Frederick checking in on me.

Warwick gazed at me like a lamb leaving the farm, unaware of its fate. He held a bunch of flawless violet roses wrapped in sky-blue cellophane, which he sniffed before offering to me.

"I thought I'd never see you again," I said.

"I was a goose yesterday."

I nodded. "You said it, not me."

"I know you're not going to invite me in, so allow me the liberty."

He humbly entered my abode and made his way to the kitchen. From the cabinet next to the oven, he fished out a scarlet clay vase and artistically arranged the bunch. I leaned against the wall, not quite sure how I felt. Guy's snoring still resonated like the engine of an old car.

"Who's been sleeping in my bed?" Warwick asked. "Papa Bear?"

"Well, it sure as hell ain't Goldilocks! And what's this 'my bed' crap? You've been straddling the writer's *pen*!"

"Not anymore."

"The ink has run dry?"

"No, Allan. I found out you were right. It was scribbling on a different notepad."

"So you've come running back to second best. Perhaps the thorns on the roses aren't the only pricks in the room."

"Okay, I deserve it. Give me your best shot. Tell me I've been distant, self-centered, and perhaps just bloody stupid."

"No, Warwick, I'm sorry. I shouldn't lash out at a man offering gifts." I reached for a canister, which sat on the bench. "Peppermint tea?"

"Yes, please."

I picked up two tea bags and went to put on the kettle. He too, reached for the kettle, touching my hand accidentally. We didn't pull away.

He blew a waft of air toward my ear. I wanted to lose myself in his soulful eyes and savor his precious maroon lips, but that little voice inside me whispered "not yet." His rich black curly hair glistened from the sunlight streaming through the window, waiting for me to rub my beard through its locks before pressing my body against his. I'd reach around to the buttons on his short-sleeved cotton shirt, taking little nibbles at his neck. I'd unhook the lowest button, nonchalantly, working my way to the top, but stopping halfway. My hand would slide under his top and caress the small silky hairs that encircled his navel. I'd nonchalantly run my finger around the rim before I gently tickled its small crevice.

"Allan, the kettle's boiling."

I moved my hand from his and promptly made the tea. Warwick seated himself on the kitchen bench, sipping the hot brew, while I leaned with my back against the pantry, relaxed by the minty aroma.

"How did you broach the subject with Pedro about his relationship with Samantha?" My friend looked into his tea, gently blowing on its surface. "You don't have to answer if you don't want to. It may be too soon to talk about it."

He continued peering into the cup.

"It's okay. I don't mind talking about it. You see, after I left Maudi's place, I went back to Pedro's where I stood at the front door. I heard Samantha's voice inside. I couldn't make out what was said, so I opened the door just enough to hear. She was telling Pedro that you knew about their relationship and challenged her about it in front of me."

"That must have been hard for you to listen to."

Warwick looked at me as his mouth quivered.

"I marched to the bedroom and began packing. I didn't want to face them. I sort of knew something wasn't quite right for a while, but it was easier to be in denial."

"So you never confronted them."

"They heard me as I was leaving, and then all hell broke loose. They kept denying it, and well, if you thought my scene at Maudi's was bad, you should have seen me rip into Pedro and Samantha. They denied it all, of course, but when I quoted the conversation I eavesdropped on moments before, they froze like statues. I questioned them on why they did what they did, but all they uttered were vague syllables. I got so pissed off, I left."

"They didn't say anything intelligible?"

"I asked them what their problem was with you. Why they sabotaged Pedro's own play with preplanned accidents, which, I will admit, Allan, I don't believe was their doing, but I asked nevertheless. Finally, I asked if Pedro ever loved me or if it was just all part of their twisted plan."

"He had to answer that one, at least."

"Not even a lame excuse. He just stared at me, so I left." I moved forward to hug him, but he politely shooed me away. "I appreciate it, Allan, but I made my bed. Now I'm lying in it."

"It doesn't mean I can't cuddle you."

"I'm finding comfort in the tea."

I shrugged, bringing my cup to my mouth. "Hey, wait a second." I lowered my drink. "If you walked out of Pedro's place last night, where did you sleep?"

"Gloria's son and his flatmate let me crash on their couch."

I strode to the living room, darting my eyes around before returning to the kitchen. "I'm guessing your suitcase is in the hallway outside my apartment." Warwick looked as guilty as a boy who'd been discovered with his father's porn stash. "Yes, you can stay. It will be nice to have you back."

He extended his arms, so I returned to the kitchen and embraced him.

"Thank you, Allan."

His spicy manly scent took me back to when we were briefly lovers. I desperately wanted to nestle my face into his neck and breathe him in.

"Oh, by the way," said Warwick, "I thought of somewhere you can screen your film."

"Really?"

I pulled away and settled back against the pantry.

"The Community Hall. I walked past it after I left Pedro's place. The caretaker was there so we checked the diary. It was clear for the night you wanted to screen your film, so I penciled you in. We just have to go back today and make it official."

"Thank you, my oldest and dearest friend."

"Well, I kind of got us into this mess. It was about time I did something to get us out of it."

"It wasn't your fault. Guy and Maudi told me that Samantha was jealous of me before we even arrived in the hereafter."

My friend leaned forward, looking me up and down as if he were Sir David Attenborough studying the face of a baboon.

"What's the matter?" I asked.

"Allan, do you remember why we left Port Macquarie on our little trip?"

"Yes, my boss was getting to me, and I needed a sanity break."

"And that's all you remember?"

"We visited Uncle Bryant and Pamela in Melbourne, and then we were off to Tasmania. Yes, Warwick, I do remember!"

He slouched back, shaking his head.

"What?"

"Allan, remember how you introduced me to acting and the small theater scene in Sydney, and how we both got involved in the local amateur group in Port Macquarie?"

"So?"

"And how you scored that role, so we had to travel back to Sydney?" Now I had the baffled expression. "Allan, we didn't just leave Port Macquarie for a holiday. We left because I was sick and tired of you bitching about Mr. Incompetent not giving you time off to star in that Fembots sequel!"

"Huh!"

"You have no idea what I'm talking about, do you?"

"I think Pedro and Samantha's lunacy has rubbed off on you, Warwick. Maybe there's a Psychosis Quarter here for the deranged?"

"Allan, you spent a year going through the motions in a relationship that never really started. Do you think you would have gone back to Sydney to do the film? No! That's why I got you to leave home on a whim. Travel around a bit so your mind could break out of routine. Remember? Otherwise, you would have been too caught up doing the *same old same old* in Port Macquarie, clutching job security instead of a chance at cult stardom!"

I still stared at Warwick as if he was talking Swahili. He looked up at the ceiling shaking his head.

"Listen, Allan! After Tasmania, we were going back to your uncle's to pick up the car and drive back to Sydney so you could take up your role as Professor Smitten in *Fembots Back from Hell*."

"Warwick, that's the campest title since, er, since..."

"*Faster, Pussycat! Kill! Kill!*? *Queen Kong*? *It's Dead, Let's Touch It*? Since what, Allan? Since what?"

The memories started hitting me on the head like a jackhammer.

"I can't believe you didn't remember your big break," he said. "Didn't you say you could mainly remember things about you and me?"

"Yes, about you *and* me. I haven't really been thinking about just me."

"I got you to call your agent before we left home. He nearly wet himself because he thought he'd have to find someone to replace you. You were going to be one of the leads, just because you had a growing fan base overseas from the first Fembot flick!"

"Yeah," I replied. "Professor Smitten was now married to one of the Fembots, but when others come back from outer space, it causes havoc in our relationship. I remember reading the script in the car. How did I forget that?"

"Buggered if I know, Allan, but we fantasized about the LA premiere and doing the rounds at sci-fi conventions around the US and Japan. Somehow, it's what got us here in the first place!"

He sipped his tea. Here was the only person who truly lived in my past, and now would share my future. I couldn't have been happier if I'd been covered in lubricant.

"Warwick, how did Pedro ever have such a hold on you?"

"Allan, I originally ran off with Pedro because I couldn't deal with all of this."

He gestured in the general space around him.

"You couldn't deal with this apartment?"

"No, with the Limelight Quarter and the Carnival of Lost Souls and all of it. Someone was comforting me, and even though it wasn't Mr. Right, it was Mr. Right for however long it needed to be."

"But I was here for you as well. Maybe I needed you?"

"That's my point. I've held your hand through a breakup, through a bad job, through fun and laughter in the gay scene, and onto a possible movie career. It's always been me. I'm your security blanket, Allan."

"I could have been here for you, Warwick, dealing with our shared dilemma."

"Allan, the best you could do was to have sex with me. When I already had Pedro to help me through this, you tried to take me away from him so *you* could deal with it. You already had Maudi and Guy in your life; you didn't need me. I had to let you move on, even if I did it with tough love. I had to leave you after the run of Pedro's play, but not let you in on my plans. Otherwise, I would never leave, and you would never grow. But then you were cast in Gloria's son's play."

"Warwick, I didn't court you because I needed to deal with my divorce from mortality! I courted you because I was in love with you."

"I think I was just your rebound when we were alive, and here in Limelight I was simply 'comfort from an old friend.'"

"And what comfort do you have now, Warwick? No Pedro! No Samantha! Who have you got?"

"I have an old friend who found his spunk! Who stood up and produced a film by himself. Who can not only look after himself, but hopefully, look after me for a change."

I wanted to scream. How dare he get it so wrong!

"Tell me something. When you cooked Sunday lunch at Pedro's, did you always intend to break up with me, or was it something your fairy-tale prince talked you into?"

"The first time he said anything about our affair was at the dining table. You were there; you knew that."

"So did guilt have anything to do with our breakup?"

"Yes, it did. That day, I felt like a real heel pretending to be running lines for your imaginary play." I scrunched my lips. "Honestly, Allan, it's the truth."

"That's not what's worrying me. Remember when we kissed and we were sure he caught us? He didn't bat an eyelid. And if you consider..."

"Yes, yes, yes. I get it, Allan. Hindsight comes with twenty-twenty vision. I was the pawn in their evil plans. I should've realized earlier. I should've picked up on the signs. At first, Pedro was there for me. Then there was the night I spent alone, not knowing where he was. Gradually, he seemed to have his own life, catching up with Samantha more and more. Once he started writing his current play, I could have worn lederhosen and masturbated, and he wouldn't have noticed."

"You could have talked to me about it."

"I almost did a few times, but our lives were on different paths. You had Guy and Maudi, and I had Pedro and Samantha. So I talked about it with Samantha a couple of times, and it seemed to work. Pedro showed me more attention, at least in the short-term."

He tightly clasped his teacup in both hands. His brown eyes had lost some of their soul.

"We really have switched roles," he noted.

"Was I actually that *needy* back home?"

"Do I have to answer?"

"I guess you've already told me."

"Allan, I didn't mind if you were needy or not back then. You were my friend. But here at Limelight, I wasn't sure I could be that strong for you. I was busy putting on a brave face while hiding my fears in my sham romance."

I let his words sink in before a gentle smile painted my face.

"Warwick, you were my hero, once."

"I'd like to be your hero again. I miss being your best friend."

"I miss being yours."

He put down his drink and hopped off the bench. His arms reached out as I placed my teacup down and embraced his broken spirit. I was hugging my best friend. We had an adventure to continue, an adventure that started when we jumped in the car and left Port Macquarie.

TWENTY-FOUR

SEVERAL DOZEN FRESH prawns made my mouth water as I inspected the catering at the Community Hall. Their pink shells lay on a red checkered tea towel inside an earthy clay bowl. Warwick searched the markets at the Medieval Quarter to find the best seafood for my screening that evening. He had also gone to the trouble of whisking together a tart dipping sauce for these delicious creatures.

Guy had been baking sweet treats while Maudi and Frederick were on refreshment duty, gathering and mixing all sorts of alcoholic beverages for the night. I had been banished from any kind of food preparation, being strictly told that my job was to make sure the film was ready for projection.

We had laid out about a hundred seats, but with the starting time twenty minutes away, only a third were occupied. Even resident theater critic, Wilma, who never missed the chance to be entertained, was absent from my important event.

Toward the back row, a pleasing group of young men and women sat laughing in well-mannered tones. One of the males had brown shoulder-length hair and an intriguing purple tie-dyed T-shirt. His girlfriend wore a creamy white cardigan and sported a quaint burnt-orange handbag. These were friends of Gloria's son, here for support. I was observing the fashion and behavior that reigned well before my own years. A girl in the aisle seat lit a joint. As she shared it with her friends, familiarity returned.

Soon Maudi and Frederick sat near them, in similarly relaxed clothes. Her flowing auburn gown would have matched a campfire sing-along, with her strumming the guitar to the tune of "Kumbayah."

"You definitely know how to put on a good spread."

I turned to face an attractive man who'd dyed his hair copper red since we last met.

"Tarquin, what are you doing here?"

"I heard this film is a twisted love tale. I couldn't resist."

"So twisted tales are your thing?"

"Allan, it's been a long time since I was in love. Romantic stories, no matter how bizarre they are, fill the void."

"That's kind of sad. It must mean that guy you were married to was definitely 'the one.'"

"You mean Kent. Yes, absolutely. I haven't felt that way about anyone else since I've been here."

"Yeah, I think I know what you mean."

"Don't tell me you still haven't hooked up with that guy."

"You mean Warwick. Well, we did, but then it came to an unhappy end."

"And now?"

"And now we're friends again, at least."

"Allan, before Kent and I finally tied the knot, we had a very rocky start."

"I don't believe that. You spoke about him with so much affection the morning after we met."

"And to speak about Kent with so much love, we had a lot of growing up to do beforehand. We argued about trivial things every second week. We betrayed each other because we were too scared to commit. We took each other for granted because it was easier than giving a little of yourself away. We did so many things wrong we made the Old Testament look like a kindergarten play."

I was lost for words. The kindhearted Christian gently took my hand.

"Allan, at some stage, you need to trust him enough to let him in. It's scary, I know. You have your independence, and you're in control, but it's important to understand his viewpoint and forgive. In time, his love will warm you like a big thick comfy coat, giving you room to grow into the best version of yourself you could ever be. Just make sure you do the same for him."

He kissed my cheek and took his seat. Warwick was at the front entrance, waiting for people to arrive so he could show them where to sit. He stood with his hands in his jean pockets, whistling cheerfully. I wanted to join his daydream and lose myself in his thoughts. I wanted to know his view on so many things, now that we had experienced the Afterlife on different paths.

He noticed me watching him, grinned, and then peered outside before shutting the old timber doors. A woman's hand pushed one of the doors back open. Her fingers spread, digging her crimson nails into the wood like a zombie scratching its way out of a coffin.

Dressed to kill in figure-hugging black, Samantha waltzed in, sporting Pedro as an accessory. They set themselves in the front row and called to me. I reluctantly strolled over.

"We thought we'd come over and lend our support," she said.

"I thought your dress rehearsal was tonight."

"Oh, we changed the time."

"It's tomorrow at lunchtime," added the lute-playing writer. "It keeps the play fresh in the mind of the cast."

"Anything helps," I replied.

I swiftly walked away and pressed the play button on the video projector.

As the movie played, I sweated it out, waiting for the audience to laugh. Although it was not a comedy, it was crucial that the crowd identified with the script's natural humor. It's the only barometer that tells they understand the film. If they laugh for the wrong reasons, you've failed as a filmmaker.

James and Simone met the young love interest at a party, scoring a few oohs and ahs from the room. The husband's musings on midlife crisis scored plenty of knowing chuckles, while Maudi's joyous interpretation of Farah and Guy's devilish version of Fabien brought out many heartfelt laughs. Ipan's concerns over the spellbound lovers made most lean forward in their seats.

The new final scene where the three protagonists finally succumb to their longings, also encouraged several oohs and ahs, but this time they were spoken with longer, gentler vowels.

The sound of thirty pairs of clapping hands resonated in my head, sounding more like a stadium than a public hall. Warwick turned and smiled, followed by Guy. Gloria's son caught my eye, grinning as I beamed from ear to ear. Maudi endorsed my art with a nod. If I could have bottled this sentiment, I would have made a killing on the black market. Champagne was now the next best thing.

To my surprise, more food came out of the kitchen. Maudi's savory brie and pear tart had guests commenting between compliments for the film. Most banded around the cast, toasting their portrayals, as others questioned them on the mechanics of a ménage á trois. Gloria's son was the only person with real advice.

"Darling, you outdid yourself," called Maudi from the other side of the room.

"Thank you," I yelled back. "But without superb actors and a superb text, I wouldn't have had a building block."

I looked to Gloria's son and applauded him.

"But a film cannot direct itself!" she replied.

I thanked her again and turned to explore Guy's homemade cakes.

"Well, it was half directed by me, of course," said Samantha.

She had crept up next to me while I was chewing a glazed donut.

"You simply directed Warwick, Janice, and Guy. We reinterpreted the play."

"You took out the magic. Where was the charm?"

"No, Samantha, we *added* the magic."

"There's no magic in adding sex. That's a cheap ploy to tantalize the audience."

She stood expressionless, clutching a cup of Frederick's warm red cinnamon wine to her lips.

"My dear fellow director," I replied, "there's a huge difference between making an adult film and making a film for adults!" She lowered her cup as her eyes darted around the hall. They finally rested on Pedro, who noticed her. "And while I'm on a roll, see how true to life everyone's acting was? It is possible, you know."

"Inspired acting? That's a matter of opinion."

"Only to those with no experience in the craft!"

"Oh, Allan, what would you know about craft?" called Pedro. He was walking in our direction.

"Listen," I replied. "That's the sound of nobody caring what you think." I turned my back on him and again addressed Samantha. "And one more thing I need to know. Why did you dress me in that moon suit?"

"It was the role! He was the man in the moon!"

"I looked like a chubby mime artist. What inspired you to dress me like that?"

"It was art. True art! Not some flick for the raincoat brigade."

I shook my head in disbelief.

"If you can't differentiate between *Dangerous Liaisons* and a Russ Meyer picture, then maybe you missed your true calling!"

The murmurs of our screening party had become quiet as our slice of reality theater played out.

"Allan," exclaimed Pedro, "for your information, the man-in-the-moon suit was my idea. Sammy did sketch the final outfit, but she originally had visions of an old man with a walking stick. I convinced her that Ipan had to be a fairy tale."

"Pedro, darling," I replied, "Ipan had to be a fairy tale?"

"Yes, a fairy tale played by a true fairy!"

Samantha smirked. Her lover's remark cut deep.

"So, Miss Baby Cakes, did it ever occur to you how difficult it would be to act in such an outlandish outfit?"

"Any good actor would have been able to handle it."

"Then it's lucky Pedro and I didn't switch roles in *your* play. Ipan's nuances would never have made it past the front row!"

Maudi yelled "Bravo" and rushed over with Warwick.

"So let me get this right," my mate said. "The blonde bombshell was threatened by my closest friend, so she conspired with my tragic Casanova to seriously hurt him on stage. When that didn't work, they tried to humiliate him in that silly costume. Finally, they tried to stop his filmmaking talents from being seen. Simple deceit, even making a patsy out of me."

"Warwick, dear, would you like some cheese to go with that whine?" Pedro said.

"Oh please! If you have something to say, then raise your hand and place it over your mouth."

"Really, my darling, you're not yourself today. I noticed the improvement immediately."

"Pedro, sweetheart, just because you're misunderstood doesn't mean you're an artist."

"And they usually call me melodramatic," said Maudi.

Warwick thumped his fist on the food table. "Pedro and Samantha, don't continue believing you pulled the wool over my eyes. I worked out long ago that there was more to your friendship—'It's our gem-collecting night, Warwick. Trust me, you wouldn't be interested. Don't wait up!'— I wasn't born yesterday, you know. I just found it hard to believe that you would hide your relationship. The more I worked it out, the more I realized your affair was older than Cher!"

Maudi applauded as Frederick came over and stood by her side. Guy followed close behind.

"And why in heaven's name would you sabotage your very own gangster farce?" she asked. "It was my production, and you ground it to a halt with slippery stuff on stage, a real gun in Guy's pocket, and a dangerous falling light!"

"The light was sort of an accident," replied Samantha. She dropped her wine before swiftly covering her mouth.

"Did something slip out, dear?" Maudi asked.

My friends and I exchanged delighted glances.

"What do you mean 'the light was sort of an accident'?" asked Pedro. His face was whiter than talcum powder. "I was on stage at the time! You told me about the slimy hair gel, and of course, I knew about the gun. You took it without asking me from my bedroom drawer. But at no time did you mention that damn huge crashing light!"

"Pedro, honey," the villainess replied, "I tried to loosen it when Allan was alone on stage, but it didn't fall. It fell later, instead. I really didn't expect anything to happen. Those screws hardly budged when I was up there."

"You could have killed me!" I screamed. "Well, not really, but you could have seriously hurt me."

"I wasn't aiming at you. I just wanted to frighten you. The light was upstage. You were downstage. Well, at least you were when I went up to loosen the screws. As it turned out, you both were downstage when the light decided to come loose."

"When the light 'decided to come loose'!" roared Pedro. "Oh, how nice of that light to decide to come loose and not hurt anyone. Not to mention me, who did, from time to time, occupy the upper part of the stage. What the hell were you doing unhooking a light?"

Samantha didn't answer. She began striding toward the front doors, picking up speed the farther she traveled. The surrounding crowd froze like ice sculptures, only moving their necks to watch her leave.

"Yes, step right up and see the freaks!" I called out. "Creatures of the limelight, devouring the harmless to feed their own pride. Performances, on and off stage, with venom splashed all over the green room!"

Pedro chased after his noxious lover. "What kind of imbecile loosens a light and not, at least, tells me about it! Oh, I forgot, there's never a moment when everything isn't about you!" His tirade continued into the distance.

"HOW DID PEDRO and Samantha become so delusional?" I asked.

After numerous glasses of absinthe, my lips weren't quite moving at the speed of thought.

"Too much ego, not enough soul searching," Warwick replied.

I proposed a toast to his insight. Maudi, Frederick, and Guy lifted their glasses.

Wearing more colors than a retina could handle was the onstage band at the Pedestal. A swing ensemble known as the Attack of the Jelly Fruits accompanied Nellie, who must have been blackmailed to stay in residency. Her lime pin-striped suit would have caused eye damage if stared at for too long. Her hair was slicked back like a 1950s teenage hoodlum, as she jumped around in hieroglyphic dance moves with the energy of a coiled spring.

"I don't know what's worse," I said. "Their outfits or her dance moves?"

"They're a perfect match for each other," Warwick noted.

The others peered at the band.

"What did happen to music in the twentieth century?" Maudi asked.

"Jazz started the ball rolling," replied the angel. His wings drooped in his inebriated state.

We sat calmly as the chocolate-colored candle on our table painted an orange glow to our collective faces. In a booth opposite sat a mature muscular male in tight denim, drinking alone. I wanted to meander over and share his nectar, but Warwick was seated next to me. His proximity was closer than it had been for some time.

"Friends, look at the man over there," he said. "The grown-up one. Is he trying to recapture his youth, or is he just young at heart?"

"Either way, I'd like to take him for a test drive," I replied. "I'm happy to do the research and give you an answer tomorrow."

Warwick nudged me hard.

"Well, my dears," said Maudi, "it looks like actions speak louder than words."

She pulled out the latest *Stage Door* and flicked to a certain page.

"Not again," I replied.

"Yes, again, Allan. You need to know your standing in the theater scene."

I grabbed the magazine and read out loud.

*

Partner swap bonanza! It's the tale of the director, the writer, the filmmaker, and the actor. Coming soon to a café or shindig near you! The new lovebirds make their nest while rumors say the jilted playwright has already hooked up with an old flame. More scandal to follow!

*

"Well, they're half-right," I replied. "Maudi, that is such a bitchy magazine! Who cares about the affairs of other people?"

"People with no affairs of their own," stated Frederick.

"I do read the articles as well," declared Maudi.

"But you seem to always know what's on the gossip page," I said.

She picked up the publication and fanned its pages.

"Yes, I know, but I need a little spice in my life."

"I thought that's what I was for," replied Frederick.

He pulled back her long hair and delicately kissed her cheek. She sighed, fluttering her eyelids melodramatically. I took the journal from her hands and studied the cover.

"Regardless of what I've just said, I'm looking forward to reading *The Stage Door*'s take on tonight's events, as I'm sure they'll hear word of it somehow." I wistfully closed my eyes. "Silly, I know, but I'm curious on how they'll paint me as the villain again."

"Either way, I'm proud of you," said Warwick. "Your film was fantastic."

The others clinked glasses.

"But only a handful of people came to see it. I'm a nobody as far as the Limelight Quarter is concerned."

"Don't buy into that crap," slurred our angel. More of his drink spilled on the table than made it to his mouth. "You are a star, Allan, to everyone with you here, at this moment."

"Guy's right," said Frederick. "It doesn't matter that only a handful of people came to see your film. You've achieved a lot by making it in the first place. Besides, you and Warwick are too good-natured to be caught up in other people's drama. Just be a bit more wary next time. Study the subtext!"

"The charming Limelight Quarter," Guy added. "Too many freaks, not enough circuses."

"This is what I hate about this place," I said. "Veteran thespians like Frederick and Maudi should account for more brownie points than delusional artistes."

"So should newcomers who take initiative," replied Frederick. "Look around, Allan, talent doesn't count around here. Self-image does."

"It's not about expanding the plight of art," added Maudi. "It's about keeping the status quo."

"Self-worth tied up in self-image," I pondered. "What an ugly cycle."

"You know, they're both trying to prove themselves with hobbies they're not suited for," said Warwick. He nuzzled closer to me.

"You're so right. Yet if they did it for the love of art, they may be content. They may actually create something they can be proud of, learn from their peers, and move on. They'd be better off."

"And you'll be better off once you drop it and move on as well," said Frederick. "Both of you deserve so much more."

He held Maudi close to him.

"Yes, Allan and Warwick," she replied. She caressed Frederick's hand. "It's time for you both to move on, and not just in your artistic achievements."

TWENTY-FIVE

I JIGGLED MY key against the lock to my front door. Somehow, it leaped out of my hand so I reached to pick it up. Warwick was literally crawling up the stairs behind me, and as I tried to unlock the door again, he latched onto my legs, causing me to shriek. The door sprung open so I jumped from his grip and staggered to an armchair.

He entered on elbows and knees, rolling over on his back like a helpless cockroach. Better judgment should have told me to grab the fly spray, but I watched my powerless mate cradle his aching head. He slurred something incomprehensible, which made me mutter in reply something equally unintelligible. He rolled across the carpet, eventually making it onto his knees and dragging himself toward me.

"What are you doing?" I asked.

My friend reached for my left foot, pleasantly caressing it. It caused me to groan so loud, Emmanuel would have blushed.

"I love you, Allan."

I fluttered my eyelids like Gidget ready to moon my doggie. He rested his hands on my feet and sniffed between my legs.

"What are you doing?" I asked. "You're not going to mark your territory?"

He nibbled at my crotch before pushing upward with his chin, exploring my length. It tickled in a pleasing way. After a while, he stopped and peered at me.

"Gosh, I love you, Allan." His speech pattern had the elegance of a wayward fart.

"Why did you stop?" I asked.

"You're giving me that look."

"What look?"

"A toddler waiting for red cordial."

"Yes, Warwick, and like that sugar-crazed toddler, I also have an addiction."

I grabbed his limp arms and hauled him to my lips. My tongue brushed against his mouth, waiting to be let in. Soon he opened his jaw, welcoming my warm guest. I explored his mouth, sliding in a fevered trance, pushing farther into my beautiful man. His familiar musky scent had me craving for more of what I currently had. My arm slid up his back as I pushed him harder against my mouth.

Eventually, he broke away, so I nuzzled into his neck, tasting his masculine skin. My goatee beard brushed against his jawline. The odor of sweat wafted around us. I licked his earlobe, taking it into my mouth, chewing gently, and then wildly running my tongue into his ear. Its sensual grooves were explored with ease.

He lowered his head to my chest, licking my nipple through the fabric of my checkered shirt with his moist tongue. He eased away and purposely popped the buttons. I greeted his devilish grin with a passionate sigh. I felt the cool air on my chest, which he rubbed before he tasted once more. A wet trail drifted back and forth between both my nipples, causing me to shut my eyes and rub my erection against his stomach. He reached down, massaging it through the denim with his palm.

I ran my fingers through his curly ringlets, each one sliding past my skin like a wedding ring. We had made love previously, but somehow I felt more connected. The few times before were just a dress rehearsal, but here and now, we knew each other's bodies—nothing new to discover physically but so much to explore emotionally.

My ethereal thoughts ended abruptly as his tender mouth slithered over my cock. His saliva drenched me. He pulled at my jeans, dragging them to my feet. He cupped my balls, squeezing gently with each forward motion of his throat.

"Warwick, stop!" His rhythm was faster. I clutched his temples, forcing him to pause. "I'm so close, and I haven't returned the favor." I kindly pushed him away.

We stood up, and I reached for his T-shirt, carefully slipping it off before undoing the buttons on his jeans. I lowered them, caressing his ass on the way down. We kicked off our pants, and he took my hand and guided me to the bathroom.

The hot water traced down our bodies, splashing the tiles below. Our bodies rubbed, sliding and throbbing together; skin against skin. I clutched him on the ass and weaved my fingertip toward his warm tender opening. Soap glided me inside, slipping back and forth as my Warwick let out a belly-deep moan. He turned, bending slightly while reaching for the shower taps.

"Now, Allan. Do it now."

I didn't. I crouched and tasted his sultry chasm. My tongue reaching as far as it could, relishing its addictive flavor. Savory, manly, and meaty. A Pandora's box to be cherished, both tenderly and ruthlessly. Its demanding nature ready to come to life, once it was no longer tense.

"Allan, stop teasing."

I entered. Like a snug woolen sock, it swallowed me. He pushed back, devouring my knob like he was going to keep it forever. I was in the warmest part, his innermost depths. My cock was held private and secure, loved and treasured in a special space by my loving Warwick.

Streams of water parted across his butt cheeks. He pushed harder. I pulled away. I grabbed his thighs and seesawed him back and forth against me. We groaned in unison. I thrust. He pressed back. I rammed again. He forced me inside him, begging me to grind away any thread of gracious human behavior. We were stripped back to our basic urges, beasts of raw emotion. The world, the hereafter, the theater, our friends—nothing existed but us in this moment.

Sweat and steam permeated my senses. I lunged and pushed and attacked his glorious ass. I pulled right out and shoved myself back in, again and again. My full length digging into the void, darting in different directions and then aiming squarely in the spot that would make him quiver.

Warwick howled like a werewolf in the light of the moon. His creamy fluid oozed its way across the charcoal tiles before water washed away the evidence.

"Come on, Allan."

He pushed back, twisting his neck to meet my eyes. My knob expanded against his fiery clenched hole, shooting my juice deep into his body. I roared in relief. My man watched as the shower splashed down my face.

*

After drying each other with towels, we wrapped ourselves in bathrobes and made our way back to the living room. Before we sat down, Warwick noticed an envelope under my front door.

"Do you think it was there all the time?" I asked. "I mean, maybe we were too drunk to notice it when we got home and just stepped over it. At least, I hope so. Otherwise, someone might have been entertained by the sound of us grunting."

"The shower would have drowned out the noise, Allan."

"Are you sure? We came pretty loudly."

My lover scrunched his eyebrows before picking up the envelope and quietly reading its contents. His eyes widened halfway through the letter, as if he'd read an obituary.

"What?" Warwick didn't respond. He kept reading. "So, what's it say?"

"You're not going to believe this."

"Tell me, you might be surprised."

"Samantha and Pedro have given us a double pass to see their play tomorrow night, as a peace offering."

"You're right. I don't believe it."

He handed me the tickets. Printed on them was a picture of the evil blonde in a director's chair, in a figure-hugging red dress that pressed together the poached eggs that passed as her cleavage. The useless playwright took up most of the space on the opposite side, looking dowdy in a minstrel outfit a size too big.

"Wow," I replied. "What a charming couple. Rushing to meet us when we arrived at the Limelight Quarter. Plotting to screw up our chance to fall in love. Shamelessly causing crises during Maudi's production. Making a fool of me on stage in that baby sumo wrestler suit. Faking a romance with you to strain our friendship. Causing dramas during my shoot. Trying to run my screening out of town. And after all that, they *want* to be friends!"

"Maybe they realized we're not the enemy?"

"Soon they'll be asking us to dinner. Don't worry if you can't find all your cutlery, Sammy and Pedro. You left the steak knives in our backs. Oh what's that? You were just practicing acupuncture on us. You confused your implements. A bit nearsighted, are we? My, my! I wouldn't want to be around when you're getting kinky. You might mistake the corkscrew with the dildos!"

TWENTY-SIX

"I KNEW YOU'D be back," said Monique. She held open the flap to her tent. "Although I have to admit, I thought it would have been sooner."

"Sorry, I was too caught up in my own affairs, or lack of them."

"Come in."

I walked in and made myself comfortable on a carved wooden chair. The slight murmur of the marketplace outside drifted in as she shuffled her tarot deck.

Only moments before, my love affair with the Carnival of Lost Souls made me wander rather than rush to visit Monique.

Outside the crowds were faint, as I focused on how much I loved this neighborhood of the hereafter. Several young girls in pink fairy costumes had twirled around me before finding another punter to have fun with. A debonair older man played the harp, which seemed to charm passersby while making all other melodies and sounds disappear into the ether. I couldn't wait to move here and explore its magic.

"So what is it exactly that you've come to see me about?"

"To be honest, I'm not sure. I've been chasing love for so long, I guess I just want to know if I'm finally on the right track."

"Why aren't you sure?"

"I've meandered, then loved, and then lost love. When I lost all hope, he came back. I guess what I really want to know is if this will work out. Is our journey coming to a happy end?"

"You held back on love last time so are you set to know it all, next time?"

"Yes," I replied. "Like on that crazy Monopoly board you showed me, the last time I was here."

She gathered her cards from the table and put them to the side in a neat pile. She muttered something about the fact that I loved music before pulling out an exquisite wooden box from a shelf to her side. It was lacquered with a rose stain and wreaked of dust. As she wiped it with an old hankie, she instructed me to close my eyes.

"Oh, okay," I replied.

I shut my eyes. I heard a latch open. I peeked. A figurine of a ballerina sprung up from inside, spinning slowly as the chimes of the same melody the harpist played filled the tent.

"Now, now, no peeping." Monique cautioned me with her finger. "Otherwise, I'll never get you into a trance. You're about to witness your next life."

The tune was simple and spun around in my head as much as that ballerina. She was intricate, but almost felt like another person in the room, not unlike the harlequin money box at home. I closed my eyes again.

As the song played in the background, I saw a vision of two middle-aged men making cups of ginger tea. Somehow I knew I was one of them.

As we let the fern-green teapot sit to infuse on the blood-red and black granite bench, I took in the scent of fresh basil and lavender from the windowsill.

"Why is there lavender growing?" I asked.

"To keep away the mosquitoes, Adam. Remember?" replied my bald but distinguished-looking partner.

What a strange place for lavender. Which one of us kept getting bitten while cooking? And how did I get a reincarnated name so close to my own?

As I poured the tea, he sauntered over to the balcony, gesturing for me to follow. It must have been the weekend. We were dressed in baggy old T-shirts and matching tracksuit pants. The sound of someone named Filippa Giordano was coming from the swanky stereo system. From the balcony, I noted the minimalist black modular lounge and glass-top coffee table. Large homoerotic prints of men's torsos towered above the furniture, what little there was. Two of the prints had walls all to themselves. Personally, I would have shot the interior decorator.

"Adam, they're at it again."

"Who are?"

He pointed to the high-rise across the street where an attractive couple—one blond, one redhead—were going at it like rabbits. The bedspread had been thrown to the floor as they thrust a bit too energetically for this time of the morning. The blond reached out to something that was obscured from our vision. We shuffled over to the opposite side of our balcony to make out what he grabbed.

"It's Clark from upstairs," exclaimed my husband.

A bulky figure being pulled by his appendage came into view.

"Sex for breakfast. Maybe we should follow their lead."

"Shall we invite one of the neighbors to join us as well? Jason is chomping at the bit to join us."

"How do you know that?"

"Remember? He's the one who brought over the lavender and popped it on each windowsill just so you wouldn't get bitten." Then my partner mimicked Jason by raising his shoulders and flapping his arms about in a tizz. "I can't let my little Adam and Wade get bitten to death now, can I? You can't get away with using makeup to hide the spots on your arms."

"Is he cute?"

"Adam!"

Wade, who again strangely had a reincarnated name close to his own, grabbed my tatty T-shirt and pulled my mouth toward his. I lost myself in this romantic gesture. There was a spark of connection that was eerily familiar. His outpouring of love was just like Warwick's, only on a deeper level. It was the same soul. His sweet body odor was stronger. My body ached and creaked in different ways, but I was me and he was he, older, wiser, and much more of a couple.

I was about to nestle my face into Wade's neck, when I heard another gay cliché enter the room. It meowed.

"She wants to be fed," my partner said.

"A cat?"

"Well, yes! She is why we're here looking after Brent's apartment. Remember?"

"Thank heaven!"

"Thank heaven what?" said Monique's voice from the ether.

"White picket fences and Californian bungalows are *my* perfect fantasy. Not sterile furnishings and pets."

I opened my eyes.

"Is it what you wanted to see?"

"Better than I expected."

She closed the music box, brushing a little dust off the lid with her fingers.

"Remember, Allan, nothing is written in stone. Stay on this path and your journey will be completed."

TWENTY-SEVEN

EVEN THE HARLEQUIN money box couldn't taunt me as we made our way to the kitchen to unload the uneaten remnants from our picnic basket. Warwick and I were giggly from sparkling Shiraz, but we held it together to neatly unpack the hamper.

"You know, Bub, part of me doesn't really want to watch another play written from Pedro's pen of pathetic plots," I confessed.

"Or should that be the typewriter of tedium?" replied my companion. He crunched on a slice of garlic bread before placing the rest in a container.

"Either way, don't wake me if I get so bored I slip into a coma."

"Now, now, Allan, it's not the end of the world," he said with garlic breath. "It's just a few hours out of our lives."

"Yes, a few hours I'll never get back!"

I snapped shut another plastic container, which held two white-chocolate mousses we were too full to eat at our intimate lunch. Warwick opened the fridge door as I crouched to find a place on the top shelf. As I reached forward, my inebriated legs gave way, hurling me back onto my butt at the base of my lover's feet. I eased my back onto his legs, my shoulder blades resting against his knees. The cold air from the fridge was overshadowed by the warmth I felt as my lover crouched to kiss the back of my neck repeatedly.

"We could make up some excuse not to attend the play," I whispered. "I'm sure we can find at least one thing we'd rather do."

He stopped his show of affection and held me tight.

"Allan, I want to go. I spent more time with Pedro and Samantha than I have with you, so I want to see how they'll extend the olive branch."

"I think you have some unfinished business, Warwick. I don't mean to be harsh, but I feel you want to connect with Pedro. You want some evidence that your affair wasn't all a sham." There was no answer. I twisted my neck to read his face. He looked lost. "Sorry, that was a bit blunt."

"No, it's okay. You're right."

"But I guess a peace gesture is a peace gesture. If they didn't want closure, they wouldn't have invited us. Besides, even though we're leaving Limelight, if we decide to return, we have to be on good terms with them. They hold too much power."

He began to stand. His bent knees pushed me slightly forward, so he looped his arms under my shoulders and pulled me to my feet. I shut the fridge, turned, and gave him a loving peck on the mouth. He wrapped his arms around me and rested his head on my shoulder. We stood for a while. The silly play was starting in an hour, but I didn't want to move from this spot. I caressed his thick black hair.

A short while later, he pulled away and led me to the bedroom.

"Darling, what did you expect the Afterlife to be like?" I asked.

"That over-the-top room we first saw when we got here sort of fits in with my vision."

"Renaissance gone mad!"

"Yeah, Allan, but the rest of it seems a little earth-like for it to be heaven."

I opened the wardrobe door and flicked through our shirts. One particularly outlandish top caught my attention. I pulled it out, admiring its gaudy colors offset with black sleeves.

"Maybe we're in limbo?" I said. "We have to absolve the sins of bad fashion."

"If that's the case, we'll be waiting till eternity to get to heaven."

I popped the shirt back on its hanger. I flicked through more clothes as we both took verbal note of our preferences.

"A single-colored T-shirt and suit jacket," suggested Warwick. "It's not a fashion I see you wear, Allan, but it's a formal touch to your usual casual look."

"Lovely idea." I considered the jacket for a moment before admiring some older clothing. "Maybe for me it's a retro night instead. Something nostalgically consoling." I pulled another jacket and offered it to my boyfriend. "Maybe dapper is more your style?"

"Perhaps," replied my soul mate. He felt the texture of its sleeve. "Gosh, picking out each other's clothes. It's like the old Allan and Warwick but with a new lease of life."

"Tonight I feel like the new Warwick and Allan, with that familiar old lease on life. Enough history to build a solid foundation."

With jacket still in hand, I slid toward my standing partner, cradling my back into his chest. He reached around and hugged me from behind. I tenderly bent my head back so my cheek could nestle against his.

"I love you, Allan. Why did it take so long for us to get together?"

"True. It took a journey to the Afterlife to finally find heaven."

MAUDI TURNED HEADS as she entered in a curve-hugging black dress, making us comment on her buxom figure. Frederick matched her style in a black suit jacket and trousers, topped off with a mauve shirt.

Warwick, Guy, and I attended together. I fished out that vintage new-wave shirt with the buttons to one side while Warwick took the street-cred approach with the suit jacket, white T-shirt, and jeans. We stopped off at Guy's and helped him choose an outfit. I made him follow my partner's sense of style with a sexy black T-shirt, classic long coat, and tight jeans. I told him he looked like the "angel of love," which he responded to by rolling his eyes.

Renowned theater critic Wilma was there, kissing the director on both cheeks. Samantha showed the journalist to her front-row seat.

"I'm so glad we're moving to the Carnival of Lost Souls, Warwick. Try as I might, I just can't be that fake."

"Allan, they think they're the jewels in the crown, just because they live in the Limelight Quarter."

"And I'm sure they're the only ones with that opinion."

My lover hugged me tight, smooching me in public view.

"I can't wait to read what my theater rag says about that kiss," said Maudi. A stagehand rang a large rusted bell. "I think they want us to sit down."

"Are we ready for lifeless dialogue and paper-thin subtext?" I whispered.

"Now, now, Allan," reprimanded my favorite angel. "You should be moving on."

It was a full house. As we were shown to our seats, everyone was handed a glass of pink champagne. A female usher sat me next to Wilma. I smiled in her direction, but she didn't turn to acknowledge me. I said her name, but she began talking to a wiry old man behind her.

Next to the man was an amiable forty-something guy with short dark hair and rectangular glasses. His academic style made me sneak a second look. He winked at me, but I rested my chin on Warwick's shoulder. The man gave me a comic frown as the curtain rose.

The first act was predictable enough. No real surprises in the plot. Pedro flounced around in tights with a lute, explaining that the king desires ultimate power, while a princess from another land was adept at wrapping suitors around her little finger.

A seduction scene in the second act stopped me from slapping my own face to stay awake. The king and the princess meet, but it's the king who has the upper hand, or so we think. Toward the end of the act, she instigates a fight for love over her between the king and her current lover, whom she is tired of.

The swordplay picked up the pace at a juncture when I was considering leaving at the interval. The actors pranced about the stage and clanked swords with the grace of Katharine Hepburn trying to crochet. This was a new reality TV show screaming out to be made—*When Choreography Goes Wrong!*

"Love is blind in your case," said the king. He thrust his sword into the air, leaving himself open to a fatal blow.

The lover swung his weapon across his body, trying to slash the king's ribs, but the king brought down his sword so fast it leapt from his hand.

Pedro watched me from upstage with a sinister grin, while Guy began to panic. Pinning me to my seat was the king's sword. I screamed out in pain for a minute or so before I felt nothing. I was saturated, but not with blood—with champagne. I glanced down and saw its clean incision through my favorite retro shirt. I looked to the stage as my consciousness started leaving the scene of the crime. I heard muted footsteps as a thousand thoughts entered my mind. Would I see Warwick again? Could I have consoled the backstabbing duo? Can you actually die if you are already dead?

Pedro was no longer on stage. Sorrow engulfed me as I realized the life with Warwick as my romantic lead was now just a lost plotline. He grabbed my shoulders and gazed in shock. Guy knelt in front of me, praying. His panic was gone, replaced with confidence. Warwick gave me a soft lingering kiss as I felt his tear caress its way down the back of my neck. Guy placed his hand on my forehead and observed me. I swear I heard his mind ticking over.

I closed my eyes and heard bewildered chatter, along with the echo of footsteps. I wasn't scared. I had that contented feeling you get when someone does something thoughtful for you.

I felt myself rise like a hot-air balloon, so my eyes flicked open. The ceiling was coming closer, and my fingers explored its coarse surface. Behind me were the subdued tones of an audience calming down. My body rotated with ease as I peered below.

Warwick clutched my lifeless body. Maudi and Frederick caressed his back in support. They were speaking to him, but for some reason, the sound from the theater had become a distant hum, even though I was right above it. Those footsteps were haunting me instead, yet none of the shocked audience were pacing. Guy was still praying, before shooting a direct stare straight at my raised vantage point. He freaked me out. I clenched my eyes shut.

*

The sound of footsteps was more pronounced. There was a pair of stilettos and a family of sensible shoes. I looked toward the noise. To my left was a brilliant white light. Its illumination formed a tunnel, from which bewildered individuals tottered toward me. The high heels belonged to a trim woman in a short black dress. In one hand, she clutched a small straw, while staring back at me with bug eyes and a bloodied nose. I guessed it was too late for her to find a trustworthy dealer.

It was the family of four who made me shudder. The father embraced a twisted steering wheel as if it was a major artifact of his former life. His wife gripped his arm for dear life, while their two toddler girls spun their heads, taking in as much as they could. For the youngsters, this must have been all part of the trip. I once understood how they felt.

I began missing Warwick. He had looked so handsome as we entered the theater that evening. I'd never be soothed again by his smile or listen to his gentle voice. We'd never grow old together.

Last time we missed the boat
We shared our lives
Held back on love
But finally, we sailed

I was beaming. It's not often that you're busy greeting the deceased when a voice you know recites poetry to you. There he was. The being who had helped me through so much.

"Why now?" I asked my angel colleague.

"Because life lessons are for the living, and wisdom is for the dead."

"Cryptic but effective." I moved forward to kiss Guy. "Do I get to say goodbye to Warwick?"

"He won't be too far away."

"Why can't he join me now?"

"Warwick's got to miss you for a while. If he doesn't have this period of grief, he might forget what you mean to him."

Guy pointed to the tunnel, urging me to walk through it. Ms. Party Girl was getting clucky over the two toddlers. One of them took her straw and asked why there was no milkshake in her other hand.

I looked toward the theater. There was no stage, no seats, no ceiling or floors, and no building. In fact, there were no backdrops or props of any description, just ghostly souls going about their business. My sad friends were translucent, huddled around me even though I could not see any sign of my body. Several others who I thought were in the audience didn't seem to be there anymore. From my peripheral vision, I noticed my hand. It too was see-through.

"What am I looking at, Guy?"

"This place in its purest form."

"My friends think they can see me, but I'm not there."

"Allan, they also think they can see a theater, wayward swords, and all the realities of their former lives."

"So I didn't die?"

"A while back, yes, but not just now. You can't die if you're already dead, but you can move on to your next life."

"But Warwick probably thinks..."

"Like I said, he needs to think that, so he doesn't leave you again."

"But after everything I went through to get him, now I'm losing him again. For goodness sake, Guy, my life was just starting."

"Allan, it started a lifetime ago. Look at the person you've finally become. You're confident and strong. You were a friend to me, and finally you were a friend to yourself."

"So what? All I wanted was Warwick."

"And you got him, when you grew into the person he was waiting for. The person he always knew was there and tried so hard to bring out." I crossed my arms in frustration. "Allan, listen. The universe doesn't bring us what we want; it brings us what we need."

I didn't know what to say. The angel's kind eyes were summing up my soul.

"Guy, I have a confession to make. Lately, I haven't been sure that I've always loved him." I slid my hands into my pockets. "He was the convenient distraction to my pointless relationship. He was the friend I needed to show me my gay self. But was I really in love with him then? I know I love him now, but maybe I was just infatuated when we first met? Maybe I was in love with the idea of being in love?"

"I see. Allan, when people truly find their soul mate, they're often the last people to notice. Their friends and family see it and gossip. You just had to love yourself before you were ready to love someone else."

"I guess. So can't I go back to Warwick now, just for a day?"

"Like I said, let him miss you."

We stood silent as inner peace began replacing my fear of loss.

"Guy, do you mean what you said before?"

"About what?"

"About being a friend to you?" He stepped forward, reached out, and embraced me. His cheek was moist. "Guy, you're crying."

"Warwick's not the only person who's going to miss you."

I began to weep too.

"You said that Warwick won't be far behind me, but what about you, Guy? Will you be far behind?"

My special angel didn't speak. His wings cocooned me, and I closed my eyes to make this moment last as long as possible. This had been the place of too many faded memories.

The murmuring of the newcomers was getting louder. They needed an explanation, and I was holding up proceedings. But I had so much more to ask.

"Guy, is there more to your past than you're letting on? I mean, um, how do I say this?" I paused and took a breath. "Guy, an angel technically can't be an orphan. Their relatives are of *this* world."

"Allan, dead people don't technically need to eat and drink either, and I'm not even sure they can technically get drunk."

"Touché. Now I'm even more confused."

"I'll explain it all the next time we meet."

"I'm so looking forward to the next time we meet."

We kissed under his wings, mouths closed but lingering. I didn't want to let go. After a while, he pulled away and gave me a peck on the forehead.

"Guy, one more question. What's Gloria's son's real name?"

He theatrically looked over both shoulders and brought his lips to my ear.

"Allan, I have no idea."

I chuckled and kissed my angel once more. He took my hand and guided me to the mouth of the luminous walkway. The others were chatting about their last mortal moments. I strode past them, still teary, and waved back at Guy one last time before I marched into my fate.

The thought of being a baby again somehow wasn't that daunting as I made my way through the tunnel. I was about to view my own tiny fingernails, hear my new mother's voice, and get whacked on the butt by some enthusiastic doctor.

My glowing surrounds were blinding me, although they didn't hurt my eyes. I was compelled to stay on course. Soon I would face a new beginning, so I held on to my memories of the Afterlife. Wayward swords. Wayward lovers. What lessons had I learned? What lessons would I take into my new life?

I thought about Warwick and how much time I'd wasted not showing him my feelings. As a distant doorway came into focus, I told myself I was unique, charming, and worth loving. I was determined never to have the same regrets and decided that the next time I wouldn't hide my emotions, trusting they were part of my journey.

After all, you're a long time dead.

About the Author

Kevin lives with his long-term partner in their humble apartment (affectionately named Sabrina), in Australia's own "Emerald City," Sydney.

From an early age, Kevin had a passion for writing, jotting down stories and plays until it came time to confront puberty. After dealing with pimple creams and facial hair, Kevin didn't pick up a pen again until he was in his thirties. His handwritten manuscript was being committed to paper when his social circumstances changed, giving him no time to write. Concerned, his partner, Warren, snuck the notebook out to a friend who in turn came back and demanded Kevin finish his novel. It wasn't long before Kevin's active imagination was let loose again. The result was *Drama Queens with Love Scenes*, the first in a series of Afterlife tales.

Kevin is looking forward to thumping the keys on his laptop and churning out stories until it's time for him to gain first-hand experience of the hereafter.

Website: www.kevinklehr.com
Facebook: www.facebook.com/DramaQueensWithLoveScenes/
Twitter: @kevinklehr
Goodreads: www.goodreads.com/author/show/4298144.Kevin_Klehr
Vimeo: www.vimeo.com/companionmedia/
YouTube: www.youtube.com/channel/UCcJrnpZjgSjbpCiBp-pA3Jw/

Also by Kevin Klehr

Actors and Angels Series
Drama Queens and Adult Scenes (coming soon)
Drama Queens and Devilish Schemes (coming soon)

From Top to Bottom

Nate and Cameron Series
Nate and the New Yorker (coming soon)

Both Cameron and I had Hawaiian shirts to wear, while Rowena sported a tie-dyed sarong and an afro wig. And around us, interesting guests wore chic little skirts, James Dean–style jackets, hippie gear, and mod wear.

"You haven't introduced me yet," said a middle-aged woman to Cameron. Her rust-colored coat had a masculine cut. Yet she elegantly held a long-stemmed cigarette holder with something that smelled very much like a joint burning on the end.

"Sorry," said my charming American. "This is my friend, Nathan. And this well-dressed lady is my aunt Beverley."

"Nice to meet you," I said.

She took my hand and kissed it. "I hope you don't think me too forward; it's just that you've got such fascinating features."

"My aunt likes to flirt."

"It runs in the family," she replied. She gave me a measured wink. "Now, nephew, where have you been hiding this handsome Englishman?"

"I'm Australian."

"It's your accent. I never can tell the difference."

"I need you!" yelled a girl in a flower necklace. She was the drummer of the band and was addressing our host.

"It's time," Cameron said.

"Time for what?" I asked.

He kissed me on the cheek and then headed for the microphone stand.

"You're in for a treat," whispered Aunt Beverley, her voice raspy from years of smoking.

"He sings?" I asked.

"He sings," she replied.

A laid-back strum of the bass guitar started the song, followed by a drum beat. Then the vocal. And before I knew it, I was being serenaded in front of a room full of acquaintances. But, wow! What a unique experience.

"I've never seen him go out on a limb for someone like this before," said his aunt.

I smiled politely, then closed my eyes. He was crooning. His honey voice made my soul rise out of my body and search for a dream. And in the hip nightclub that appeared in my mind, he wore a gray suit with a crimson tie, standing tall in front of the trumpet section who were waiting for their cue. And I was the only one in the club.

"Where are you?" asked Aunt Beverley in a low tone.

I wanted to say I was in love but stopped myself. I realized it was rude to have my eyes closed during Cam's song. I opened them. He had me in his sights. I wanted to jump into the waves on his Hawaiian shirt and end up on a deserted island with just him and me.

"Would you like a toke of my cigarette, Nathan?"

"No, thank you. I think the fumes have already hit me."